Allan S...

May 2023

THE NOONDAY DEVIL

ALLAN STEVEN

Copyright 2022 Allan Steven

All rights reserved.

This book or parts thereof may not be reproduced in any form, stored in any retrieval system, or transmitted in any form by any means – electronic, mechanical, photocopy, recording, or otherwise – without prior permission of the author.

For permission requests email:
fruitymetcalfe@me.com

This is a work of fiction. Names, characters, businesses, places, events, locales, and incidents are either the products of the author's imagination or used in a fictitious manner. Any resemblance to actual persons, living or dead, or actual events is purely coincidental.

"When a man stops believing in God he doesn't then believe in nothing, he believes anything."

G.K. Chesterton

For Mum and Dad. Xx

Cover artwork by Martin Gorst

Author's note

'Shift yourself'

'The Noonday Devil' is properly termed 'Acedia'. In Chapter 6, the Reverend Rufus Coleridge says:

"You can be busy, but still be infected with Acedia. It's a combination of weariness, sadness and a lack of purpose. You feel empty, and that life is without meaning."

Collins' dictionary defines Acedia as, *"Spiritual sloth, apathy, indifference."* We observe that it says *'spiritual'*, not *'religious'*. However, it was applied in Christianity, with especial reference to the monastic life. It was in use between the 13th and 16th centuries.

I chose Rufus Coleridge's definition to explain the title of my novel, as it identifies the zeitgeist plainly. This is the malaise that infects the life of the United Kingdom, if not the entire Western World to varying degrees.

We have a twofold problem. Whilst we may be thankful for living in a society where our every need is catered for, the consumerist obsession has deprived us of our identity. When the mobile 'phone we have is out of date, because there's a new one a nanosecond faster; when fashion changes, what are we left with? 'FOMO' – the fear of missing out. We set off, yet again, in breathless pursuit of novelty to add to our already multiple identities. It is chasing a chimera. When we realise that we are rootless, who then can relieve us of our anxieties and depression - permanently?

That is the second part of our difficulties. We try to overcome our dissatisfaction by comfort eating on abstract notions . Mythology is created around groups of people, so we can categorise them into good and bad. It is a self-centred act designed to make us feel noble. In this case, the sun doesn't just shine on the righteous; it gloss paints the self-righteous.

'The Noonday Devil' does not spare anyone. The facile notion that people are automatically good or bad, because of their gender, race, sexuality, politics, religion or class receives a good taste of the lash. Journalists get an especial mauling. The arrogant and conceited Fourth Estate (I didn't mention the BBC), which has come to believe that it possesses an inalienable right, not just to report but, to manufacture the news. Thereby manipulating the population into unceasing oscillation, between crisis and outrage. Dr. Josef Goebbels of infamy could not have done better.

Perhaps the most uncomfortable part of the book is displayed in the characteristics and behaviour of teenager Barry Corrigan. Four decades in the teaching profession taught me that children are not sugar and spice and all things nice. Parents know that you never have to teach a child to be bad. Sadly, the present low quality of parenting in our nation means that too many of them abdicate their responsibility to nurture civil and civilised behaviour in their children. Corrigan's actions may be extreme, but it won't take the reader long to relate them to shocking real life incidents.

I suppose that, as a Christian, I should now proselytise, but I will refrain. Let me, instead, quote an atheist friend of mine:

"I may not believe in God, but it's a pity that the Church of England doesn't have influence any more. At least it gave us good values when we were growing up."

Acedia – the Noonday Devil – permeates our society. We have spent decades examining our own entrails. The consequence is that we believe there is nothing greater than ourselves. Subsequently, our actions are motivated by rampant selfish individualism, and devil take the hindmost. An explosive recipe that may well cause us to implode.

The panoply of characters and situations in the book may also provide you with '*a reet good laff*'; a phrase common in the part of the North I was brought up in. Well I would say that, wouldn't I!

Allan Steven, Stratford-Upon-Avon, November 2022

1

'Aye, 'appen'

Alfie Starkiss' passion for words teetered on the brink of adoration. He paused before fastening the third button down on his cassock. Worship of words, like worship of anything, qualified as idolatry; inappropriate to his calling. He continued to dress. A scene from his boyhood in Liverpool fluttered across his retinas. He'd once overheard his mate's mum gossiping to Mrs. McNulty, as he pumped up the tyres of his bike. The brick wall dividing the backyards hid him from view. Terry O'Reilly's mum hadn't mastered the subtleties of public address; she had a gob like the Mersey Tunnel, and just as filthy.

"Did ya 'ear 'im, Treesa? 'e was 'avin' a fuckin' eppy!"

"What was it this time, Josie?"

"Same as fuckin' usual. He didn't like the way she cooked 'is dinner."

"Did he…"

"Na, not this time. Lily kept her trap shut. You can still see the bruisin' on 'er arms from last time. Twat!"

"What would yer do if your Billy give you a backhander, Josie?"

"I'll tell yer this fer fuckin' nottin. He'd wake up next mornin' with 'is bollocks fer earrings."

"Ah, 'e's oright, your Billy. He's a great laugh down the club."

"Oh yeh…'e's still a fuckin' divvy. Eh, did ya 'ear wot 'appened to Jesse O'Connor's gerl? Knocked up at fourteen. Dirty little cow couldn't keep 'er legs together. Like mother like daughter."

Alfie tugged the surplice over his head and the sight of the Vestry notice board obliterated the childhood scene. 'Eppy', an abbreviation of epileptic fit. Scouse shorthand for someone going off at the deep end. He snorted, and addressed the A4 sheet announcing the forthcoming Harvest Festival.

"Goodhearted folk in Liverpool, and such a wonderful sense of humour!"

He was uncertain if his ironical tone amused the cheery farmer displayed on the notice, in all his bucolic glory. Years away from his native city had altered Alf's viewpoint. He was, by nature, a man who was always up for a laugh, but had discarded the humour which infested his childhood environment. He was wary of Scouse humour. It was a vicious attack dog; destructive. Predicated upon belittling and humiliating whoever was on the receiving end. In tandem with his father's aggression, it marred his growing up; force-fed into his DNA.

A combination of nature and nurture had turned him into the raging, acid-tongued young adult of yesteryear. He was not stupid, and whilst he thanked his God for moving him along a new and peaceful pathway, he was aware that the coals of anger smouldered within him.

Alfie made a pact with himself. He would persevere with the struggle not to utter angry words and profanities in public. His release valve would always be in private. Theologically, he knew that solitary cursing was also *verboten*, but eradicating secret sinning would have to be stage two of the project. Journeying with the burden of human imperfection on his back, but stepping ever closer to Christ.

The metal ring affixed to the Vestry door rattled. Alfie knew whose hand was upon it, and resisted the temptation to mutter the vulgarity aloud. By concentrating on its origin, Old Norse and Middle Low German, he justified his ill-thought as academic research. The word was short, and began with 'C'.

"What's it all about, Alfie..."

Rufus Coleridge thrust himself into the Vestry of All Souls Temple Weston with the sensitivity of a blow to the gonads. A song forever on his lips. You would have thought he owned the place. Technically, he did. Two years on from ordination Rufus had been fast tracked to Rector of the Benefice, with four churches under his angelic wings. Butter wouldn't melt in his mouth. Alfie smiled through bared teeth, and saw a vision of his mother's raised eyebrow:

"Aye, 'appen!"

"Ready for the off, Alf? Sermon all tickety-boo? Don't frighten the horses."

All Souls was hosting a Baptism. Alf christened it *'The Bumptious Baptism'* in honour of his Rector's presence. He was still serving his curacy, and his senior at All Souls was sat at home floating on a rubber ring to ease his haemorrhoids. Word reached Alf that the House for Duty priest, Colin Ambler, had been less than amused when informing the Rector of his indisposition. Rufus Coleridge had responded in song with Johnny Cash's *'Ring of Fire'*.

You had to forgive Rufus. Forgiveness wended its way seamlessly through his life. Nanny once ventured to instil a modicum of self-discipline, but his mother, Vanessa Calthorpe, née Curzon-Browne (always Browne with an 'E'), projected her through the tradesman's entrance into unemployment.

Rufus was dispatched to one of those prep schools where communing with trees was philosophically soul-enhancing, and then onward to a like-minded boarding school. At the latter he embraced the non-uniform policy with religious fervour. He also became an equally inflamed apostle of pissing into wicker waste paper baskets after lights out in the dorm'. Nary a spare thought emerged for the underpaid ancillary staff who mopped up after him and his acolytes. In fairness, Rufus' early exposure to trees and wickerwork bequeathed him his lifelong passion for carpentry, at which he was adept. His imitation of Christ's gift may have been unintentional, but when the *'Call'* came he saw it as a divine portent. Alf sometimes pondered if *'omen'* might have been the better choice of word.

Perhaps Rufus did undergo an existential moment. When he attained his mid-thirties, despite the toxic combination of booze guzzled and an entire pharmacy of drugs consumed, he had survived. He responded to his new vocation by leaving the band. Rufus Coleridge was the acclaimed lead guitarist in *'Flatulence'*, a stellar group specialising in Hi-NRG Dance Pop. High energy had been Rufus' schtick since he soiled his first nappy. It was whispered in senior circles that it remained vibrant in his current career, as an ordained minister in the Church of England. He was going places, according to *'The Guardian's'* sycophantic article, which granted him all glory laud and honour. Even Corbynites enjoy a celebrity vicar, as long as he (or she), is out of the right bag.

Rufus' decision to lead the baptismal service at All Souls appeared whimsical. Alf was qualified to undertake the sacred ceremony, and had done so on many an occasion. 'Roof', as he liked to be called, thought he should show his face in Temple Weston. It wasn't the largest parish in the Benefice, but was by far the wealthiest. Church and village housed numerous influential people. He would lead the service, but the graft of preparing a sermon devolved onto Alf.

"You lead, I'll follow…Roof'!"

"Fandabbydosey! Come on. Let's crack this gig."

"Give me a sec, I need a *'Jack McFlash'*."

"A what?"

"To micturate…take a leak…a slash!"

"Right on, bro'. I'll be outside."

Alf gathered his books and sermon, and stared at the ancient door. He couldn't contain himself, and murmured,

"You long-nosed ponce."

He closed his eyes, and stilled his breathing. Once more he heard himself speak.

"Oh well, I did promise to follow…until the end."

2

'Flatulent ducks.'

Temple Weston is east of Junction 15 of the M40. It lies midway between the motorway and the sizable village of Harbury. Most of the houses are grand, and of ancient mien. A chunk of social housing had been built behind the discreet shading of majestic oak trees. It stood like an ominous Native American encampment outside the stout fort. Benson Hargreave was responsible for that. The late and great Liverpool comedian Ken Dodd once remarked,

"You can always tell a Yorkshireman...but you can't tell him much!"

Ben Hargreave, or to grant him his full moniker Sir Benson Blackledge Hargreave, might have been the template for Doddy's ribald assertion. 'Beebie.', as he liked to be known, was in the rag trade. His principal shirt factory was on the outskirts of nearby Leamington Spa. He cast himself in the mould of the great 19th Century Yorkshireman Titus Salt, who was no mere manufacturer but also a philanthropist. He had built the village of Saltaire for his workers, and it stands to this day. Beebie wasn't prepared to go to quite the financial lengths of his hero, essentially because he was as tight as a duck's arse.

The Rector's Garden Party at St. Dunstan's, Mother Church of the Benefice in Dunsmore-by-Napton, had been an occasion to welcome Rufus Coleridge to his new Benefice. Beebie Hargreave held forth volubly. A parishioner whispered into Alfie Starkiss' ear,

"What's the definition of a Yorkshireman?"

"I give up."

"A Scotsman…without the generosity!"

Alfie was circumspect, and maintained a respectful silence. Lady Edwina 'Teddy' Bowcott, divorcee of that parish, was not to be stopped. Another arrow *'of outrageous fortune'*, whistled past Alfie's left ear.

"Your dear Churchwarden at Temple Weston Alf, may I call you Alf, or is it Alfred?"

"Alf or Alfie will be Jim Dandy."

Teddy was puzzled.

"Oh, *'Jim Dandy'*, I see."

She studied him, and Alfie felt uncomfortable, like a butterfly speared to a board.

"I think I prefer Alfie. Well, Alfie, as I was saying, when Benson Hargreave speaks, or should I say pontificate, he could power a hot air balloon for Richard Branson. Which, I conjecture, would be most appropriate, as *that* knight of the realm also prefers the sound of his own voice. I digress. Promises Alfie, promises. Your Churchwarden bears an uncanny resemblance to Satan tempting Christ in the Wilderness. He promises the earth, but exacts a price; his pound of flesh. Oh dear, am I mixing my metaphors, or just literary references? Have you visited Stratford-Upon-Avon yet? It's a cockstride across the other side of the M40. I'd be delighted to escort you around the sights."

"Cockstride! Goodness me Edwina."

"Teddy please, always Teddy to you."

Her fifty-three year old hand lingered on his arm.

"I was going to say, Teddy, that the last time I heard *'cockstride'* it came from the lips of my mother. She was from Manchester."

"My mother was one of the Fishers of Clitheroe. Do you know Clitheroe?"

"Indeed I do, Teddy. 'D. Byrne's'…"

"Oh, the wine merchant. Quite outstanding. You are a devotee of the grape?" He didn't get the opportunity to reply. "I relieved Bowcott of his wine cellar when we divorced." Her lip curled. "The least he could do for me. We must arrange a tasting." She scanned him once more. "I feel certain that you would enjoy my Grenache."

Alfie blinked, dismissing the notion that she had employed a euphemism.

"Tell me, Teddy, what sort of promises does Beebie make?"

"Oh, money for this, money for that. Some of it dribbles through, but the big bucks never materialise. He's a windbag."

Alfie's response was reflex, and accompanied by a laugh.

"I see. A case of, *'we've heard ducks fart before'*.

Teddy's roar brought him a sigh of relief. He was wondering if he had gone too far.

"Priceless my darling, absolutely priceless."

Beebie Hargreave was displeased by Teddy's raucous laughter. It took the attention of the new Rector away from him. To regain it he looked Rufus Coleridge in the eye, and declaimed loudly,

"I've a passion for shirts, but I draw the line at shirtlifters."

His howl of self-approbation was mimicked by one or two sycophants. Most of the company looked askance, and those in the know were embarrassed. Later, in the privacy of their drawing room, his wife informed him of Rufus Coleridge's sexual preference.

"How the hell was I to know, Freddie, I leave all that arty-farty stuff to you. Anyway, no harm done, I expect the bugger has a sense of humour."

Frederika 'Freddie' Hargreave showed him her back, whilst pouring another Tia Maria. She had long since misplaced her sense of humour. Freddie was an intelligent and well-informed patron of the arts, and the recent *'Hamlet'* she had seen in Stratford rose to the forefront of her mind.

"I have of late – but wherefore I know not –lost all my mirth..."

Prince of Denmark! Mollycoddled little sod. He'd know what suicidal thoughts were if he had to live alongside the philistine and heathen she had married.

The garden party was winding up.

"Your home is *'The Manor'* isn't Teddy?"

"Been in the Bowcott family since the 1470's, somewhat modified these days. Of course, it came with far more land than I now possess.

The estate was granted to Rufus Bowcott when he was knighted by Richard III for services rendered. Typical Bowcott, choosing the wrong side."

"Rufus! Same as our new Rector."

"Oh yes, I hadn't clocked that."

"Clocked! Bit of Clitheroe still there, Teddy."

"Don't let my fragrant youth, and designer frocks fool you, Alfie. Some ladies of my station prefer to draw a veil over their origins. I couldn't be arsed."

She had assessed the man in front of her. He was down-to-earth, despite his dog collar.

"You can take the girl out of the North, but you can't take the North out of the girl, eh Teddy?"

Her unfettered laughter once more reverberated around the garden.

"Spot on your Reverence."

"Not yet."

"Pardon me?"

"I'm merely a curate. It's Rufus – Coleridge of that ilk, not Bowcott – who has risen to the dizzy heights in HS2 time."

"Well yes, naturally. The Church of England latches on to the fashionable with alacrity. They delude themselves into thinking that the young are naive."

She threw herself into acting mode.

"Oh look, a pop star turned vicar. I think I'll turn to Jesus. The root of our current problems lie with the Archbishop. He may have attended public school, but he has no 'bottom'."

Teddy linked Alfie's arm and drew him into the lee of the rhododendrons.

"What do you think of our new Rector?"

Alfie cast a carapace of caution about himself.

"Rufus and I trained together, and were ordained at the same time." He told a white lie. "We were good friends throughout the three years of study."

They had, in reality, been friendly acquaintances, but no more. Teddy's non sequitur took him by surprise.

"It's about time *The Manor* took a hand in church affairs once more."

She flashed him an angelic smile from beneath the war paint.

"I'd be ever so grateful if you could squeeze me on to the PCC."

Teddy peered into the distance, letting her eyes settle upon Rufus Coleridge.

"I do believe we might be living in exciting times, Alfie."

Her attention returned to Rufus, and she giggled.

"I shall call him Sister Wendy!"

Alfie clocked the reference immediately. His lower lip quivered in amusement, as a vision of the toothy television nun from days of yore floated past the greenhouse.

3

'All my eye and Betty Martin?'

"Do you turn away from sin?"

"I do."

"Do you reject all evil?"

"I do."

"Do you turn to Christ as Saviour?"

"I do."

The mobile 'phones clicked with frantic regularity. It was a photo opportunity around the font. When Alfie led baptism services he asked family and friends to refrain from photography until the ceremony was complete.

Alongside Holy Communion and the Marriage service, Baptism is a sacred act. Anyone can take a funeral service (not in church), but only ordained ministers can 'hatch' and 'match'. The Eucharist has a slight variation. Licensed Lay ministers can give *'Communion by Extension'*, if an ordained priest is unavailable and has blessed the Host.

Even so, the words are rendered in an alternative format.

Sorrow rippled in Alfie's breast. Parents and godparents affirming their rejection of evil, and acknowledging Jesus in their lives. He tried to refrain from silent judgement. None of us knows the secrets of another's heart. Clergy understand only too well that regular congregations are what might, euphemistically, be called 'compact'. The extra forty or fifty who pile in for a Baptism are Sherlock Holmes' *'Baker Street Irregulars'*, with a twist. The Meerschaum-piped detective called upon London's street urchins to ferret out information in the pursuit and defeat of evil. In the 21st Century the majority of the public clamour for the services of the Church when an atavistic urge nudges them in the solar plexus. Sloppy sentimentality propels them into an ignored building. Their self-imposed entrapment in the cell of religion exposes them, for a short while, to thoughts of good and evil that might discomfort them; if they can be bothered to listen. Births, marriages and deaths…hatch, match and dispatch…then on to the highlight of the day…a good piss up.

Rufus Coleridge recited,

"This is the faith of the Church."

Alfie disguised a wince as a smile when the response was chanted.

"This is our faith.

We believe and trust in one God,

Father, Son and Holy Spirit."

Rufus concluded proceedings around the font, allowing a further minute for additional photographs. A cocky wag shouted,

"Don't be shy Vicar, we want you in the pics as well. The star of the show."

Rufus did not correct the young woman in her theological blunder. Alfie made a mental note. He sought the inspiration of the Holy Spirit when he preached, and was confident that guidance would be forthcoming to enable him to explain who was the one and only centre of attention.

He trailed Rector, parents and baby along the central aisle of the Nave, standing to one side at the Crossing while Rufus made his closing remarks. Alfie watched the congregation. Excited eyes were glued to the minister. They were in the presence of a real life celebrity, and were awestruck. Unconsciously, he hummed the first verse of a hymn.

"Our God is an awesome God

He reigns from heaven above

With wisdom, power, and love

Our God is an awesome God."

An uncomfortable thought crept insidiously into his head. Was he jealous of Rufus Coleridge? He compared lives, and found himself wanting. Did he too want to be adored?

He was caught off-guard.

"Alfie…Alfie…"

He realised every eye in the house was on him, and Rufus was intoning his name.

The Rector chuckled,

"We must forgive my curate. He is no doubt occupied by listening for the voice that will lead him through his peroration. We await your pearls of wisdom, Alfie."

The congregation laughed while Alfie collected his notes and stepped forwards. His swept the Nave with a look of authority, and the noise dissipated into silence. He digested a proliferation of fake-tanned summer legs, extending below the short frocks of young women, complemented by ill-chosen orange/brown shoes on the feet of young men. They clashed with the shiny blue of their regulation too tight suits. Footwear christened in northern climes as, *'a pair of shagging shoes'*.

A slight murmur arose when the notification of text messages bleeped twice from different parts of the church.

"May the words of my mouth, and the meditations of all our hearts, be acceptable in your sight. O God, our strength and our Redeemer.

Rufus spoke the truth. Any wisdom imparted will come straight from our Father. We priests are only his agents; occasionally James Bond, more often Johnny English."

Appreciative laughter swirled around the Nave, and the atmosphere relaxed. They had recognised the reference to Rowan Atkinson's portrayal of the dim-witted English spy. Self-deprecation is a reliable weapon for disarming potential adversaries.

"May I also welcome Shania, Courtney, Kylie, Lou-Lou into the Christian family. We at All Souls will always be here for her, and her family, as she follows in the footsteps of her Saviour, Jesus Christ."

Talk about putting a damper on proceedings. The collective sinking into lethargy was almost audible. Alfie girded his loins, and positively exuded energy. He cast a look over his shoulder at Roof, who was slumped in his seat. A wicked thought arose. Perhaps he had tapped into his Rector's fabled grid, and drained him.

"Further congratulations are in order. Our reading, from Luke's Gospel, was beautifully delivered by Freddie Hargreave."

He caught her eye, and she smiled modestly. Looking up from his notes he saw Teddy Bowcott beaming at him. She projected an outrageous wink in his direction. It encouraged him no end.

"Now I know that you were all giving Freddie your rapt attention when she recited Jesus' parable of the lost sheep that was found. What about that marvellous ending,

'…there will be more rejoicing in heaven over one sinner who repents than over ninety-nine righteous persons who do not need to repent.'

And Jesus Christ and His Father always keep their promises."

Inadvertently, his eyes rested upon Beebie Hargreave. The merest flicker of a smile passed across Alfie's features. The knight look uncomfortable, and stuck a finger inside his collar. The Yorkshireman didn't wear his own shirts, and once boasted that his came from Saville Row. Perhaps the prick of conscience had disturbed his repose.

"Did you know that Luke was a doctor?"

Two-thirds of the assembly looked at each other in bewilderment. Who was this Luke? There wasn't another baby due to be dunked in the font was there? Oh no, how much longer did they have to put up with this?

"Luke, as in he who wrote what Freddie read."

Alfie steadied himself. He was enjoying himself too much, and waltzing on the ice owned by the patronising.

"Seems rather appropriate to a baptism. Did you have good doctors and nurses at Shania's birth, Bianca?"

Under normal circumstances Bianca Bailey was never short of an opinion or two. In this formal public arena she became shy, so her husband piped up.

"They were 'Boss'."

"Thank you Kyle. Did you know that I am originally from Liverpool? 'Boss' is a term used widely in that fair city, meaning *'the best'.*"

He refrained from adding that it was normally employed for the purpose of self-aggrandisement, as in,

'We stayed in this Boss hotel.'

Meaning, *'We're better than you.'*

He couldn't resist temptation.

"I sincerely hope that when you went into labour, Bianca, you didn't have to go through a receptionist to arrange a telephone call back from the G.P."

The entire congregation rocked in their chairs. No part of the United Kingdom was untouched by the feeling that G.P.s had ducked and dived throughout the Covid Pandemic, and hidden away behind their telephones.

"I'm being very naughty, and my Rector will chastise me after the service."

Roof stirred in his majestic chair at the thought of chastisement in general.

"Our hospitals did a sterling job throughout the Pandemic, God bless them. They brought the lovely Shania safely into the world...but what sort of world do we want for her...what sort of world do we want for ourselves...?"

A mobile phone began to sing, and its owner shut it down rapidly. He was red-faced when everyone stared at him. Alfie recognised the song. It was Ian Dury and the Blockheads performing *'Plaistow Patricia'*. The owner of the 'phone had been slow off the mark. The first two words of the lyrics ping ponged off the church walls,

"Arseholes, bastards…"

"To create the world we want is to create the world God wants. It means medicating ourselves repeatedly. We need antibiotics that cure selfishness, and promote healthy consideration for others; we need vaccines that enable us to persevere, and overcome the sickness of evil doing. You may have heard of the *'Seven Deadly Sins'*: pride, greed, lust, envy, gluttony, wrath and sloth. They are the fearful viruses that infect every wrong we think, every wrong we speak, every wrong we commit. They are the diseases that whisper into our ears the dirtiest words known to mankind,

'You come first, and everyone else can go hang. You are the star.'

We need to cultivate self-control that enables us to think of others, as well as ourselves, and perseverance for the struggle to maintain that attitude. Others can help and support us on that journey to full health, but it is essentially an act of self-surgery. Then we heal, and that is our contribution to the renewal of our world. Renewal of ourselves, but also for Shania, and for all the Shania's and Shanes yet unborn. Mighty oaks from little acorns grow.

God gives you these thoughts to take away. You might, when today's celebrations are done, want to ask yourself,

'Am I that lost sheep, and do I want to be found?'

We hope to see you again. Whoever you are, whatever might happen in your lives, you are always welcome here at All Souls. You now know something of the way of Christ, the Prince of Peace; the brightest star in the firmament, and the only one worth worshipping. God bless Shania and her family; God bless you all."

Tension was palpable in the Vestry. Rufus changed rapidly, and picked up his case.

"For the foreseeable future Alfie, would you be kind enough to forward your sermons to me in advance of their delivery?"

"Is there a problem Rufus?"

The Rector was six feet three inches tall. He looked down his lengthy proboscis with a magisterial air.

"No, no, not a problem. Perhaps more the need for ongoing education. Whilst I, and the congregation, enjoyed the humour with which you leavened your sermon, I sensed that many of them were ill-at-ease with the force of your assertions."

"Did they discomfort you, Rufus?"

"Baptisms are such sensitive occasions. Most of those present have never seen the inside of a church. Surely you see that it is our responsibility to step lightly. We look to save souls, to recruit for Christ. Perhaps a gentler approach, a coaxing, is required if we are to see them enter through our doors again…"

"Matthew 7:7."

"Absolutely Alf! '…*knock and the door will be opened to you.*"

"Is it your view that soft soap and a load of old flannel will motivate the godless to even take hold of the door handle?"

"That's putting it a bit strong…"

"It's an outdated gambit…a play…the Church of England policy that's in tatters. We've been trying it for years and it's got us nowhere. The Holy Trinity doesn't vote Liberal Democrat; they don't put themselves forward as candidates for election, not even against the opposition of Satan. I…I…I…the best I can come up with to explain myself is to echo Martin Luther.

'Here I stand, I cannot do otherwise…'

And if it's not presumptuous, isn't that where God stands?"

The temperature had risen, and without thinking Rufus blurted out,

"He doesn't have to minister to a half empty church week after week!"

The moment it was out of his mouth he looked stricken.

"God forgive me for saying that."

Pity filled Alfie's heart. He wanted to ask, *'Are you tired of your vocation already, Rufus?'*, but held his tongue.

"May I share another verse from Matthew, Rufus?"

The big man was downcast, and heavy clouds filled his eyes, as he nodded.

"If anyone will not welcome you or listen to your words, shake the dust off your feet when you leave that home or town."

Rufus cast an enquiring look at him.

"All we can do Roof is offer, but doing it in an equivocal way just makes us look like Uriah Heap. The public is ignorant in so many ways, but that doesn't mean they're stupid. When we hum and hah – *'on the one hand, on the other hand'* –they see through us and lack all respect; not just for us, that's bearable, but for the Word, and that's intolerable."

Alfie wanted to leave it there, but thought it best not to part on poor terms. He smiled.

"I hesitate to mention that God-awful woman – no blasphemy intended – the Blessed Margaret T, but you know what they used to say about her?"

Rufus cocked his head to one side.

"I don't agree with her, and I don't like her, but at least she knows what she stands for."

Rufus stood like the Rock of Ages, and turned his thoughts inwards, before his energy returned.

"Glad we've had this conversation Alf. Forget what I said about future sermons, but do walk carefully. Any time you want to mull things over with me the door is open."

"Thank you, your offer is reciprocated."

"Right on, brother. Must dash. Got a friend at home waiting for his lunch."

Alfie clambered into his civvies, and tidied up the Vestry. He closed the door behind him. A few minutes prayer at the High Altar, for Roof and for himself; for their churches and for their parishes, full of pitiful lost souls.

He heard voices in the Nave, whilst he prayed. Probably the usual sightseers inspecting the monuments, and writing in the visitor's book,

"Beautiful church, and so peaceful." Ron and Doreen, Nether Wallop.

An apologetic cough made him turn his head. Bianca Bailey loomed above him; her swaying husband stood behind her.

"Sorry vicar, we forgot the Baptism Certificate," she waved the document, "it was on that table. Special day."

Kyle started to whine.

"Come on Bianca, we've wasted enough time 'ere."

Alfie rose.

"You consider it a waste of time, Kyle?"

Husband and proud father was already well oiled. The words exploded angrily from his mouth.

"You...you...you talk a load of bollocks."

Alfie looked at him with compassion.

"You know Kyle, sometimes I think you may be right."

Bianca grabbed Kyle by the arm.

"Come on, everyone's waiting for us to cut the cake, and you're supposed to make a speech. Keep it clean."

She led him through the Chancel. Looking over her shoulder she mouthed,

"Sorry!"

Alfie watched them disappear, and then the superb acoustics of the church picked up his words.

"So am I Bianca, so am I."

4

'Get out of my road.'

"Good!"

Never was the word used more inappropriately. Well, that's a mite hyperbolic, given the substantial list of ne'er do wells, reprobates and evil sods who have contributed to the history and misery of the world. Nonetheless, Beebie Hargreave deserved his place on the Roll of Dishonour.

Microwaves of concealed disdain generated heat in a product lower down the food chain, who Beebie had bought up and gnawed on with regularity. Kyle Bailey knew what his boss thought of him, but suppressed his genetic disposition towards anger in favour of the backhanders he received.

"Good boss? Your foreman's trying to start a union in the factory, and that's good?"

"Jack Corrigan's got problems of his own with that lad of his. If I'm not much mistaken he'll up before the Bench soon, and I sit on that Bench, as you well know Kyle."

He grinned as he spoke his next words.

"Don't you fret lad. If Jack has to go I've you in mind to step up from Charge hand."

"Thank you Mr. Hargreave…"

"Sir, lad, Sir. I was knighted by Wales himself. Would have preferred Her Majesty, but *'number one picaninny bilong Mrs. Queen'* sufficed."

Kyle managed to work out the reference to 'Wales'. Papua New Guinea was off his radar, as was the fact that when Prince Charles had visited the country he had introduced himself in Pidgin English as,

"Nambawan pikinini bilong misis kwin."

Of which, Beebie had given a rough translation.

"Titles are important, young man. You'd not want to be called Chargehand if you were Foreman, would you Kyle. Who knows, one day it might be Sir Kyle Bailey."

Kyle kept his trap shut, and simmered. No need to take the piss.

"Right young man. I'm paying you extra brass to keep your eyes skinned on what's going on in the factory, and what's brewing on the estate. I didn't build those houses out of the goodness of my heart. You've done well…so far. Don't bollocks it up. There's plenty of others short of cash in hand."

"Not you, you tight-fisted Tyke," Kyle thought…and he didn't care for being called *'young man'*. It reminded him of that old football manager his dad went on about. Who was it? Oh yes, Brian Clough. Patronising, pompous git was his old feller's trenchant view of the former Derby County manager.

"Yes sir, I'll remember."

"Righto, to recapitulate your mission Mr. Spock…"

Kyle got that one, and was rather pleased.

"Who's getting into debt, who's knocking off whose missus, whose kids are causing grief, and who's rocking the boat generally. Got it?"

"Got it Skipper, er sir."

Beebie's belly shook like a jelly on springs.

"Nice one, young man; humour with deference. You'll do. Off you trot. Oh Kyle, didn't know you and your missus were members of the God Squad."

The current lesser foreman had a gormless look on his face.

"You were in All Souls on Sunday for the child's baptism. By, she's a lovely looking little lass. Takes after her mother does she? You've a handsome missus there, young man."

Beebie leafed through a file on his desk.

"Nobody pays much attention to what the Church has to say these days, but it's wise to keep right side of all the Establishment…can't say telling one of them he's talking bollocks falls into that category! Close your mouth lad, you'll be catching flies."

The file slammed onto the desk with a resounding slap.

"We live in a small community lad. If you're to be of any use to me I don't need you shaking the maritime vessel with anyone. *Capisce?*"

Kyle didn't speak Italian, never mind the pseudo-variety, but Beebie's meaning was clear.

"Yes sir."

"Here lad, something to wet the baby's head."

"Thank you, sir." He thrust the twenty-pound note into his overalls.

"Off you trot."

When the door closed they simultaneously exclaimed,

"Dickhead!"

Hargreave pressed a button.

"That reminds me, Maggie…"

"What does, Sir Ben?"

"Never mind. Get Jack Corrigan up here, pronto love."

He asked himself why he employed Corrigan. The answer was simple. He was good at keeping the workforce in order, but that force of personality of his could work against Beebie. Bloody Scousers. There was no love lost between a citizen of Leeds and a Liverpool bucko.

Kyle gnawed away at it all day. Who had opened their mouth about his abusive remark to that vicar? Could only have been the vicar himself…oh hang on a minute. He'd hardly crossed the threshold before he started on Bianca.

"'ave you been opening your big gob?"

"What?"

"It was you, wasn't it?"

"What the frig are you on about?"

"You know, what I said to that vicar, wotsisname?"

"Oh 'im. His name's Alfie Starkiss. Funny name 'i'nt it? I like it, I think it's all lovey dovey."

"Fancy 'im do you?"

"Don't be so friggin' daft, an' stop shoutin'. I've only just put baby down."

"Did you tell anyone what I said to 'im?"

"Who?"

"Alfie bleedin' Starpiss, you dozy bitch."

"Eh you, I'm not friggin' dozy. I'm not the one who shouts bollocks in church."

"So you have been mouthin' off."

"I might have mentioned it to Marie Corrigan at baby's party. What's it matter?"

"To her of all people. You've dropped me in the shit with the gaffer. Somehow it's got back to him, and he's not chuffed. Do you know how much extra he gives me for being his man on the ground?"

Kyle regarded himself as a bit of a *'Jack Reacher'*; Tom Cruise by proxy.

"Eh, hang on a minute. Is that old Yorkshire bugger playing both ends against the middle. Says he's got me in mind for Foreman…"

"Oh Kyle, that's brill…"

"Shut the fuck up! He could be keeping me sweet to do his dirty work, and he's got Jack Corrigan watching me. The sly Yorkshire bastard."

Bianca sidled up to him, and clasped him in her arms.

"I am sorry, Kyle bab, but there's one bit of good come out of it."

"What?"

"At least you know about Corrigan. Eh, I tell you what, I'll keep my eye on Marie. Agents together. Mata Hari and Jack Reacher."

"Who's she when she's at home?"

"Famous woman spy, yonks ago. Tell you what, she was a dirty cow, an' all."

Bianca dropped to the kitchen floor. Kyle stood erect, with his overalls round his ankles. His mind was in two places at once. Latin and the name of the Roman satirist Juvenal were not familiar subjects on his curriculum, but instinctively he asked himself,

"*Quis custodiet ipsos custodes?* Who guards the guards?"

Self-satisfied moron. Lady Freddie Hargreave peered at her husband, seated at the far end of the dining table. He was shovelling food into his mouth like a gravity feed hopper. In public he behaved himself, but as soon as they entered the privacy of their home his inherited traits leapt at you like a *'Jack-in-the-Box'*. Hargreave, as her scorn insisted she called him, went on like a bloody toothache about his working class origins. His second favourite boast was,

"I went to the University of Life."

The gold medal was reserved for,

"…and studied in the School of Hard Knocks."

What she learnt, over the course of their marriage, was that he was the one who administered hard knocks to others. The only institution he should be going to was prison…for life! She did not pass draconian judgement upon her husband because he was financially corrupt, because he wasn't. He sailed close to the wind, but was too canny to step across the line. No, it was his moral corruption that appalled her. Beebie Hargreave epitomised the age; rampant selfish individualism, which had already torn the fabric of civilised society to an alarming degree.

Freddie sat on numerous committees, but the one that disturbed her most was as a school governor at the local Primary. The head teacher was a waste of space. She recalled an argument with her at the last meeting.

"The children are never in the classroom. You have them outdoors at the drop of a hat. Physical education periods are appropriate, but there seem to be an endless array of projects that require sitting on the grass scribbling and drawing in their books, with their handwriting going to pot. This is not good training for adulthood."

Lucinda Patterson's patronising smile smothered Freddie.

"Perhaps you are unfamiliar with modern methods, Lady Freddie?"

Freddie had long since asked everyone to drop the title when addressing her. However, the headmistress was of that upper working class ilk who can't resist reminding themselves that they are on terms with the *'aristocracy'*. Freddie shared her contempt for the woman with Beebie.

"She reminds me of that police inspector in *'Bleak House'*. However many times he's told not to he keeps bowing and scraping and repeatedly calls his host SIR Leicester Dedlock BARONET! Ludicrous."

"Bleak who Freddie?"

"House, Hargreave."

She studied his bovine, nonplussed features, and sighed.

"Dickens my own, Charles Dickens!"

"Oh aye, Oliver bloody Twist. In my opinion the child got everything he deserved."

"You've read a book? You astound me Hargreave."

"Noooo, don't be so bloody daft. Do you not remember? You made me go to see that nephew of yours in the school play…years ago. They were doing *'Oliver'*, and I mean doing…to death. Worst two hours of my life. I don't know what you see in these theatricals. Bunch of slippery *'Backstairs Billy's'* if you ask me. Bloody Shakespeare."

"What do you mean by that?"

"Well I ask you. He nivver uses one word where forty-six'll do. Needs a bloody editor. As for that Romeo and Juliet, they should do what their parents tell them. If I'd been their father I'd have given him a backhander, and her a smacked arse. Mind yer, I did enjoy that *'Tit-us Androneekus'*. He's the lad for me. Didn't let no-one stand in his road. Was he Greek?"

She noted the lapse into bits of dialect, and his Yorkshire accent becoming more pronounced. Par for the course when over-excited. No, he was about as working class as the characters in *'Eastenders',* pulling a fast one on the public. Marx's lumpen proletariat, the lot of them. Freddie was a Labour voting middle class girl from Leeds, who had worked hard and studied PPE at Warwick University. She knew her onions, and the one that made her eyes water most was Marxism. Under their rod if you wouldn't work, or thieved, it was straight into the camps; that's what they did with the underclass. Freddie gave Beebie the once over. She had no doubt he would have survived their inhumane treatment; there's always a call for informers.

She had lost her appetite.

"Are you not eating that dessert? Skop it down this end of the table."

She hoped that her utter contempt was apparent, as she shot the dish along the polished surface in his direction.

"Bloody good shot, my love. You should be in the Scottish Curling team."

"You seem to be in an especially good mood this evening, my own."

His dark eyes shone with predatory intent, beneath bushy eyebrows and a low forehead.

"Not bad, not bad."

She knew that all she had to do was wait. Benson kept his business cards close to his chest, but everyone needs to offload, and his wife was his confessor.

"Incipient trouble at the factory...have I used that word right?"

He surprised her at times. Hargreave possessed a penchant for picking up useful information. She nodded her approval.

"Jack bloody Corrigan trying his union antics again. If I let them start one in this factory they'll want one in the other three. I had him in the office. Said nowt about unions, or any other business. Gave him a bit of fatherly advice, like."

He gulped mounds of trifle down like it was going out of fashion. Freddie collapsed inwardly. Where was he in the world? Their son Mark. It was so-called fatherly advice that had driven him out of the home. Four years of university, and never to return or communicate. Hargreave's voice shattered her reverie.

"That lad of his…"

"Who's?"

"Jack Corrigan. Are you listening to me?"

"What about the boy?"

"Right bloody tearaway, and he's only fourteen. I had to advise Jack that the lad could be heading for a court appearance, and I didn't want to have to pass sentence on him, and…"

A lump of trifle wobbled on his spoon and they froze, gripped in anticipation. Avalanche to the table top. Despite her disgust, Freddie pressed him.

"And what?"

"Oh aye, I had to remind Jack, sadly, that under the very generous terms of my tenancy agreement with the residents of the *'Sir Benson Hargreave Estate'*, it could lead to them losing the house."

"How did he respond?"

"Silence of the Lambs!"

"That's a film, Hargreave. Do you mean silent as a lamb?"

"Indeed I do my own. What would I do without you? Would you bloody Adam and Eve it, a Scouser lost for words. Quite a red letter day. Then…"

He scooped up a blob of trifle from the table with his middle finger and sucked on it.

"Hargreave, this is not a thriller with cliff-hangers. Though if you don't come to the point it may turn into a murder."

"Just saving the best bit for last. You know I've got my Chargehand on a leash…"

"Remind me."

"The Bailey lad, Kyle Bailey. Him and his missus had the babby christened last Sunday."

"Shania Courtney Kylie Lou-Lou!"

"You've a good memory my love." A grin came over his fizzog. "Nice names."

"Hargreave!"

She saw the naughty schoolboy look, and couldn't help bursting into laughter with him.

"You are wicked at times, my own."

"Let me finish my tale. I felt it my duty to inform Jack Corrigan of the rumour doing the rounds, that Kyle Bailey is leading his lad astray. I may have implied something about *'county lines'*. Can't quite recall."

Freddie was more shocked than usual. Enticing children to carry drugs across county lines was not a gambit for businessmen to play with.

"I've got the pair of buggers where I want them. At each other's throats, and I don't even have to pay Jack Corrigan a penny. Nothing like a bit of rivalry to keep folk on their toes."

She was singularly unamused, and poured a third glass of wine. His oleaginous voice oozed down the table, and she knew what was coming.

"I was wondering, my love, would it be possible for me to pay a visit to your room tonight?"

They had slept in separate bedrooms for the last two years. Principally, out of convenience. She drained her glass.

"Apologies dearest. I have an appointment with my gynaecologist in the morning."

"Still troubling you, is it?"

"Improving, but not quite there."

An awkward silence weighed upon them. Beebie couldn't bear it, and he was tempted to joke,

"Not going to the dentist are you?"

He knew it would not go down well, so to speak. Always wise to keep in with the Establishment.

5

'Bob's your uncle, Fanny's your aunt, and Dick's your best friend!'

The Maybird Shopping Park in Stratford-Upon-Avon is a boon to motorists. It's provides free parking on its vast site, and is only a short walk from the town centre. Stratford is blanketed in machines for liberating you from your money, for the privilege of parking closer to the shops and theatre. Plus, the council appears to employ more traffic wardens than the East German Stasi had informers.

Rufus didn't want to risk getting a ticket. His trips to Stratford would end up on record. If the press found out they would pursue him like a rat up a drainpipe. He wished he'd never joined *'Flatulence'*, it would follow him throughout his life. He discovered that if he parked at the far reach, where *'Asda Living'* is located, the boring part of his walk would be short. You could hop a few hundred metres and, between the Premier Inn and the out-of-town McDonalds, descend onto the towpath of the Stratford-Upon-Avon Canal and head towards Wilmcote.

It was pleasant to stroll by the water on late-August evenings, indeed at any time of the year. Narrow boats queued to pass through the flight of Wilmcote locks. Rufus perched on the grass for a while, watching families celebrate life together; the children eager to help mum and dad with the lock gates. He smiled at the sight of retired couples sharing responsibilities without regard for gender. Women steered the craft into the locks, while hubbies applied the winding handle to the rack and pinion mechanism, and vice-versa. The click-clack sound varied according to the patience or impatience of the operative. Sometimes a steady and measured beat, and occasionally frantic, as someone went at it with a will. Rufus preferred the former; he'd had enough of the latter.

Beyond the locks, and still short of Wilmcote, there is a bridge. It was here that he went for his encounters. A little conversation with fellow walkers, most of whom moved on with a cheery 'Bye', and then longer congress with a man who was keen to linger. They would part with a nod, after a short period together in a nearby declivity smothered by trees in leaf.

Rufus would always finish his walk to Wilmcote. He would go as far as the gateway to *'Mary Arden's Farm'*; the homestead of Shakespeare's mother. Without fail the same thought recurred,

"Did you ever regret leaving this place for London, Will Shakespeare? Wasn't there love enough for you here?"

Later, he stood by the river's edge on Waterside, the bustling town behind him. To his right the Royal Shakespeare Theatre loomed. Shielding his eyes with his hand, to mute the vivid light playing hopscotch on the river, he looked intently at the spire of Holy Trinity Church; Shakespeare's burial ground. Rufus wouldn't have minded being the vicar of what was reputed to be the most visited parish church in the world. A few more bells and smells than the low-church habit worn by the congregation of his parish; St. Dunstan's in Dunsmore-by-Napton. He would revel in leading a full and thriving church, but it's difficult to get a job in a museum.

He cast the desire away with a *"Get thee behind me Satan!"*

Rufus looked at his watch. Oh heck, he was due at Teddy Bowcott's in an hour. The car was on the other side of town. His long legs ate up Sheep Street, galloped along Ely Street, and soon he was in Rother Street; halfway there. An ambulance clattered by as he negotiated Arden Street, and he said an involuntary blessing upon its occupants. Five more minutes and he was starting the engine. A right at the roundabout would take him to the A46, the quickest route, but he wanted time to think. Left took him parallel to the town centre, and along to the Warwick Road. A pleasant drive up to the M40.

He knew why he'd abandoned his music career, despite the benefits of stardom. It was Ronnie. They met on Hampstead Heath.

"No pun intended, Roof, but you lot ain't 'alf up your own arses."

"I beg your pardon?"

"You're all so *'look at me'*. Do you know, when we were doing the business just now you were too busy looking at yourself to give me a second thought. You could give Mick Jagger a run for *'Preening Ponce of the Year'*.

Rufus told him to 'F' off, and strode away in a huff. Ronnie's parting shot cut him to the quick,

"Try loving others, and not just yourself."

It shook his complacency.

Not long afterwards he attended his mother's marriage ceremony. If at first you don't succeed, try, try again. It was her third go. The classic 1 Corinthians 13 had been selected for the reading. When he heard,

"If I speak in the tongues of men and of angels, but have not love, I am only a resounding gong or a clanging cymbal…"

he started to weep openly. Everyone nudged each other, and whispered,

"Ah, isn't he sweet. He must really love his mum."

Rufus did love his mother, and she worshipped him; it was none of that Oedipal shit. He had seen enough of that at public school, with friends and enemies alike. Ferocious mothers, who lived their lives through their sons. The wedding was an epiphany for Rufus. He no longer wished to be mothered and smothered, ingrained with the notion that he was the best thing since sliced bread. At the reception he took his first tentative steps towards ministry; a quiet chat with a very surprised vicar.

The car climbed the hill. Round the bend was the garden centre, with the speed trap just beyond.

The Church didn't make a song and dance about his sexuality. It was, of course, explored in depth. They even made it clear that if he should wish to enter into a civil partnership, should such a loving relationship occur, it was unlikely that there would be any difficulty. The celibacy rule would, however, remain in place.

A loving relationship? No, just ships that pass in the night. Why? Why? He looked to right and left. This was the Heart of England; he loved it, and he loved the people. Why couldn't someone love him?

Alfie Starkiss came to mind, and a wan smile crossed his features fleetingly. They'd been on nodding terms throughout theological college. He hadn't any sexual aspirations towards Alfie, but he would have liked to have him as a friend. Sadly, he felt that his curate was repelled by him; nothing to do with his sexuality, but more woundingly his character. He wondered if the Bishop had been right to move Alfie from St. Dunstan's when he had been appointed to take over from the retiring Rector. Probably right, odds were it would have only been a matter of time before their relationship reached a crisis point, if they were sharing the 'shop' together.

The lights were on red at the M40 roundabout. He turned on the radio. The Communards began to sing,

"Don't leave me this way..."

Rufus' tears blinded him.

"Are you sure you won't come, my dear?"

"I'm so awfully sorry to leave you on your own, Hargreave, but my gynaecologist was firm on the matter; rest until tomorrow. It was a rather harrowing examination."

"Aye, well, I'll get gone."

He took his pocket watch out of his waistcoat.

"Just right, I shall be fashionably late. Teddy'll appreciate my grasp of social niceties. I'll tell you something for nothing, Freddie. Wouldn't it be grand to live at *'The Manor'*?"

She was distracted by her magazine.

"I'm sure she will, my own...oh, Hargreave."

"Yes my love?"

"Do be careful what you say in front of the Rector."

His eyebrows knitted.

"I told you, how was I to know that he's as queer as four-speed walking stick?"

"Perhaps if you were a little more *au fait* with matters of an artistic bent you would be better informed."

"I'm not bent about nowt. Don't wait up."

The door shut forcefully.

"That'll be the day," she said to herself, and wondered if he'd heard of Buddy Holly. Had Hargreave ever been young?

Freddie skipped a fandango down the stairs. A Mojito was critical to her well-being. She laughed noisily. Gynaecologist indeed, her husband would swallow anything she told him. The only person in this household in need of uterine expertise was him – the twot!

She settled herself on the sofa, drink in hand and telephone in the other. Freddie was overcome by anxiety. She had spent an hour in the office of a private detective, hired two months previously.

"My son, I want my son," she said to her glass.

They assured her that progress had been made. In fact, they promised her that a telephone call was imminent. The odds were that it would give them a result. She was advised to stand by her telephone this very evening.

Unlike the umbilical cord between Rufus and his mother, Freddie and Mark enjoyed a more emotionally stable relationship in his childhood. If required, he received a good, if compassionate, telling off, and any resentment passed swiftly, as it does with most children. She loved him dearly, but not at the expense of his father. Her disenchantment with Hargreave grew exponentially as the remorseless years advanced, because of his insensitive and coarse behaviour. The person you see throughout the courtship ritual is not the one revealed in marriage.

Freddie's first inkling of *'Mr. Hyde'* came at the end of their honeymoon. The sex was not bad. The night before flying home from Mauritius they had gone at it like knives, as he rather inelegantly put it afterwards. When he ejaculated he shouted over her shoulder that crass and vulgar expression. It was doubly offensive. She had an uncle named Robert and an ex-boyfriend called Richard, who she certainly wasn't best friends with.

Whilst doing a jig with the cocktail shaker she mulled over the merits and demerits of sex. She wasn't averse to it, but not with Hargreave. Oh, he treated her well enough. He'd even been pleased when she told him about her new job, as secretary and administrator to Rufus Coleridge.

"Can't say I'd normally approve of my missus going out to work, but under the circumstances I think you've made a good choice. There's a certain...what do you call it...social...social something attached to assisting a cleric of his station."

"Cachet, social cachet, my own. Is that what you were thinking of?"

She took a test sip of the freshly made Mojito. Yes, she wouldn't mind a little affair of the heart with someone. She wondered who. Certainly not Rufus Coleridge, the stall would never open for that prospective mount..

"Alfie Starkiss!"

She startled herself by exclaiming his name aloud. Mmm? What was he, maybe thirty-seven. Not classically handsome, but there was something about him. He emanated an aura of danger. A frisson of excitement tingled in her dormant regions. She wished she had gone to Teddy's drinks party; he was going to be there and she could have assessed his merits. Mind you, she suspected that Teddy might provide competition. She sighed. It would be nice to be cuddled, nice to be loved.

The telephone rang, and her heart throbbed.

"Yes? I see, yes…and you've spoken to him…he will. Telephone or face to face?"

She heard friendly laughter at the end of the line, and was thrilled when the voice said, *'face to face'*.

"Where? I'll travel to the ends of the earth if necessary."

Gentle laughter burbled again.

"Banbury! He lives in Banbury, but that's barely forty minutes away. Thank you, oh thank you so much Mr. Gorst."

The telephone remained in her hand, but she put down her glass.

"My son, my darling Mark. I'm going to see my son."

She wept tears of joy, and walked to the kitchen. The contents of the cocktail shaker gurgled down the plughole. Kettle in hand, she looked rather quizzical. What on earth did Hargreave mean,

"Wouldn't it be grand to live at the Manor?"

The source for her tears this time was uncontrollable laughter. Surely he didn't have designs on Teddy Bowcott?

The unfortunate recipient of Alfie's ire was Paddy McGuiness, presenter of *'A Question of Sport'*.

"BirmingUM! Commonwealth Games in BirmingUM. It's BirmingHAM, you Mancunian halfwit!"

Frightful use of the English language, written or spoken, was something against which he fulminated with tedious regularity. Fortunately for others the static clouds of ennui hovered over him alone; he lived a solitary life.

Why, oh why, oh why, he grumbled. Whatever happened to aspiration, bettering oneself through endeavour and the cultivation of your gifts and talents. It had been the bedrock of his working class existence in Liverpool. Unsettling memories clung to him about his father, but he was eternally grateful for the encouragement and discipline he received.

"You don't want to end up doing manual labour like me, son. Pay attention at school, do the best you can, and you'll stand a chance of having an easier life."

He turned to God.

"Fifty pounds, Lord, to your favourite charity, if McGuiness' school reports are anywhere near as good as mine."

He knew God didn't have favourite charities; he was Charity – Love.

Yet McGuiness had made good, and it pulled him up short. Was he wrong? No! Nowadays you were rewarded for being cocky, and having a loud mouth…or for relentless mockery of others. Wear clothes a peacock would be ashamed to be seen in, and plaster yourself in tattoos, and you were one of life's winners. If you could become the sensei of sexual innuendo, or even plain filth, you were sure to be a hit on television. That's why he mostly watched programmes on the iPlayer, otherwise he would have been in a permanent rage.

Alfie looked out of the window, and his hand rested on the table. Fingertips brushed the telephone, explaining the trigger for his outburst; there was always a trigger. His ex-wife had called. As per usual, it was about money. She received her due every month without failure. Alfie would have regarded it as moral and practical dereliction of duty not to support her and his son Luke. More, she always wanted more; she had always wanted and expected more. Debbie never understood why he gave up his teaching career to become a clergyman. Money was the principal motive for her grievance, but her contempt for religion didn't lag far behind.

He tried to preserve their marriage, perhaps even their love, with a painstaking explanation.

"Schools are just dreadful, Debs. The children are constantly pandered to, and they see it as their right. The handful that rise above it do so because they've got good parents behind them with traditional values. Most don't want to learn; they want to be entertained. I loved the job when I started, but it's become a millstone round my neck. If I don't get out now it will turn to hatred. I can't bear the thought of that."

"Okay, okay, I can sort of get that, you always were a bit antwackie when it came to modern teaching methods, but why a bloody vicar? Don't think I'm going to spend my life serving teas in the vicarage garden, and waiting on others."

That's when he realised that he had stopped loving her, because he was called to serve others. He gave her a medley of loosely connected ideas and events; childhood church, a few Christian colleagues and their influence upon him. Most of all attempting to articulate to her how teaching had engendered pity in him.

"They're pitiful Debs."

"Charming way for a Christian to speak."

"I don't mean it like that…"

"Your father did."

She was absolutely right. His Dad nursed a bellyful of disdain to hide the disappointment in himself. Almost everyone and everything was pitiful. It was a word he used until the end of his life, and always to condemn.

"I mean it in a purer sense. People are so adrift that they're drowning themselves and each other, trying to grasp for meaning in falsehoods and fripperies. They deserve all the pity we can give them, and the help that goes with it. You claim to be a Socialist so…"

"Yes, but not a Christian Socialist. Utter waste of time."

So that was that. She was gone before he was accepted for training, taking his beloved Luke who he missed dreadfully. If Debs' absence bothered him at all it was in the evenings. He once ran into Tony, his best mate at school. They swapped stories. Tony turned out to be well-travelled, and single.

"It's great in the daytime Alf, but come eight o' clock you sit alone in a restaurant with loads of couples and families around you, and you feel...I don't know what."

"Lost, bereft?"

"They'll do for starters, and not very appetising ones."

The clock chimed in the hallway.

"But not tonight. Thank you, Teddy Bowcott, I shall enjoy your company, and your wine."

He strolled through the village, toward the Manor, exchanging pleasantries with parishioners and neighbours alike. The couple up from London, for rest and recuperation in their weekend cottage, jogged past together. A brilliant smile from the stunning young lady lit up his evening, and when she waved to him over her shoulder he almost levitated. Alfie became preoccupied with her tight *'buns'* in lycra sparring with each other. Every step she took bounced them into the distance. He approached the Bowcott residence, and spoke quietly under his breath.

"Wonder what the talent will be like tonight."

Clergymen and women are human, believe it or not.

6

'Who do you think I am, Croesus?'

"Old Clarence still going strong, I hear. What is he now, in his eighties?"

"Eighty-three Chad, and strong as the proverbial ox."

"Marvellous. He keeps your grounds a picture Teddy."

The hostess accepted the compliment with grace, and gave due deference to Clarence, her gardener. Rufus echoed the sentiment of Sir Chaddesley Corbett, High Sheriff of Warwickshire. Benson Hargreave bobbed on the spot, not quite knowing how to make small talk. Teddy took the initiative.

"You know that Benson is a native of Yorkshire, Chad?"

"Are you indeed. Which bit?"

"Leeds, just outside Leeds, Chad."

Only Teddy noticed the imperceptible stiffening. Harrow, Cambridge, the Guards, and innate breeding had trained Chaddesley in good form. He was Chad to his friends, not to first-time acquaintances.

"Don't suppose you know North Yorkshire all that well?"

"I've done business in York quite frequently."

"Fine city. What about Richmond? Yorkshire that is, not London. Don't expect you're that fond of *soft southerners*, eh Benson."

Rufus caught Teddy's eye, and their mouths shaped a simultaneous 'Ouch!'.

"Are you a Hargreave of Roundhay, Benson. You must know Bobby and Madge Flexington. Their estate is on the outskirts of Richmond, but they have strong charitable associations with Leeds."

Benson squirmed, but had commonsense enough to get himself out of a hole. He knew of the Flexingtons. They had been his parents' landlord, owning the whole terraced row where he had been brought up in Normanton; nearer Wakefield than Leeds.

"Their names are familiar to me Sir Chaddesley. I believe the Earl and his Lady are great benefactors throughout Yorkshire."

"No need for formality. Chaddesley will suffice."

Corbett eyeballed Hargreave.

"You know, old Bobby Flexington is the most avid collector of sayings. Last time we dined at the club he had us in fits with his latest.

'Everyone's queer except thee and me…'

He clapped a hand on Benson's shoulder.

'…an' I'm not too sure about thee!'"

Benson managed a strangled laugh through gritted teeth. Rufus unintentionally set the cat amongst the pigeons.

"A corruption of the original, if I'm not much mistaken."

He accepted their enquiring looks as encouragement to continue.

"All the world is queer save thee and me, and even thou art a little queer."

They looked none the wiser.

Rufus added, "Robert Owen, champion of the working class, and foremost in the development of cooperatives and trade unions."

"Of course, Rufus, thought it rang a bell. Didn't he subscribe to Utopian Socialism?"

Benson's banger had been lit, and it exploded.

"Socialism! Dead as a duck in water. Was always meant to be a hand up, not a hand out."

"Benson has a point."

Four heads swivelled, and discovered Alfie Starkiss port side.

"Sorry to creep up on you. Was admiring your blooms Teddy when I overhead Benson reciting his creed."

Chad gave a raucous laugh.

"Heard it before have you, Mr…?"

"Permit me to introduce my curate, Chaddesley. Alfie Starkiss…Sir Chaddesley Corbett."

"Thank you, Roof the Rector. In mufti, Alfie, or may I call you Alf?"

"Alf will be Jim Dandy…and you appear to be in mufti Chaddesley, or may I call you Chad?"

The knight looked puzzled.

"Left your six shooters at home, Sheriff."

The booming laugh resounded.

"You may certainly call me Chad. And pray, if that's not an inappropriate word, what is Hargreave's point?"

"Socialism's roots are in Christianity. Equality of rights and opportunities was its founding creed. As such it had an innate faith and confidence in the ability of people to flourish through their own efforts, once those opportunities were no longer unjustly held from them. The corruption emanates from the 1970's when certain politicians and trade union leaders became more intent upon their desire to be the governing class."

"Fascinating Alf, fascinating. Some of your thinking was doing the rounds of the Civil Service, just before Margaret took office. Who are you thinking of Alf?"

Corbett glanced at Hargreave, with a mischievous smile on his chops, and whispered,

"A Yorkshireman? Scargill? Apologies for the melodramatic tone. You never know when the *'Noonday Devil'* is listening."

Rufus picked up Chad's theme.

"*The Noonday Devil*. Now there is a notion long forgot. Acedia, the *'Unnamed Evil of our Times'*, according to Abbot Jean-Charles Nault."

Teddy Bowcott reverted to the patois of her Lancastrian mother.

"Who, or what, is Acedia when he's at home, Rufus?"

"He is the Demon of Acedia; the vice of sloth…"

"Oh, laziness."

"Not at all, Teddy. You can be busy, but still be infected with Acedia. It's a combination of weariness, sadness and a lack of purpose. You feel empty, and that life is without meaning."

Teddy looked mystified.

"So what then is Benson's point, and come to that Alfie, what is yours?"

"That, ironically, corrupt Socialism has no faith in people. It says, *'poor you, you're so useless and inept that you must rely upon us to do everything for you'*. No longer a hand up, but dependency and helplessness."

"Who are they that emasculate the people, Alf?"

"Those who assume the guise of Socialists to gain power and govern, Chad"

Corbett whispered once more.

"Corbyn perhaps? Oops, there I go again."

Hargreave was encouraged.

"Aye that carrot munching numpty, and his fruitcake brother. He'd have had us all in the poor house."

"And *did* Alf understand you correctly, Hargreave?"

The latter shifted uncomfortably from foot to foot.

"Not precisely, Teddy. Too many folk with their hand out these days. That's all I'm saying. A fair day's pay deserves a fair day's work; not skiving."

Rufus bristled.

"2 Thessalonians 3: 10 '*If a man will not work, he shall not eat.*'"

"Aye, that's what I said..."

"No you didn't. Too many of those in work these days are having to rely upon benefits, because they're not paid a decent living wage. The only unwarranted aspect of those benefits is that we, the citizens, are subsidising employers. That's a handout to the employers..."

Alf chimed in,

"...and it says WILL NOT work. What about those who CANNOT work? It remains our civic and moral duty to support the weak and helpless. That isn't a hand out."

Teddy grasped the opportunity.

"Which brings me nicely to the Auction of Promises; the principal reason for our evening."

She considered asking Alfie to take her arm, but it would look a trifle obvious.

"Rector, would you escort me to my podium? Chad, Alf do join us."

The microphone gave a squeal.

"My lords, ladies and gentlemen, may I introduce to you our very own High Sheriff of Warwickshire, Sir Chaddesley Corbett…Chad to most of you."

Hargreave had a front row seat, and seethed. Had Teddy aimed that *'…most of you'* at him. That snotty bugger Corbett was speaking.

"The charity to benefit from your generosity has been selected by my wife Letitia. It is *'The Temple Weston Women's Group'* who, I understand, will begin their meetings in the Church Hall in one month's time. The proceeds of the auction will contribute to the redecoration and equipping of the hall, but mostly will provide ongoing resources to assist young mothers, children and families who live on the…er…yes, here it is…on *'The Sir Benson Hargreave Estate'*. Give generously, and give freely. Isn't that what the Good Book says Rector?"

Benson was incandescent. Hadn't he done enough for those families already, with jobs and houses? Wasn't he being made to look a fool? He conveniently forgot the minimum wage he was paying, and the rents he was charging. There would be one successful bid, at the bottom end of the financial scale, and then he would make his excuses. He hadn't come here to be insulted.

When he drove away, he swore that he would be back, and he'd take the smile off of their collective faces.

"Walk with me Alf?"

"Sure Roof?"

They strolled towards Rufus' modest vehicle.

"Really enjoyed what you said about helping those struggling to make ends meet."

"And putting my Churchwarden in his place?"

Rufus grinned.

"Christian charity must prevail. Great idea, the women from the estate meeting every Tuesday. Do you have sufficient help?"

"Certainly have. The formidable duo of Teddy Bowcott and Freddie Hargreave have taken the reins, with backup from half a dozen other ladies."

"That will be a dynamic duo. If there's anything I can do to help, please ask."

Rufus pressed the car key, and the click of unlocking seemed to boom across the stillness of the village. Neither clergyman made a move.

"I say Alf, we seem to have got off on the wrong foot. Is it something I've done?"

Alfie felt ashamed.

"You've haven't done anything Rufus. It's me being silly. To be honest, I suppose that I'm a bit resentful of your meteoric elevation."

"Ah, I did wonder."

"And…"

"Go on, I won't be offended."

"And probably of your rather interesting past."

Rufus smiled. It combined understanding and pain.

"Not all it's cracked up to be, Alf. A bit of a bloody burden to tell you the truth."

"Really?"

"Listen. I'd like us to work more closely together. I understand why the Bishop shunted you out of St. Dunstan's when I arrived. Give her credit, she almost certainly deduced that tensions might arise. With your permission, I'd like to approach her, and request a rejigging of your time. Say twenty-five to thirty per cent at St. Dunstan's, the rest here in Temple Weston. What do you say?"

Alfie felt a weight drop from his shoulders.

"What I say, Rector, is lock your car, and come and share a bottle at my house so I can resent you in comfort."

Freddie was propped up against her pillows, serene and unruffled by Hargreave's grumbling. Soon she would meet with their son, her son, and nothing could disturb her composure.

"If any other bugger uses the words 'queer' or 'bent' to me I'll give them the rounds of the kitchen. I was born with a right hand thread, as you well know Freddie."

"Calm down my own. I'm sure there was no intention to imply that you are anything but an Alpha male."

"What's one of them?"

"Top dog, top banana…king of the castle."

"Aye, too true, and I'll not be insulted by some toffee-nosed public schoolboy who probably bends for Britain."

"Really my own, you should try to keep on the right side of these people…"

"Why should I? Who the hell do they think they are. I've made something of myself; made my own way while they've had it handed to them on a plate."

He glared into the dressing table mirror, and grew in size by force of will. The soft and quiet tone of his voice sent a chill along her spine.

"Beautiful place. Solid place like. Not too grand mind, but refined and dependable. A proper and permanent home, fit for an Englishman."

She knew that he was referring to *'The Manor'*.

It was a serpent's hiss when it came.

"I want it, and I mean to have it. Then they'll know who *mester* is!"

"Super evening Teddy."

"Thanks awfully, 'titia."

Teddy was not the genuine article, but she had cultivated the right manners and correct forms of address.

"What did you think of our clergymen?"

Before Letitia could reply her husband chipped in.

"Your pop star Rector is sounder than I thought. Schooled at King Eddy's. The interesting chap is his curate."

"Interesting, Chad?"

"Mmm? More a case of sensible, and fully committed to the cause. Not to be underestimated, Teddy."

"I thought there was tension between those two, but I think our enthralling political discussion was a turning point. I'm confident they'll pull together, and put some life back into this Benefice."

"Can't say I warmed to your shirty shirt manufacturer, Ted. *'Put not your trust in Princes'*.

"Gosh Chad, never knew you were a devotee of Psalms."

Letitia reached for his hand.

"Oh, when Chad is weary of the world he rather fancies the cloister, don't you darling."

"Only if you're bunked up with me. Which reminds me, Teddy. Our Tyke has taken a shine to you."

"Really Chad, be serious."

"I'm telling you. I watched him watching you. Think he fancies getting his hands on your assets."

Letitia shivered.

"Ugh, repellent little man. I shook his hand. It was slippery."

Teddy drank in the words of her old and intimate friends.

"I say, you two, it's been quite a while."

Her guests beamed in understanding.

"Shall we, for old times' sake?"

Chad proposed a toast.

"For auld lang syne."

"For auld lang syne!"

Three glasses smashed into the fireplace. Chad offered and each Lady took an arm. The triumvirate mounted the fine wooden staircase with style.

7

'You'll wonder 'til the birds build a nest up your arse, then you'll wonder how the twigs got there.'

Police sirens didn't bring the entire street out of doors; they were already there when the police arrived. Those adjacent to the Corrigan and Bailey households enjoyed the fracas, before the constabulary broke it up. Sunday mornings were usually quiet in Palmerston Way, but a right ding dong was going on between Jack Corrigan and Kyle Bailey.

"You keep away from the lad, Bailey. I know you la'; friggin' trouble at the factory, an' friggin' trouble here."

"What the fuck are you talkin' about you Scouse twat?"

"Mind yer *'luggage'* in front of my missus, you melt."

Jack was old school Liverpool. From a period when bad language favoured the lower end of the obscenity scale in front of children and women.

"Come 'ere you."

Fourteen year-old Barry Corrigan shuffled forward.

"I've told you, I've not dun nottin'…"

"Not done anything. Speak properly. What the hell do they teach you at school these days!"

Kyle stood there shaking his head. He faced Bianca.

"He's lost it, the dickhead has finally lost it. Do you know what he's talking about?"

Bianca screeched. Her choice of word was deliberate.

"Not a *fuckin'* clue. What I do know is what that bitch has been sayin' about me."

Her finger extended in the direction of Marie Corrigan, as if saying,

"Yes, I recognise the accused, m'lud."

"What's she been sayin'? What 'ave you been sayin' about my wife, Marie?"

"She's not your wife yet…"

"Bollocks! She will be in a month's time, and you two can bin your invite cos you're not welcome. Anyroad, don't change the subject. What 'ave you bin gobbin' off about?"

"I'm sayin' nuttin...apart from neither of yer are any better than you ought to be!"

Bizarrely, Kyle lapsed into a bit of Liverpudlian.

"Go ed then, spit it out."

"I'm sayin' nuttin...our kitchens are at the front of the 'ouse, in case yer didn't notice."

Kyle was in a state of bewilderment.

"No shit. Who do you work for Barratt's? What are you goin' on about?"

"You should pull your blind down when you an' 'er are...well you know."

That was what necessitated the arrival of the police. Bianca flew at her neighbour.

"You dirty, disgusting, spyin' nosy cow. Is that 'ow you get your rocks off? I suppose you 'ave to livin' with that long streak of paralysed piss."

Jack Corrigan winced, the abusive reference to his elongated stature didn't bother him. He was offended because, as a lifelong Labour man, he had used precisely the same epithet about Conservative politician Jacob Rees Mogg. The comparison rankled.

Marie choked his response at birth.

"My Jack's worth twice wot your drug dealin' *'partner'* is, getting' kids to work for 'im!"

Kyle and Bianca advanced upon her in a fury.

"You wot, you fuckin' wot. Drugs? Kids? Yer out of yer fuckin' mind, yer troublemakin' Scouse bastards."

By the time the boys in blue arrived most of the residents of Palmerston Way were engaged in the rumble. Sides were taken on the basis of who got on with who in the workplace, and who didn't. It took a dog handler to calm things down. Jack and Kyle were taken into custody, but discharged with a caution.

"Where's this come from Bianca? I've never been into drugs."

"What about the kid?"

"Eh?"

"Barry Corrigan."

"I've never had owt to do with him. Oh yeh, I did catch him once knockin' Tony and Sandra's boy about."

"Little Arthur. Aw, he's a lovely lad. What did you do?"

"Cheeky little bastard eyeballed me, and said, 'Wot are you lookin' at'?"

"And?"

Kyle grinned. He loved his film quotations, especially Clint's.

"I said he looked like a sack of shit in cheap trainers…"

"And?" she persisted.

"I might 'ave said something about tearing him a new arsehole, if he didn't leave Arthur alone."

"That's it then. He's made up this story about you getting him to flog drugs to get back at you."

Kyle rubbed his designer stubble.

"Could be…could be. Naw, I'm not convinced. Corrigan shouted something about a reliable source when we was scrappin'. From the rows we hear through the walls, it doesn't sound as if he thinks his stepson is reliable about anything."

"Who then?"

In the Corrigan kitchen next door a similar debate took place. Barry Corrigan brought it to an end.

"I've told yer, I don't sell drugs to no-one."

"Then why did…?"

Jack cut himself short. He had shared the information with his wife, but it would be best not to let the lad know his well-heeled source.

"I'll bet it was Bailey himself who made it up?"

"Why would he do that, soft lad? You 'eard him out there. He denied it until he was blue in the face. Kept denyin' it even when the bizzies asked him over and over about it."

"Ow do I know? Anyway, he's always pickin' on me."

Marie leapt to her son's defence.

"Said he was gonna give Barry a good hidin'."

Jack squinted his eyes in suspicion, as he looked at his young wife.

"Why would he do that? I know I don't like Bailey, but he doesn't strike me as the sort o' bloke who'd 'ave a go at kids."

Marie hugged Barry to her.

"He was only messin' about; he didn't mean nuttin."

"Go on…Not you, 'im."

"I was just 'avin a laff with little Arthur. Bailey saw us, an' said 'e'd tear me arse'ole in two."

"You were bullying the little lad."

"I never…"

"Shut it! You're grounded for the day. Get to your bedroom."

Barry flounced out of the door with a parting shot.

"You're not my dad. I don't 'ave to do wot you say! An' I wanna change my last name back to my dad's."

Jack stared through the kitchen window, at the now peaceful street. He knew Marie was watching him. Sometimes he ruminated on why he'd married her, and taken all this on. He'd been forty-five at the time, and she was twenty-one with a baby in tow. They'd honeymooned in the Lakes, in a caravan. He got chatting to the bloke parked next to them, and mentioned that they were newlyweds.

"Congratulations mate, you've got yourself a young cracker there."

The reply slipped out of his mouth without thinking.

"There's plenty of that in Liverpool. So long as you don't mind the kid."

Thirteen years on, and he'd come to mind the kid in spades.

The only detached house in Palmerston Way stood in splendid isolation at the entrance to the road. Its occupant was the matriarch Mary Jessop. Her late-husband Eddy preceded Jack Corrigan as foreman at the Hargreave factory. Beebie regarded himself as the epitome of benevolence. The houses were constructed after Eddy's death, but he spotted an opportunity for a P.R. exercise. To great fanfare and publicity, Mary was installed in the premier property. It was she who had called for the police.

While the tea brewed, she stood in the kitchen with her wedding photograph in hand.

"All those years, Eddy, building a respectable life and bringing John and Lily up properly. Now this, fighting and swearing in the street. How have we come to this? I'll tell you what, Eddy, I won't put up with it, and I'll tell you another thing. I've remembered what you said to me near the end. Don't you worry love, I wouldn't trust him as far as I can throw him."

8

'The devil makes work for idle hands.'

Mark Blackledge Hargreave gripped her chin twixt fingers and thumb. The naked girl tried not to wince at the pain. She was hypnotised by the glint of delight in his eyes.

"Now you be a good girl. There's a day's work to be done. I can't afford to support lazy workers."

In a rare moment of insight he realised that he sounded like his father.

"But I love you Mark. How can you keep asking me to do this?"

"Maisie tells me she's booked in four clients for you today. Be good to them, and I'll be good to you."

The redoubtable Maisie functioned as his 'Madam' for the brothel he ran outside Banbury; known euphemistically as *'The Country Retreat'*. He had always loved making words work for him, and at thirty-two years of age retained a fondness for his days as President of the school debating society. Mark's boarding school, in Hertfordshire, enabled him to hone his values and instincts to perfection. Regrettably, they were not simpatico with the ethos of the famous old institution.

"But…"

"Daisy, Daisy, Daisy, my tainted goddess."

His hand transferred from chin to left breast. He fondled it, as if touching it for the first time.

"You are, and you always will be, my special girl. The others are just drones."

He observed her to see if she understood, and added, "Workers," in case she thought he was referring to a pilotless aircraft. Mark glanced at his expensive watch, and tapped the dial.

"Tempus fugit, my angel."

He didn't bother to translate.

"Got to fly; important business meeting. If I receive a good report from Maisie we'll have a trip to London next week."

He gave her a long and luxurious kiss, then headed for the door.

"Oh yes, Maisie informs me that one or two clients have left disgruntled."

Daisy's gormless expression revealed her incomprehension.

"They were pissed off! Make sure you put your back into it."

The engine of the Audi TT burbled, and he held the gear stick whilst mulling over the pros and cons for putting up with the girl. Well, you don't get to play with a stunning seventeen-year old every day. The attraction would pall eventually, and then it would be a case of open the front door and shout *'next please!'*

Mark was excited. Partially at the prospect of seeing his Ma, but the real frisson came from the opportunity to forward the project he had formulated. His mind flipped to his schooldays. Only one teacher had come close to understanding his true persona, during the seven-year sojourn in Herts. The image of his old housemaster appeared on the windscreen.

He addressed the glass.

"Wonder if you got remission for good behaviour, you cadaverous old fuck?"

Mark laughed, savouring the thought of how he and Martin Scott-Bowen had stitched the old boy up, and got him sent down for seven years. His face resembled the volcanic ash of an Easter

Island statue when he recalled the housemaster's damning report, word-for-word.

"Mark is noted in Lucan House for his sublime use of English, especially when dominating the debating society, and also for his exquisite skill whilst wielding the sabre. The latter has brought him county honours, and we anticipate with pride his eventual elevation to national recognition.

It is, therefore, profoundly disappointing that he uses his gifts to travel less salubrious paths. I hesitate to use the word litany when recounting his misdemeanours. His perverse actions strike one as being of a more diabolic nature. We recall his cheating in the geography examination, at the tender age of eleven, as a mere test run for more serious infractions. Bullying has, of course, been his every day meat and drink. One addresses his destruction of school lockers with philosophical reflection. Discovering that he manipulated the circumstances to apportion blame to another pupil in his form - one of unblemished innocence– afforded an unsettling insight into his psyche. It would be invidious to single Mark out as the only boy in the school to have dabbled in the arenas of drink and drugs. That he manifests himself as the lynch pin holding together his errant cabal of acolytes in these extramural pursuits is worthy of comment.

Mark is a talented boy who relies too readily upon his 'winning ways'. It is crystalline clear that he cherishes the belief that his gifts are of sufficient eminence to achieve his desired outcomes, without expending too much energy. For all his acute and masterful use of the English language, he remains obtusely unfamiliar with the commonplace words 'hard' and 'work'.

With a degree of ennui I raise the subject of his recent attempt to smuggle an air rifle into the country upon returning from the school skiing trip..."

It wasn't the sarcasm that still bridled with Mark, but the ineluctable truth of Jasper Pluck's observations about his character. He still smarted, if only metaphorically, from the thrashing his father had given him. Seventeen! He'd been seventeen-years old, and a strapping lad, but Sir Benson Hargreave was bigger. He had flown from the room, to return in a trice with a leather belt in his hand.

"I've never forgotten the sense your grandfather knocked into me with this, and I'm going to hammer some into you!"

The belt slammed into Mark's body twice before his mother got between her boy and her husband.

"What are you complaining about you old bastard? You got your name on the Sports Hall in one of the most prestigious schools in the country."

"Old bastard! Old bastard! I'll give you a bloody good hiding…"

"…if you so much as lay another finger on him we're both out of here, and the whole of Warwickshire will know that you're a wife-beater!"

Benson hesitated. He wrapped the thick belt around his hand, before placing it beside the whiskey decanter.

"Cost me a bloody fortune, preventing you from being expelled. I'll tell you this lad, you've two terms left. You'll get your head down, and finish your studies, and then straight on to university."

"I'm not going to university."

Freddie Hargreave intercepted another grenade from her husband.

"We were going to tell you. Mark and I have discussed it, and we think that it would be good for his development to undertake two years' VSO…that's Voluntary Service O…"

"I know what it is, and I'm expected to get my hand down again, am I, for him to fart around in Africa or somewhere."

Mark knew that the tide now flowed in his favour.

"South America, actually, Pa. I'll be up and down the Amazon, ministering from village to village."

"Ministering! Who do you think you are, Mother bloody Theresa? I'll tell you this for nowt, you cock up again and never mind the Amazon, you'll be up shit creek without a paddle. Cos you'll not be welcome back here. Bloody Amazon, the way you're going on you'll end up driving a bloody van for them."

"And I will finance Mark from my father's estate."

"Aye, well…"

"May I bring him in to speak with you?"

Freddie Hargreave bit her lip, and waited for his answer. She and Mark had lunched together, and she just knew that he was a changed person from the one who had returned from his VSO experience in disgrace. A decade or so had matured him, and she was so moved by his honesty.

"A psychiatrist you say, Freddie?"

"Yes Benson, Sir Jeffrey Fennimore. PTSD was the diagnosis. That's…"

"I know, I know…post-traumatic stress disorder. By God, if I could get my hands on that nonce I'd happily cut his knackers off myself."

For once, Lady Freddie did not find the coarse terminology unacceptable. It harmonised with her feelings about Pluck the errant, if unjustly punished, housemaster.

"Bring him in then. No, I'll fetch him myself."

Benson strode into the hall, and she clasped her hands together, before throwing her arms wide and exclaiming, "Thank you God!"

"For me lad, for me?"

Father and son bustled into the room.

"Will you look Freddie; will you just look what the lad has brought for me?"

"It looks like a bottle of whiskey, my own."

Beebie threw his arm around his son's shoulders.

"A bottle of whiskey, she says. It's nothing less than a bottle of *Lagavulin 26 years old Special Release 2021'.*"

He realised his good lady was none the wiser.

"This must have set you back a pretty penny, lad. Certainly four figures…and you did that for your old Pa."

"By way of a long awaited apology Pa. I know it's rather inadequate, but…"

"I'm very touched son. Now you sit yourself with your mother, and I'll pour us a drop."

"It's for you Pa…"

"No, I insist we share the first glass together. Will you have one Freddie?"

"Perhaps a teensy drop, with water."

"Water! Bloody sacrilege. Aye, alright."

"Let me Pa. You sit with Ma. She was telling me that you had a heavy day at the factory. You must be exhausted."

"Thank you son, I have. Bloody union agitators."

"Here we go. May I propose a toast? To my dear Ma and Pa, to family."

They settled themselves to savour the scotch.

"Your mother's brought me up to speed. I suppose that explains everything. I can understand now why you were dabbling in young ladies up the Amazon…"

"Benson!"

"It's alright Ma. Sir Jeffrey encourages me to talk about it."

"You're still seeing him, I understand. Very eminent figure."

"Just occasionally Pa. Nearly out of the woods. It was he who thought I should seek reconciliation with you…and Ma."

Mark added his mother hastily. He didn't want to create the impression that the family hiatus was solely between him and his father. Beebie hastened to the drinks trolley, and waggled the bottle in the air. His offer was declined, so he poured another for himself.

"Thinking of taking up residence with us, I hear?"

"If that's agreeable, Pa?"

"Of course, of course." He gestured at the cut glass in his hand. "How are you fixed on the financial front?"

"No worries there. I'm not Croesus, but doing well, thank you."

"What line have you been in these last few years?"

"Cryptocurrencies, Pa. Made a packet. I keep a small office suite in Banbury, with all the necessary tech, and Bob's your Uncle, Fanny's your Aunt and…"

"I'm going to leave you two alone for a while. Papers to look over for tomorrow's governors' meeting."

The gentlemen came to their feet. Freddie embraced her son, and kissed him on both cheeks. She thought it politic to give Beebie a peck.

"See you later, my love?" he whispered hopefully.

"Of course, my own."

Her gritted teeth were unseen, as she exited.

"Now then, lad. I understood that the cryptocurrency business was in a bit of trouble."

Mark swallowed the last of his Lagavulin. The old bastard was still cute when it came to sniffing out money.

"Quite right, Pa. Which is why it's time to diversify. Would you mind awfully if I were to outline a little project I've been thinking over? Not only would it be a nice little earner, but it would be of service to Temple Weston, and Sir Jeffrey says it would be good for my mental health."

"Fire away son, fire away!"

Beebie was folding his trousers meticulously. Freddie watched on from the bed; her detachment was commendable.

"Clever lad we've got there, Freddie. Come up with a cracker of a scheme. It'll do me a bit of good, as well as improve his mental health."

Freddie was astonished. Beebie's views on mental health were usually akin to those of a 19th Century muscular Christian; cold baths, a stiff backbone, and keep your hands away from your privates. However, her interest was aroused.

"What scheme would that be?"

"Promised the lad I'd let him tell you himself. My lips are sealed. Now, how about yours?"

9

'What fuss there is when beggars meet.'

Tuesday mornings in the Church Hall were going well. Young mothers, single and married, got together for two hours with the ladies of All Souls for chat and advice. The residents of the *'Sir Benson Hargreave Estate'* were grateful for a meeting point. Despite the pleasures of their cosy new homes, many hankered for a livelier environment. Temple Weston was beautiful, and lovely for the children to grow up in, but the sap of life still flowed strongly in those who didn't work beside their husbands or partners in the shirt factory. There were days when they longed for the company of bustling urban streets.

They were also pleased to be pointed in the right direction for Universal Credit claims, medical matters and such. Teddy Bowcott and Freddie Hargreave avoided being intrusive, but occasionally inserted advice about child rearing in a roundabout fashion. Old Mary Jessop, who lived amongst their guests, tended to be somewhat more forthright, but not unkind. There was an inadvertent quid pro quo. The titled ladies learnt about the habits and psyche of women outside their experience.

"I heard the ambulance arriving. Saw you getting into it with little Shania. I was destroyed for you."

Marie Corrigan was part-time at the factory, and this was one of her day's off. She was addressing Bianca Bailey in a tone worthy of Eastenders at its most nauseatingly melodramatic. They had long since patched up their differences, following the fracas in the street. Within a week, Marie was once more pencilled in as Matron of Honour for the Bailey wedding. The reconciliation occurred when they chanced upon one another in the Ladies loo of the village pub, *'The Cock with Two Balls'*.

Landlady Kelly Hampton faced fierce opposition when she renamed the pub from *'White Horse Inn'*, and it went before the local magistrates. The old stagers in the village were torn, because the pub had been closed for eighteen months, and they were desperate to see it reopened. Close the local boozer and a village is on the slide. Surprisingly, Beebie Hargreave did not take sides; his wife was outraged.

"Really Benson! It lowers the tone of the entire village."

"I think it's bloody hilarious, especially as the landlady's name is Hampton."

Freddie looked at him quizzically.

"Hampton Wick!"

The puzzlement on her face didn't alter.

"Anyroad, I think you're wasting time and money taking it before the magistrates. I know what Kelly Hampton has up her sleeve. You've no chance."

When it came to court Ms. Hampton's solicitor produced the design for the pub sign with all the aplomb of magician Paul Daniels.

"As you can see, your worships, the image presents a fine portrait of an English cockerel rampant, astride a football and a rugby ball. You may agree that it bears a certain heraldic quality.

The Chairman of the Bench addressed Kelly Hampton.

"Ms. Hampton, were you aware that the choice of name for your new premises might have had…ahem…unfortunate connotations?"

Kelly was a Brummie lass through and through, and had flattened a bit of grass in her time, but you'd have thought she was the Virgin Mary.

"I had no idea what it might mean until all this fuss and palaver blew up."

"Would you consider changing it to something else?"

"I'd rather not, your Grace…"

"Your worship, I'm not a bishop yet."

"Oh, I am sorry. See…your worship…I've always supported Tottenham Hotspur, and I love the French Rugby team. It sort of expresses the *entente cordiale*, and celebrates it in the sign. After all, Temple Weston's a wonderful English village, ain't it? I think it embraces the perfect value of good neighbourliness. Anyroad, I don't wish to be rude…your worship…but don't you think that these smutty thoughts are in the minds of them that think them, not in an innocent name for my business? I hope to make the pub a thriving social point for the village, especially as loads of new houses have been built. Build a community spirit, like."

There was a brief conflab on the bench.

"There is no need to retire to consider our verdict; we are agreed. Whilst recognising the concerns of some residents of Temple Weston, we feel that the clarity of the sign is sufficient to dispel any injurious influence that might arise from a childish misconstruction being placed upon it. We find for the defence, with costs."

"Eh Marie."

Marie Corrigan was touching up her makeup in the mirror. She didn't turn.

"What?"

"I was thinking like. We've been ever such good friends. How about letting bygones be bygones. All that fuss over nowt last week."

Bianca failed to elicit a response.

"Marie."

"What?"

"You know me and Kyle have put the wedding back to the end of October. I was wondering, will you still be my Matron of Honour?"

Makeup adjustment complete, she turned to face Bianca.

"You must be fuckin' jokin'!"

Bianca flinched, and Marie burst into laughter.

"Matron, fuckin' Matron! What do you think I am, ninety fuckin' three? How about Maid of Honour?"

"You cheeky bitch. Maid, you? You've had more pricks than a second-hand dart board. On the other hand, why not – all the blokes have made you."

"You should talk, Bianca. I heard when you went to school you had a mattress strapped to your back."

All was forgiven, and the girls strode out of the loo arm in arm.

"Eh Bianca, that Kelly behind the bar she's a right fuckin' laff. Know what she told me?"

"What?"

"I asked her if she really didn't know how people would take the pub's new name. She said, 'Do you think I came over on the fuckin' banana boat. Have you seen how many tourists are coming to the village, just to take a pic of the sign. I'm raking it in'."

"The crafty cow. Eh, know what I heard about her? They reckon she used to be on the *'Game'* years ago in Brum. She wouldn't pull many punters now."

"Oh yeh, under that ton of makeup she's destroyed. Mind you if she put her prices on her arse in Braille she could still get the blind punters!"

Freddie Hargreave overheard the conversation concerning baby Shania's trip to A & E , whilst collecting mugs. It had resulted in advice from the doctor on duty to keep a bottle of Calpol in the house for minor sniffles, and tiny rises in temperature. Every week she picked up snippets about this crisis and that crisis, which never turned out to be a crisis at all. She said to Mary Jessop,

"They seem to live their lives as high drama, and relish every moment of it. It puzzles me, Mary?"

The sage old lady didn't hesitate.

"They're empty; their lives are empty. They don't cook or bake; the garden is an alien planet to them. No interests, and what's worst of all no faith."

"In God you mean?"

"Aye, in God, in Jesus, but also no faith in themselves. Oh, they think they have, but when there's no more telly to watch, and the latest takeaway cartons are strewn around the house, and the bottle's finished they don't know which way to turn. You know something Freddie?"

Freddie smiled. She had finally managed to get Mary to drop *'your ladyship'*.

"What should I know Mary?"

"Folk shouldn't worry about this lot turning the world upside down; they're too busy turning on each other. It distracts them from having to face up to themselves; what they are, and what they're afraid to be."

"Afraid to be? I'm sorry, you've lost me."

"I know you think that I'm hard on them, Freddie, but it's because they break my heart. There's not a one of them that couldn't do better for themselves."

"Then why don't they?"

"Because we've had nearly sixty years of clever so-and-so's patting them on the head, and telling them that if they find something hard to do they should just give up. Do you remember a TV programme called *'Tomorrow's World'*? With all the wonderful gadgets being invented we were going to spend our time on the beach with our feet up, sipping champagne. We swallowed the nonsense, and what's worse we handed it down to our children. Work Freddie, work and perseverance; running the race and not giving in that's what…"

"Hello everyone!"

The loud and elegant voice was met with a gooey rejoinder,

"Hi Mark."

Cow eyes splashed desire all over Mark Hargreave, who was standing in the doorway.

"With your permission Mrs. Jessop, Teddy, Mummy. This week's goodies are outside in the van. A carrier bag each. Not yet produce from my market garden, but the great day is not too far away. Soon have the winter crop for distribution. My man Jim is outside waiting for you."

Bianca whispered to Marie.

"What's a market garden? I thought it was called a smallholding."

Marie giggled.

"Bet it's not that small a holding."

Mary Jessop may have been ancient, and her hearing was none too good, but she heard that. She cast a disdainful look in their direction.

"Perhaps we might say our customary closing prayer before the ladies depart, young man?"

"Ooo er, Mary, what about me and Eric?"

Alistair and Eric Ball also attended with their adopted baby son.

Despite her austere demeanour, Mary smiled. She had a soft spot for her boys. They'd invited her to tea more than once, and their house was immaculate. Eric's Spotted Dick was to die for.

The Tuesday gatherings were run by the church, but were not an occasion for force feeding the attendees with Bible bashing and hymn singing. However, everyone was comfortable with a closing prayer.

"I think that's an excellent idea, Mary."

Alfie Starkiss had popped in, and was standing beside Mark.

"A prayer then…"

"I say Alf!"

"Yes Mark?"

"Would you consider it terribly forward of me to offer up today's prayer?"

"Great idea. When you're ready."

Mark clasped his hands into the classic prayer position, and espied tears of pride trickling down his mother's face.

"Dear Lord and Father, we thank you for this time of fellowship and friendship; for the joining together of our good people in community. We thank you for the efforts of those who make it possible, and we ask for your blessing upon them, and upon all those who attend. May their lives grow in fruitfulness, and in the image of your Son, our Saviour Jesus Christ. Amen."

A ragged chorus of 'Amen' resounded, and Alfie patted the young man on the back. Freddie Hargreave came bounding over, and dragged him to her bosom.

"Darling, that was wonderful."

"Thanks Ma, sorry to be a nuisance but I need to catch up with a few people before they go."

"How's it all going, Mark? I see the trucks keep coming with the flat packs."

"Yes, yes, lot of acreage to cover Alf, and a lot of experimental work going into those greenhouses. Pa's become quite hands on; some great advice and input. Really sorry, I must just have a word with someone."

The hall was almost empty by the time Mark's enquiry was answered, and he'd been pointed in the right direction.

"Hi ladies. I know one of you is Bianca, but not sure which."

"That's me…"

"…and who is your charming friend?"

"That's Marie."

"So it's you whose wedding is coming up, Bianca. What about you, Marie, are you planning to tie the knot?"

Marie sat there, blushing and tongue-tied, whilst Mark surveyed her with undisguised lust.

"Nah, she's already wed. Anyway, how do you know I'm getting married?"

"My father, Sir Benson, mentioned it. I understand that for baptisms and weddings he's always generous towards his employees. Your husband-to-be is his Chargehand, isn't he?"

"Oh yeh, that's Kyle. We've chosen the whiskey decanter and six glasses from the list we was given."

"I know, and I thought I'd add a little something to the kitty. Here, this is for you both in advance."

"Oh eh, thanks. What is it?"

"Take a peek."

"Two bottles of whiskey. Oh, I see, for the decanter."

"One for the decanter, and one to make a start on. You won't find that in the supermarket. Only the best for Bianca and Kyle. Think I deserve a kiss for that."

The ladies giggled, but Bianca leapt to her feet and gave him a smacker on the cheek.

"Suppose that will have to do. Can't go upsetting Kyle. Shame I didn't bring a bottle for you Mrs…?"

Marie found her voice.

"Corrigan, Marie Corrigan."

"That name has a familiar ring. Any relation to Jack Corrigan, my father's Foreman?"

"He's my husband."

Mark was tempted to say, "Don't you mean your father," if what his old man had told him was correct.

"How do you know my Jack?"

"My Pa talks about his work sometimes. Full of praise for your Jack…and Kyle as well."

The lie was accepted without demur.

"So what does the rest of the day hold for you two?"

"Me and Marie have got a fitting this afternoon for our dresses. Before that we've got to cut Marie's bloody great hedge, pardon my French."

"Yeh, Jack's a stickler for keepin' things in good order. If it's not done by the time he gets home he'll get a monk on."

"Ah well, won't take long with a good hedge trimmer."

"You mean shears."

"Oh dear. Tell you what Bianca, you get some lunch on the go for yourself and Marie, ready in say an hour. Is that okay? And I'll give Marie a hand. We can use my tool. Have you ever used a battery-operated one Marie? It vibrates quite a bit, but I'm sure you'll keep a firm grip."

"Thanks Mark. I'd love to try it out."

He bent down and whispered into her ear.

"It will be my pleasure. I'm sure we can trim your bush to your husband's satisfaction."

"Will you come and have lunch with us, Mark?"

"Would love to, but I have business to attend to."

"Tell you what. Will you come to my reception after the service?"

"Why thank you, I most certainly will. If I may, I'll attend the service as well. Dresses! What role do you play in this star-studded occasion, Marie?"

"She's my Maid of Honour."

"Positively Maid Marian. Come on Marie, let's go and attend to your bush."

10

'You look like prick at balls wedding.'

When you look out upon the great unwashed, to see them flailing their way through life in a state of confusion, it is a grave error to conclude that they are irredeemably hopeless in all things. Alfie Starkiss knew this from experience; not merely as a Church of England minister, but from the fruits of his childhood being reared in a working class community.

He looked at the eager and excited faces of the wedding congregation, and gladness filled his heart. At least for one day they could set cares and sorrows aside, and celebrate an act of creation. They were in best bib and tucker, and looked splendid. Haircuts and hairdos, smart suits and fine dresses, not to mention polished shoes. The Bridegroom – never Groom, they look after horses – Kyle Bailey was resplendent in his hired morning dress, along with his Best Man and Ushers.

Alfie's heart went out to them. They were day lilies in bloom, but he knew that it would pass too quickly. The beauty drawn out of them for the wedding would soon drain into a stagnant pool of puzzlement about life, and a resignation fed by a plethora of aimless activities. The petals of loveliness adorning them would decay. Some would be fortunate, and only gentle breezes would occasionally disturb the equilibrium of their lives. Many would find themselves bent double, trudging remorselessly into fierce gales and storms; heads down and battling to remain on their feet; bewildered by an absence of help.

"In the presence of God, and before this congregation, Kyle and Bianca have given their consent and made their marriage vows to each other. They have declared their marriage by the joining of hands and by the giving and receiving of rings. I therefore proclaim that they are husband and wife.

You may kiss the Bride."

Hands clapped, and cheers echoed through a packed All Souls. The Rector had played his part, and he gestured to Alfie. The happy couple were rather embarrassed when they had asked Alfie.

"Would you mind? It's not that we don't think you're very good, but he christened Shania, and it's like…like…"

Alfie helped them out.

"Continuity?"

"Yeh, yeh, sort of like that," they mumbled.

The smile on Alfie's face relieved them. What they couldn't hear were the words going through his head, *"And you wouldn't want me talking bollocks!"*

"Consider it a done deal. I'll ask the Rector tomorrow at our staff meeting."

They shuffled in embarrassment once more.

"We've already asked him."

"I assume that he has said yes?"

"Sort of…he said we was to ask you first, but he wouldn't do it if you felt uncomfortable."

"Well I don't. We want your big day to be happy, happy, happy, and your long married life to be filled with good memories."

Rufus frowned when Alfie brought the matter up at the ensuing staff meeting.

"Don't look like that Roof, you did absolutely the right thing. Gives me a day off."

"Ah well, I was wondering about that. I'm not happy having the village think that you can always be set aside when they feel like it. So, how about doing the sermon?"

Alfie grinned.

"Do you want to read it first, Roof?"

Rufus grinned back at him.

"Christian charity prevents me from answering that, but the second word is *'off'*. How would you feel about delivering it after the vows, instead of before?"

Alfie walked to the centre of the Crossing with a few crib notes in hand. How many of them might come to Faith today, as a result of his words? He prayed fervently that the Holy Spirit would rest upon him, and inspire.

"Let's have a quiz. Where did Jesus do his first miracle?"

Silence.

"Come on, surely someone knows. Winner gets a drink out of me at the Reception. Yes sir?"

"The Marriage Feast at Cana."

"Spot on, and do you know, er...?"

"Jack."

"Do you know, Jack, what that miracle was?"

"Changed the water into wine."

"Thank you Jack. I owe you a pint. Isn't that my hometown accent I hear? We'll enjoy a bevvy together later. Scholars have calculated that Jesus changed somewhere between 120 and 180 gallons of water into wine; that's960 to 1,440 pints of wine. It was of a quality you won't find in Yates' Wine Lodge. Jesus was a partygoer, not a party pooper.

Marriage is a great celebration in Christianity. It fulfils God's plan to bring men and women together to create and build families, generation after generation. Families to live in union, in mutual respect and happiness. The source for that joyous state is love.

Kyle and Bianca chose our good old favourite for their Bible reading, 1 Corinthians 13. You heard that great long list of what love is: patient and kind; not putting yourself first and being angry when you don't get your own way; protecting each other, and trusting each other, and always living in hope. There's another word in the reading which I think a loving marriage can't do without. Anyone? No? Well, it would be unfair of me to expect you to memorise thirteen verses *'just like that'.*"

He gave a passable imitation of comedian Tommy Cooper to deliver the last three words, and raised a laugh.

"Kyle, Bianca, this is your special day, but – and I don't want to be the party pooper – you've got years ahead together… Do you know, I've just remembered something. A guy from Liverpool wrote a play about poor kids having a day out in the countryside. One little girl loves it so much that she sings a song called, *'Why Can't it Always be Like This'.*"

Alfie repeated the title to himself, quietly, and stood mute.

"Sorry folks, I was just asking myself the same question. The answer's simple. We're human, we make mistakes, we mess things up occasionally, but – and here's that special word – we can persevere. We persevere by being patient and kind; by sharing and remaining calm; by protecting and trusting each other, and by living in hope. We Christians live in the hope of Jesus Christ, who wants us to succeed in all things, and Rufus and I can tell you that He is always with us; He never leaves us; He is our Rock.

Kyle, Bianca, I hope that this day has been wonderful for you so far, and that it will continue to be so. Perhaps take a teensy weensy moment to consider how the thousands of days ahead can be equally as wonderful. Maybe it would help to have the last verse from your reading pinned up around the house.

'And now these three remain: faith, hope and love. But the greatest of these is love.'

God bless you both, and Shania."

Alfie turned away swiftly to hide his distress. The abject failure of his own marriage had drenched him in a monsoon, and he thought that his legs would be swept from under him at any moment.

Kyle and Bianca postponed the wedding to October 31st so they could afford a better venue. They decided that the Church Hall wasn't good enough for their reception, and needed time to raise extra funds. If they were going to do it then they would do it *'large'*.

The disco resounded from the marquee at the rear of *'The Cock with Two Balls'*. Kelly Hampton promised she would do them proud, so long as they paid in cash. After a sit down dinner in the marquee the tables and chairs had been rearranged for the evening bash.

"Here you go Jack, one pint as promised. Got me out of hole; a miracle to identify a miracle."

"Cheers Alf."

"So how come you're a whizz kid on the Bible?"

"Altar boy, mate. No insult intended, all that crap is behind me but it never leaves you."

Alfie was determined not to rise to the bait.

"What brought you South, well to the West Midlands at least?"

Jack took a long satisfying draught from his pint and winced as the rear door to the bar opened. A blast from the disco intruded. He looked Alfie in the eye, as if to say, *'I dare you to condemn me.'*

"Suppose you'll have a go at me for leaving the greatest city in the werld."

"Hardly Jack. I'm in no position to throw stones. What makes you think Liverpool is the greatest city in the world?"

Jack's truculent manner didn't leave him.

"Course it is mate. We had The Beatles, and football, and Alan Bleasdale and Willy Russell; nominated for an Oscar he was."

"The operative word is *'had'* Jack. All that was half a century ago. Somebody else's turn now. That's the way of the world. When Liverpool was a village Chester was the big player. The tide shifts Jack."

"Still the best."

"Why don't you go back?"

Bitterness clouded his features.

"Her kid!"

"Who?"

"Barry – Marie's lad. He's not mine. A toddler he was when I met her, and that was a bad day's werk."

Alfie trod on eggshells.

"Barry, or both of them?"

"The kid certainly."

His demeanour suggested that the jury was out on his wife.

"He's the reason we had to leave the 'Pool. Aged ten he was, and in trouble with the bizzies since he was six. Then there was a stabbing, and he blabbed. We're in witness protection…no one else knows in these parts, so I'd appreciate confidentiality Vicar."

"You have my word. So you ended up at Hargreave's?"

"Don't get me started on that old bastard."

"Everyone says you're his right hand man, Mr. Foreman."

"That's the image he puts about, but it's just to undermine me while I'm trying to get the werkers to join a union. I've tried to get JC interested, but he's a busted flush."

Alfie knew exactly who Jack was referring to, but decided to play dumb.

"So you think Jesus Christ is all washed up?"

Jack saw the wry look on his face, and managed a mirthless laugh.

"They're both washed up."

"Funny thing you know, mate. If it wasn't for Christians there wouldn't be a Socialist movement. Our Methodist friends in particular had a big hand in that creation."

"So what?"

"I think you guys have ditched the baby with the bath water. The Christian element was the glue that binds. It's what I was talking about this afternoon."

"Love!"

"That's right. Thank you dear Lord, at least one person was listening."

"How can love be the boss for Socialism?"

"Because without it you've all splintered into your factions, and sectarian in-fighting. That's why it's become a busted flush. You only love the people who agree with you. That isn't a basis for brotherhood, or should we call it *'personhood'* these days?"

Jack slammed his glass down, and knocked his seat over as he stood.

"You talk a load of bollocks! An' where did you get that posh accent from?"

He was gone. Somewhere out back his wife and stepson were enjoying themselves.

Alfie looked at the pub clock. Half past ten. He'd arrived after the dinner, at six o' clock. The lengthy stay enabled him to make his face known to the denizens of the Hargreave estate. Without a dog collar on he was just a normal guy. He'd overheard a few people describe him as *'not such a bad lad'*.

"Thanks Alfie." She popped his money in the till.

"No problem Kelly. What time are you shutting up shop?"

"Long way to go yet, and we might have a bit of a lock-in. Got to keep the cash register tinkling. No problem eh? Looked to me like there was."

"Oh, you mean Jack. Political discussions, always doomed to end in failure. I should know better."

"Doomed to end in a barney with that miserable sod. That's the trouble with idealists, they're like Freddie Mercury."

Alfie looked blank, and the landlady sang,

"I want it all, I want it all, I want it now…"

She received a round of applause and a loud cheer.

"You may be right, my love…"

"Eh, don't get fresh with me Vicar. Mind you, twenty years ago I'd have had you on toast for breakfast…and lunch and dinner."

"And I'd have considered myself the most fortunate of men. Mind if I use the old right of way, and nip through the hedge."

"Mind how you go, Alf, there's wicked women out there."

People were milling outside the marquee, with the odd person puking in the rhododendrons. They were assembling for a firework display. A demon burst out of the nearest bush.

"Trick or treat, mister. Oh, it's you. Sorry mate."

"Is that a werewolf, or Barry Corrigan?"

"Both."

"It's getting late. I think your dad's gone home."

"He's not my dad, and my mum says it's alright."

"Where is she?"

"Dunno. Enjoying 'erself I suppose. She was pissed three hours ago."

"Take care Barry, and God bless."

Barry ran away whooping to join the other devils and demons cavorting around the lawns. Flickering shafts of light from the marquee and a collection of torches created a vision from the cannibal imagination of Hieronymus Bosch.

Alfie was about to slip through the hedge when he heard a low moaning. He recognised instantly that it was of pleasure, not pain. A thunderous crack rent the heavens, and an immense burst of brilliant light made night into day. He saw them against an ancient tree, twenty metres away. Marie Corrigan had both hands on the trunk, and her maid's dress was bunched around her waist. The naked backside of the man behind her was pumping against her furiously. Alfie surmised that throughout his entire life *'the young master'* had always had his wedding cake and eaten it.

11

'Up before the sparrow farts.'

Lady Edwina Bowcott's slumber was interrupted at one in the morning by the police siren. The stout yeomen of the law were summoned to deal with Barry Corrigan's gang of witches and warlocks. The feral youths had decided to play 'knock and run' throughout the older part of the village. They persisted in disturbing the peace for over an hour. When the siren approached 'Commander' Corrigan dispersed his shock troops to their homes with a succinct order, worthy of Field Marshal Bernard Montgomery,

"The fuckin' bizzies. Leg it!"

Teddy stood naked before her full length mirror in the dressing room. She was fifty-three years of age, and a very attractive woman. She recalled her older brother with a smile. When she was sixteen he had entered her bedroom on an errand from their mum. She was clothed up top, but still in her knickers. Louis had stared at her long legs, and she exclaimed,

"Yes Louis, they go all the way up to my arse!"

Bad language wasn't tolerated in their home; a three-bedroomed bungalow in Clitheroe named *'The Pantiles'*. After her experiences of life with Bowcott, she wasn't sure that there was much wrong with a soupçon of middle class pretension. At least it demonstrated aspiration. Her mother and father had worked tirelessly to fulfil those hopes, for themselves and for their children.

Her meeting with Bowcott completed their master plan. She had been home from university for the summer holiday, and was doing a spot of waitressing. It was the County Show, and she was assigned to the Lord Lieutenant's tent. Bowcott was up from the family estate, and guest speaker at an evening dinner. In those days he had a raffish charm, and happenstance brought them together twice in the same day; Teddy was also waiting table in the evening. Her parents had no objection to their liaison, and were thrilled when Bowcott proposed. He may have been much older, but wasn't there a substantial age gap between Charles and Diana? Edward and Margery Walsh had always wanted their daughter to land a rich one; the title was a bonus. Hey ho! Days of yore long gone.

The curtains were drawn. Daylight was breaking, and an early Sunday morning walk was one of life's pleasures. Teddy risked a final peek into the mirror. The threesome with Chad Corbett and Titia had scratched an itch, but it wasn't like the old days when *'The Manor'* hosted a carnival of carnality. She had stepped away from that when she realised that Bowcott was using her acquiescence to sex with other men to get his rocks off. It was her brother Louis who had made the inelegant assessment when she confided in him. Teddy regarded those gatherings with disgust. She rarely called upon her degree in French, but when thoughts of Bowcott slithered through her mind the word *'souteneur'* popped up. Yes, that's what he was, a pimp in plain English. Thank God he was gone. She sighed heavily, because she still ached for a man; a loving companion beside her forever.

"Morning Teddy."

Her heart was in her mouth. She hardly ever encountered anyone out and about at this time of day.

"You put the fear of God into me, Alf."

"Think that's rather the point of my vocation."

Companionable laughter sparkled on the autumnal air, but not a net curtain twitched in response. A few folk were out of bed. That was obvious from the smoke emerging from chimneys. Log burners had been fired up. More than likely they were enjoying a pot of tea, and listening to Radio 3. Teddy knew her villagers.

Alfie closed the lych gate behind him, and joined her.

"What are you doing in your place of work so early? I thought the eight o' clocker was last Sunday of the month?"

"A bit of prep. Got the ten o' clock here, and then over to St. Dunstan's for the eleven-fifteen."

"Really! Pray where is our estimable Rector today?"

"Ah, cross your heart and hope to die, Teddy, and I will reveal all."

He drew close to her, and she smelt a seductive musk rise from his body.

"Roof went to London yesterday, straight after the wedding. Between you, me and the lych gate, he's gone for rehearsals."

"For what?"

"Rehearsals for…wait for it…wait for it…the next series of *'Strictly Come Dancing'.*"

"Noooo!"

"And STRICTLY entre nous, a fortnight on Saturday you can watch him on the quiz programme *'Ring My Bell'*.

Teddy arched an eyebrow.

"You and Sister Wendy should change surnames. He is most certainly star kissed. By the way, where does your surname come from?"

"Not too sure. A few of us were loafing around Hertfordshire in the early 20th Century, mainly in domestic service. Hardly superstars in the making. Now when we come to Coleridge, that is Anglo-Saxon. They even have a family crest; four birds around a cross."

"How appropriate. So you checked your boss out?"

"Once a teacher, etc."

"Do you have time to walk with me, Alf?" They began to stroll. "Have you another Christian name?"

They set off down the road.

"Ahem, Clement. Dad was a great fan of Liverpool football club…and Clement Attlee."

"I think that's a lovely name. Would you mind if I called you Clem, just between the two of us?"

He gave a smile of assent.

"Actually, Clem, you are looking rather pleased with yourself this morning."

He was fit to burst.

"My son, my Luke, is coming to live with me."

Teddy set the thought aside that this might interfere with his social life.

"Marvellous! How old is he?"

"Thirteen."

His head went down, and he stopped dead before the stile they were about to negotiate.

"Something wrong, Clem?"

"His mother…his mother, Debs, is remarrying. Moving to Hampshire."

"Do you still carry a torch for her?"

His laughter was so loud that she was sure it must have alerted somebody in the nearby houses.

"Not in the least. It's just that, well, Luke no longer fits with her lifestyle. If the new husband was being awkward about him I wouldn't think twice, but it's her. Says she wants some freedom;

needs to find herself. I can't fathom how a mother can part with her child, just like that."

This time he didn't essay a Tommy Cooper impression.

"I usually take the footpath, Clem, and then do a circuit. Come out round the back of the church and home. Will you keep me company?"

"I'd like that…"

"…but only if you promise to have breakfast with me afterwards. I won't take no for answer. You have a busy day ahead, and you need to stoke up. I hope you're not a muesli and yoghurt man. Full English on my manor. Oh heck, listen to me, I sound like an East End gangster."

Alfie, 'Clem', hopped over the stile, and offered his hand. She took it, but caught her back foot on the post, and almost tumbled into his arms. While they meandered along the footpath she said,

"You were an English teacher, weren't you? I've been given a pair of tickets for *'Twelfth Night'* at the RSC, and I'm without a companion…"

A curtain had agitated at the sound of Alfie's laughter. *'The Grange'* was opposite the entrance to the footpath. Though set well-back from the road, a Yorkshire-born knight of the realm had seen them as clear as day, from his bedroom window.

"Well, I'll be buggered! She's a handsome woman. Dip your bread, lad. You'll get no condemnation from me."

Beebie Hargreave was blissfully unaware of his faint allusion to the final verse of Charles Wesley's magnificent hymn, *'And can it be that I should gain…'*. He stretched the waist band of his pyjama bottoms, and took a gander at their contents. Dare he make a dawn raid on his wife's bedroom? It promised to be a glorious morning!

The meteorology office designates September 1st the beginning of Autumn. Tradition dictates that seasons change on the 21st of the relevant month. Older folk are resigned to the blathering of those pseudo-scientists, who couldn't forecast that three hundred seconds make five minutes. Be that as it may, Temple Weston was well into autumn, and it had a stimulating effect on some.

Mark Hargreave was also out of his bed. Humping Marie Corrigan, under the spreading chestnut tree, not to mention the nose of her husband and the rest of the village, had invigorated him. A sizeable breakfast would go down well, but first there was business to attend to.

He stood inside one of the greenhouses, surveying the rapid growth. It was hot, and he laughed when he thought of the electricity bill. When he explained his project to his father he assured him that sufficient financial resources were available to last a lifetime.

"Pity you didn't play the cryptocurrency market yourself, Pa."

"Not for me, that sort of thing, but I'm proud of your success."

"Anyway Pa, we've got eleven acres to cultivate. Once we're up-and-running we'll be able to keep the community in fresh fruit and veg. Distribute it gratis for the first year, and then sell at prices according to income. Those on benefits get it for free."

"Hmmm? Not sure I approve of that, but it's your pigeon. Ee lad, I never thought I'd see the day when you'd turn your hand to charity."

"Been a bit of prat, Pa, I know that; a rather fortunate prat. Time to give something back."

"And you say you can stand all the cost? I'm willing to help out a bit. Won't do me any harm in the area. Between you and me, I'm on the brink of an announcement. A new direction in life, away from those bloody factories. Might be an opportunity for you there, son. Does a takeover appeal to you?"

"Really Pa? Not running away to sea are you?"

Beebie chortled. "Got to keep it under my hat for a while longer. Now look, I'd like to put something in the kitty."

"Well…"

"Go on."

"I've a ton of equipment to purchase, and there'll be a few chaps and chapesses to employ…"

"Minimum wage!"

"Minimum wage. Tell you what Pa, routing electricity out there is a bit of a fag. I'll pay for the set-up, but do you think you could take care of the quarterly bills?"

"Course I can, and I'll stump up for the installation. I'll not take no for an answer."

"What's so funny Mark?"

He addressed his guests. Two large gentlemen, dressed in designer jeans, Barbour jackets and Doc Marten's.

"Thinking about my dear old dad, Jason."

"And that's funny?"

"If you'd met him Tommy you'd find it bloody hilarious. So what do you think?"

Jason and Tommy exchanged an imperceptible nod of agreement.

"Let's step outside Mark, bleedin' hot in here."

"Okay Jay."

Jason opened his mouth to speak as Mark raised a hand. He pursed his lips and gave a shrill whistle. A swishing noise brushed the air, as something swept through the coppice fifty metres away. What emerged made even Jay and Tommy blanch. A pair of Rottweilers advanced upon them at an alarming rate. With only ten metres left, Mark raised an outstretched palm and they came to a halt at his feet. He flicked his wrist, and the palm faced downwards which caused them to sit in obedience.

"Gentlemen, may I introduce Donald and Vladimir. Donald is a little out of shape at present, but a strict regime will see him rise again. They are my boon companions."

"Your what?"

"Quid pro quo Tommy. I look out for them; they look after me. Why, they even sleep with me, don't you boys. In a non-biblical sense of course. Now chaps, are we happy with the agreement?"

"I think I speak for both us, it's a fair cut. You produce, we distribute."

"Thank you Jay. Now, if there's nothing else, I'm in need of my breakfast. By the way, your illegals are a bit green behind the foreskin when it comes to agricultural labour, but I'll knock them into shape. Maybe a quiet word with the one they call Rasool. Bit too fond of taking a siesta."

Mark watched them make their way to a gap in the fence. They would have to cross a field to get to the back lane. Better that than have their faces seen around the village.

"Come on boys, time for din dins."

The fierce dogs loped along; one in front of him and one behind. He walked thirty metres before turning suddenly, gave another whistle and extended his arm in the direction of a clump of a rhododendrons. Donald and Vladimir leapt into action. A cry of terror was emitted, and a teenager burst into the open. He stood stock still in terror, the dogs pressed up against him. Mark strolled across.

"My, my chaps, what little bunny have we flushed out of the undergrowth? I think he must be a very naughty little bunny, or perhaps a thieving little rat. What say you Donald?" The dog gave a low growl. "Are you in accordance with Donald's opinion, Vladimir?"

"I wasn't doin' nuttin', honest. I...I was just scrumpin' for apples!"

"Permit me to conduct a short English lesson. It will make up for all the ones you've missed. Scrumping means to engage in the illicit acquisition of APPLES! Therefore, your use of the additional word 'apples' is tautology. Saying the same thing twice, you ignorant and misguided little toad. As for being honest; you wouldn't know honesty if it jumped up and bit you on the ass."

The words came hard to him, but he said them, "Sorry mister...I won't do it again."

"You were in my greenhouses earlier, weren't you?"

"I never, I was nowhere near 'em..."

Mark raised one finger, and the Rottweilers stirred.

"Stop 'em mister, please, stop 'em!"

His palm faced downwards, and they sat. Mark knew exactly who he was dealing with. He had been present when Barry came begging money off Marie at the wedding reception.

"I know you, don't I? You're…," and he twirled a hand in the air, as if to say, *'I can't quite remember the name'."*

"Barry, sir, Barry Corrigan. You was talkin' to my mum yesterday."

"Oh yes. You know what that makes you Barry. A thieving Scouse bastard. What does it make you?"

Barry stared at the dogs, and mumbled,

"A thievin' Scouse bastard."

"What were you after? A bit of machinery, tools? It doesn't matter, Barry, because you are going to learn another lesson today."

Barry started to cry, and Mark saw the legs of his jeans turn wet.

"Now, now, my little man. Don't be frightened, because it's a good lesson. *'When one door closes another one opens'*. Ever heard that? No, I thought not. Come with me. It's alright, they won't touch you."

They stood beside one another in the sweaty greenhouse; it was vast.

"You recognised it, didn't you Barry. Bet you don't know its Latin name…"

"Cannabis sativa!"

"What a surprising young man you are."

"I like biology."

"And I hear that you are quite a force in Temple Weston. The leader of the pack in Palmerston Way. Barry, how would you like to make a lot of money?"

Mark outlined his proposal and Barry agreed, with enthusiasm.

"I want my breakfast Barry, and you have rather delayed me. Here, something on account."

He pressed two twenty pound notes into the child's hand, clutching it tightly while he whispered.

"Don't ever think of telling anyone about our deal. Donald and Vladimir won't like it…and neither will I. You're not playing with your mates now, MATE! Go on, slide out the way you came in. The lads will escort you off the premises. It's alright, they won't harm you, unless I tell them."

In Palmerston Way someone else was aroused early, or rather a part of him had swollen. Jack Corrigan wrapped an arm around his wife and fondled her breasts. Marie tried not to shrink. She was in seventh heaven after yesterday's frivolities, and she couldn't bear the thought of sullying it by having Jack bouncing on top of her.

"Sorry Jack, time of the month."

He rolled onto his back and stared at the light fitting, before getting out of bed and heading for the bathroom. The door was locked.

"Is that you, Barry?"

"Yeh, just havin' a shower."

"Wonders will never cease. It's usually sundown before you get out of your pit. I'm going to make some breakfast. Do you want some?"

"Yeh...please."

Jack's eyebrows shot heavenwards. *'Please'*?

"My God," he exclaimed to himself, "things are looking up since Pa died!"

"Okay lad. We'll have the full Monty, and you can tell me what's made you full of the joys of spring."

Barry responded to his stepfather's laugh with a manufactured one of his own. How was he going to explain his piss-stained jeans?

12

'Pull the other one, it's got bells on.'

It is never surprising to find the auditorium of the Royal Shakespeare Theatre busy. The combination of tourists, schoolchildren, and the literati ensures that a tidy sum sustains the ringing of the tills.

"Going to buy anything Clem?"

"You know something Teddy…" Alfie halted mid-flow. "May I make a request?"

"Of course you may."

"Would you mind if I called you Edwina, it's such a pretty name?"

She felt herself get hot in delight at the compliment, and laughed.

"Edwina Mountbatten and Clem Attlee out on the town. People will talk. Well are you?"

"What?"

"Making a purchase?"

"I was going to say that the RSC shop always puzzles me. The theatre is the shining city on the hill for left wing luvvies. Here they espouse the cause of the downtrodden masses, whilst running a Capitalist enterprise. Have you seen the prices?"

Edwina's attention was elsewhere.

"Don't look now Clem. Oh well, go on, everyone else is."

She placed a hand on his shoulder, and twizzled him about. Eyes met across a crowded foyer, and a voice boomed, unfazed by the multitude of eyes upon him.

"Alf, Teddy."

Rufus Coleridge excused his way through the crowd; kissed Teddy on both cheeks, and shook Alf's hand.

"How lovely to see you here."

Roof was too well brought up to display surprise at seeing them out for the evening as a couple.

"On your own Rufus?"

He grinned widely.

"I rather think you know that I'm not, your Ladyship, from the direction of your steely gaze.

May I introduce my friend, Spencer Hoffman. Spencer, this is Teddy Bowcott, Lady of the Manor in Temple Weston, and this is Alfie Starkiss, Curate of All Souls, in the parish of that ilk."

"Actually Spencer, I am Edwina and this is Clem."

Roof shot them a quizzical look.

"Incognito tonight, are we?"

She linked Clem's arm.

"Our names in private for one another."

"Then Edwina and Clem it shall be, in private."

"Thank you Spencer. You two are attracting quite a crowd."

Rufus' dapper companion chimed,

"I'm afraid that we've become the side-show wherever we turn up these days."

"Spencer is rather more popular than I, currently."

"Oh Rufus, my poor dear."

"Thank you for your commiseration Edwina, but it's quite unnecessary. I'd rather fade into anonymity these days."

Edwina and Clem shared the same unspoken thought, and Roof divined it.

"Fair silent comment from you both. If I might be indiscreet, the Church, in the shape of Her Grace, rather encourages me to pursue these public appearances. Build our profile nationally. It has its rewards; that's how Spencer and I met."

"What's your line, Spencer?"

"I'm in television."

Clem lightly smacked the back of her hand.

"Really Edwina! Spencer is the highly successful host of *'Ring My Bell'*. It's a quiz show, I told you."

In response the warning bell for five minutes rang. Spencer took command.

"Just time to get the drinks order in for half time. G and T's all round?"

'Twelfth Night, or What You Will', to grant it its full title, is evergreen and popular with schools. The *'House'* was brimming with teenagers, all on best behaviour. There's never a dull moment at the RSC, and the current interpretation thrilled not only the youngsters, but also the large and earnest lady schoolteachers, and their hefty, bearded male counterparts.

Malvolio is the Steward in the house of the Lady Olivia, and encouraged by mischief-makers he believes she is in love with him. Or on this occasion, her! In the culturally thrusting RSC modern tradition, Malvolio was played as a rather austere lesbian, with a German accent. The comic characters of Sir Toby Belch, and the fey Sir Andrew Aguecheek had a similar Woke appeal. They were portrayed as suppressed English homosexuals, with the unsubtle hint that they were using Feste the Clown as gay 'trade'. The director, in her programme note, indicated that she wished to highlight the exploitation of the workers by the effete class. It went down a storm in *'The Guardian'* review.

Spencer expressed himself forcibly, during the interval.

"Trite and banal! Less *'What You Will'*, and more a case of *'Do what the fuck you like to mangle Shakespeare'*. The costume, my dears. Sydney Pride Parade meets Hampstead Heath! Can you imagine what would happen if they ever did a production in traditional costume?"

Clem blurted out.

"Piers Corbyn would picket the theatre, and brother Jeremy would demand that Anthony Eden withdraw from Suez!"

They roared with unabashed laughter. Around them, sensitive souls smiled unctuously, and were affirmed in their creed that artistes are such wonderful free spirits. A rumour did the rounds that Edwina and Clem were Toyah Wilcox and Mark Almond.

Spencer turned very Henry Irving on hearing the summons to return to their seats.

"I go, and it is done; the bell invites me.

Hear it not, Duncan, for it is a knell

That summons thee to heaven or to hell."

Rufus clasped his chum by the arm.

"I say, Spence, we're in enough trouble as it is, don't start quoting the Scottish play."

He rapidly addressed the other two.

"A thought dear friends. Spencer is staying the night on your manor. I've booked him a room at 'The Cock with Two Balls'…"

"How could I resist, my dears!"

"Shush Spence. Kelly Hampton's arranging a late supper for us. Won't you join us, I'm sure she can rustle up something?"

Edwina jumped straight in.

"We'd be delighted."

"Once more unto the breach, dear friends…"

"Oh stop showing off Spence."

Kelly Hampton escorted them to the dining room, located in the refurbished conservatory tagged on to the side of the pub. The grounds were floodlit, illuminating the lawns and casting light upon the church tower beyond.

Spencer was an old smoothie, if a tad more fresh-faced. He was pushing a decade younger than Rufus.

"I say Kelly, this is a bit special. Gorgeous ambience you've created. Love your napkins."

Her Brummie accent was broader than usual. Lunchtime trade had rushed them off their feet. The *'impoverished'* pensioners were out and about, now that the kids were back at school after half term, and the restaurant had been full all evening. Despite the lateness of the hour, the bar was packed. Kelly was knackered, but like the old pro' she was the cheery smile never left her face.

"Aw, thanks Spencer, you're a luv. God, I luv your programme, you're a bloody scream. Pardon my language your reverences. Now, Jilly will bring your drinks in two shakes of a lamb's doodle, and chef's got your tucker on the go. Give me a shout if there's anything I can do for you."

Spencer put an hand on Rufus' knee, and said archly,

"Sadly my dear, I don't think there is, but I'm all of a quiver about meeting your two balls."

"You'll have to go to London and Paris. I've no idea where the Cock is."

"My dear, you come right out with it, don't you!"

She left with a parting sally,

"A scream, a bloody scream!"

"Do exercise a little discretion, Spence. Clem and I have a bit of a position to uphold."

"My profound apologies Roof...Clem. Mixing with theatricals always brings out the worst in me. I say, who is the grand lady in the corner giving me the evils?"

Edwina made a half-turn, whilst depositing her bag on the floor.

"Oh, it's Freddie and Beebie, and who's that with them? It's Mark."

They followed Edwina's example and waved. Rufus pushed back his chair.

"I'll have a word. Be impolite not to….good evening Freddie, Benson. Hello Mark."

Beebie boomed.

"Taking your dinner a bit late, Rector. We're just on dessert…"

"Pudding my own, pudding. Good evening Rufus. Mark is treating his decrepit parents to a night out."

"Aye, we're celebrating the completion of phase one of his grand project."

"The allotment coming along well, Mark?"

"More a market garden. Yes thank you, Rufus. Won't be long before we are dispensing our crops to the poor. God willing, naturally."

Benson chirruped again.

"Church of England should take a leaf out of Mark's book. By their deeds ye shall know them. Isn't that biblical?"

Rufus bared his teeth, but smiled benignly.

"*'Ye shall know them by their fruits…'*, Matthew 7. Actually, Sir Benson, the Christian community does contribute a little to food programmes."

He delivered his treatise with the rapidity of a spitting machine gun.

"The Trussell Trust is the major player in food banks. The organisation is based upon Christian principles, and its values are rooted in Christian teaching and practice. Of course, no-one is excluded when it comes to giving help. Between April 2021 and March 2022 it distributed more than 2.1 million parcels. We have one of their food banks at St. Dunstan's. Do enjoy your *'dessert'*."

"What are you grinning at Freddie?"

"I was pondering the word *'comeuppance'* my own."

Mark burst into laughter.

"You did lead with your chin, Pa."

"I'm a busy man. How am I supposed to know all these things? And I don't need a bloody lecture over my sticky toffee pudding. Anyroad, who's that Nancy boy with the Rector? I can spot them a mile off."

"More to the point, my own, Teddy Bowcott and Alfie Starkiss look rather hunky dory with one another. Do you see how she keeps touching his arm?"

Beebie held his counsel about his recent sighting of the pair. For his own amusement, he'd labelled it *'The Affair at the Stile'*. He was rather pleased at that. Contrary to Freddie's belief, about his reading habits, he was an avid Agatha Christie fan.

"Time we got gone Freddie. Before we love you and leave you Mark – I take it you'll be joining the lock-in in the bar – I've a surprise. An announcement is imminent. I am to be the future Conservative candidate for the Parliamentary constituency of Dunsmore-by-Napton. About time that old bugger Bernard Watlington retired, get a local man in like me."

Mark covered for his astonished mother, who sat there with her mouth open catching flies.

"I say Pa, that's bloody marvellous. You're just the man for the job. This calls for champagne…"

"Not just now son. Keep it under your hat. We'll crack a bottle before dinner tomorrow…"

"…and it will be my pleasure to provide it, Pa. Cristal."

"Come on Freddie, shift your attractive posterior. Good night Mark, and thank you for dinner."

When they passed the clerics and their companions Freddie raised an eyebrow at Edwina Bowcott, accompanied by a wry smile. Teddy held her eye boldly, but Clem blushed.

"Rather good food," Spencer opined. "I do enjoy traditional English grub. Are we having pud'?"

Mark Hargreave passed by with a gracious smile and repaired to the bar. He settled his bill with Kelly and she gave him a cognac, on the house. With his back to the bar, he surveyed the room, and his attention lit upon a gorgeous blonde sitting on her own.

"Hi, I've brought you a refill. Looks like Prosecco you're drinking."

"It's champagne."

Her reserved and disinterested demeanour did not put him off.

"You look fabulous. Work out do you?"

In fact, she was the young woman Alfie had seen the rear end of disappearing into the distance with her running partner.

"I know a great club in Banbury we could go to…"

"Or you could go on your own!"

A tall and athletic man towered over him, and Mark saw the muscle rippling under his close fitting shirt.

"Just being pleasant to the lady. She shouldn't be left on her own."

"My wife and I are rarely separated. We even work together."

"Oh yes, what line are you in?"

"Ready for home Siobhan?"

"Yes Harry. This place no longer amuses me."

Mark remained in the chair he had commandeered, and watched them leave.

"Snotty bitch," he murmured.

He felt a hand on his shoulder. Kelly Hampton loomed over him.

"A word in your shell-like sunshine. Siobhan and Harry Norton live in the village. Well, at weekends. They appear every Friday evening from London." She drew closer. "Henry is a Royal Protection Officer, and the word on the street is that she's some sort of personal secretary at the Palace. Don't go rocking the boat, or our deal is off. It's dicey enough as it is without you stirring the waters. Keep your dick in your pants."

She gathered up a few glasses, and returned to the bar. Mark resented being spoken to like that by a pub landlady who, if rumour was right, was once a bloody prossie. However, he was savvy enough to know that he'd received sound advice. He slugged his cognac down, and left.

"If it's not impertinent, Rufus, are you two an item?"

"What do you think Spence?" He returned his attention to Edwina, and tried to answer her question. "We only met a couple of months ago. So it's *'One Day at a time sweet Jesus…"*

Spencer burst into song.

"Getting to know you, getting to know all about you…"

He was a canny lad.

"And what about you two, my dears?"

Clem continued his song from *'The King and I'*.

"Getting to like you, getting to hope you like me…"

Edwina stared at him with intent.

"Really?"

"Really."

Spencer plucked his napkin from his lap.

"Right, I'm off to the Land of Nod."

"And I must get home. I told Kelly you wouldn't want breakfast, Spence. A little light repast at the Vicarage. 09:30 sharp. You can remember the way?"

Rufus caught the look that passed between Edwina and Clem.

"It's not subterfuge. He really is staying here, and I am off to my lonely garret. Come on Spence, see me off the premises. Night you two. Oh, Spence is taking care of the bill. He's a bloated Capitalist living off the fat of the land."

"Steady on Roof. I don't work for the BBC. Night."

Edwina and Clem were alone. The synchronised rhythm of their breathing was the only thing disturbing the silence.

"What about you, Clem? Back to your lonely attic?"

"I expect so."

She drew an imaginary doodle on the table cloth.

"It doesn't have to be…"

His smile was gentle and sincere.

"One Day at a time sweet Jesus. I've had a wonderful evening Edwina, best in a long time, but I rather think that Roof and Spence have set the example. Small steps, one at a time. Listen, you know I'm holding a bonfire party in the grounds of the vicarage, for the kids on the estate. After they're gone there's drinks and a bit of supper for the adults. Would you be my hostess for the evening?"

She wanted to cry, she was so happy, and just nodded her agreement because she couldn't trust herself to speak.

"Come on, I'll see you to your door."

The conversation was conducted between bedrooms. Freddie had no intention of letting the old goat loose upon her; Conservative candidate or no.

"You're making too much of it Freddie. I know I'm a stickler in some things, but even the clergy need a bit of a cuddle now and again."

"That is not the point, Benson. A gay relationship on the one hand, and the other with a woman old enough to be his mother."

"Give over. There can't be more than ten or twelve years between them. You're out of fashion; it was good enough for Charles and Diana."

"An entirely different question. Behaviour like that is the prerogative of royalty."

"You're starting to sound like your mother," he said under his breath.

"What did you say?"

"I said pull the other. What's sauce for the goose is sauce for the gander."

"Nonsense! Those two gentlemen made sacred vows."

"I can see your point about *'Nigel Nice and Teddy Tidy'.*"

Beebie's reference to Vivian Stanshall's *'Sir Henry at Rawlinson End'* revealed the inordinate pleasure he took in listening to the ancient cassette tape. It transported him to an England long gone; if it ever was. He was word perfect.

"Nevertheless, my love, the Church has got all sorts of procedures in place for shirtlif...gay priests. Quite sound actually. As for the other two, well I have to say that the young man could learn a lot from a mature woman. You set me straight a few times, in our early days."

"Benson! I am only seven months older. I really am surprised to hear these views from you. Do you think they will go down well with your future constituents?"

He stopped drying his hands. She was right there. Better keep his opinions on this subject within the four walls of *'The Grange'*.

"There will be trouble Benson. Mark my words. The village will not stand for a vicar dallying with a lady above his status. Goodnight."

My God, she was turning into her mother. Or was she…?

13

'Everything comes to he who waits.'

An unanticipated calm descended upon the Corrigan household in Palmerston Way. Unbeknownst to Jack, Mark Hargreave was responsible for his current domestic bliss. Sadly, the hardworking foreman wasn't the recipient of any rapture or ecstasy.

"The smile's never off her face, but she's gone right off sex. Do you think the two are connected?" Jack was confiding in Kelly Hampton over a pint after work.

"Ah well, we ladies go through phases, Jack. Give her a couple of weeks and she'll be as right as rain. In the meantime, you know what your right hand's for?"

He threw her a sharp look.

"I meant do you want another pint. You fellas, never stop thinking about it. This one's on the house. Put a bit of lead in your pencil."

While she pulled the pint she thought what a miserable get Jack Corrigan was. Too busy to notice that someone else was banging his missus. She didn't blame Marie. If she was married to Jack she'd stick her head in the gas oven, or more probably his.

"Here you go lovey. Where is your Marie this evening?"

"Gerls night out in Leamington with Bianca."

He really was a dozy sod. She'd run into Bianca Bailey that morning.

"Can't get a babysitter, Kelly. Stuck in tonight."

The landlady wasn't as green as she was cabbage looking. More than likely Marie was having a night in, or rather someone was having a night in her, and she knew who it was.

The cannabis plants provided a surreal backdrop for Mark and Marie's assignations. She thought it was romantic, and brought a *'Love Island'* feel to their sexual exercises. Naturally, the environment was tropical hot to generate rapid growth.

Mark leant on his elbow, pouring two more glasses of discount champagne. He wasn't wasting the good stuff on Marie.

"Eh Marky. This carpet we're lying on is rough. Look."

She crouched on all fours to reveal the friction burns on her back.

"I have to get dressed and undressed when he's not around. I don't have sex with him, you know."

As if Mark gave a shit. He knelt behind her.

"Then in the interests of health and safety we'd better go at it like this until your scars are healed. Here, take your glass."

Marie accommodated herself to his rhythm so that she could take sips of champagne without spilling, whilst he thrust in and out of her doggy style.

"Eh Marky..."

His kept his sigh inaudible. Prefacing all her comments and questions with, *"Eh Marky!"* exhausted him. He wasn't too keen on the *'Marky'* either. However, she had her uses, and it wasn't just the sex.

"Yes my love?"

"Thanks ever so much for givin' Barry a weekend job. He's a changed lad. School says he's calmed down a bit, an' 'is attendance record is better. They're a bit bothered by how many

Fridays he has off, but apart from that he's doin' well. Even Jack says so. I reckon it's down to your influence."

Young Barry had numerous Fridays off, because he spent them being drilled with instructions about his weekend itinerary, and he wasn't alone. He had recruited two boys and a girl. All came willingly, apart from 'Little' Arthur. He was a delightful twelve-year old, who wouldn't say boo to a goose, and that was why he was so useful. Arthur's normally cheerful and angelic disposition would keep him free from suspicion. Mark loved him from the minute Barry effected introductions. Nonetheless, the new recruits had to be intimidated, and they were initiated into the world of 'Donald' and 'Vladimir' for starters.

Mark was gratified that the business venture had come to fruition. The production of cannabis for sale was going great guns. On Saturdays the children travelled by bus to various places, distributing the product to middle men and women working for Jay and Tommy. Their principal destinations were in Warwickshire, with regular trips to Warwick and Leamington Spa. Those towns also provided convenient rail links. Journeys into South Worcestershire and North Gloucestershire were not uncommon.

'Little' Arthur was excused duties on Sundays. Tony and Sandra, his parents, were churchgoers, and Arthur had to attend. The others worked alternate Sundays. They would meet Jay and Tommy's drivers in the back lane, and be taken to Coventry; the hub for the day's work. It was going like a dream.

To add to Mark's delight, Kelly Hampton was shifting a small, but regular, amount of *'gear'* to a trusted few. That outlet was growing though, because her customers began to act as suppliers for friends.

Mark slapped Marie's backside.

"Come on, time for you to go."

"Aw, 'ave I got to?"

"Places to go, people to see."

She pulled her mini dress over her head.

"Eh Marky."

"Yes, light of my life?"

"When can we have that weekend away?"

"That's rather up to you. Had any ideas yet?"

"I'm not supposed to show my face in Liverpool, but I could tell him I'm going somewhere to meet my mum and sister."

"Great idea. Choose a couple of dates. I can't be free at the drop of a hat."

Mark knew all about the Corrigan's rapid departure from Liverpool. Marie couldn't keep her mouth shut if her life depended upon it. When she told him the real reason, he had worried away at it for a while. Then he had a brainwave. Young Barry was becoming cocky, and Mark needed to put the frighteners on him.

"You fuck about with me, Barry, and certain people in Liverpool might discover where you live. Understand?"

Barry understood, but he also comprehended something else. Their family predicament was supposed to be a cast iron secret. As far as he knew, Mark Hargreave had nothing to do with his stepfather, but he'd overheard some gossip on the estate. So they were right. Someone was knobbin' his mother, and now he knew who. Well, he'd curb his tongue and stop being arsey with Mark, but useful information cuts both ways.

Marie was still in bed on Sunday morning, sleeping off her hangover, and a puff or two of some stimulating tobacco Mark had supplied. Jack was up with the lark. If he couldn't screw his wife then he'd focus on shafting Beebie Hargreave.

"Brothers and sisters, the offer of two-and-half percent is an insult in these times of economic crisis. If we do not band together in comradely unity any negotiations with the employer will fall on deaf ears."

The gathering assembled on one of the football pitches bequeathed by Beebie, as part of the estate. Jack gave up every evening the previous week, canvassing from door to door. He was gratified by the response, estimating that around eighty-five per cent of the residents/employees had turned out for the meeting.

"I therefore propose that we form a staff association, from which members will be elected to make representation to management on all issues appertaining to pay and conditions in the factory."

A middle-aged man of Indian origin called out,

"You mean a trade union?"

Jack smiled broadly.

"Association falls more gently on the ear."

A wave of laughter rippled across the playing field. The piping treble of an elderly woman silenced it, as she declared with approval,

"*A rose by any other name would smell as sweet.*"

Jack looked over his shoulder. Mary Jessop was seated on a kitchen chair; upon the small platform they had erected. Though she no longer worked in the factory, she was right behind Jack in every sense. Her late husband never rocked the boat with Beebie Hargreave, but had on occasion stood up to him in that quiet but obdurate fashion of his. Eddie and the gaffer had always managed to settle their differences quietly, and keep the factory on an even keel. Mary knew times had changed, and a more formal setup was required, or pay and conditions for the workforce would be at the whim of Hargreave.

"Thank you Mary, nicely put. Now I think we'd all like to get down to some breakfast and a read of the newspaper, after a hard week's work. So, I've got some membership forms. Very easy; name, address, and signature. We've kept it simple to begin with. A few basic rules of membership, including election of officers, and your agreement that the association can negotiate on your behalf…"

"How much?"

"Eh?"

"To join, Jack?"

"Five pounds a month, just to cover admin costs. Elected officials are not paid, and at this stage we can't see the need for expenses. We all live cheek by jowl on the estate. Once we're up and running, we'll have a social committee for events in the club, and fundraising."

Jack paused. This was the moment of truth.

"If you're in favour of the association," he held out a biro, "come up and take a form. You can complete it now, or take it away and give it to me at work next week. First month's subscription on pay day."

"Over a hundred signed up, or took the form away, sir."

Beebie Hargreave tapped his desk with one finger.

"What about you, Kyle, did you put your moniker on this bit of paper?"

It took Kyle Bailey a moment before it dawned on him what he was being asked.

"Well, yes and no, Sir Benson."

"What's that supposed to mean?"

"I went up with the rest and took a form, but I'm not going to fill it in…"

"I think you are, son. You'll sign it, and stand for election to the committee. I'll give you the money for the subscription. Are you getting my drift?"

Kyle was thrilled.

"Like I'm your agent on the inside. Brill!"

"Furthermore, young man, at the end of this month you will receive a pay rise of five per cent. That's between you, me and the gate post, and pay roll of course. Harry Greenwood can deal with it personally. We can rely on Harry to make sure nobody else knows about it. Deal or no deal lad?"

"Deal sir, definitely a deal."

Beebie stared into space, and said to himself,

"Association my arse. A bloody union. If Yak herders in Outer Mongolia went on strike their bloody shop steward would be a Scouser!"

14

'It never rains, but it pours.'

Dante's Inferno could not have lit the sky so brightly, nor produced such a hellish sight. The Church Hall, of All Souls Temple Weston, went up like a Roman candle, illuminating the Primary School next door.

A crescent moon dwelt over the village, but was becoming indistinct as dawn approached. Alfie looked heavenward, wondering if its job was done. It seemed to condone the event unfolding before his eyes. His mother had been brim-full of superstition, and related many a nuance to him of this or that primitive belief throughout his childhood years. She called it the sickle moon It was appropriate, as Alfie spied the paramedics emerging from the smouldering remains. Aficionados of Moon lore hold that, in its current state, it was a sign of fertility related to life and death; pinpointing the changing seasons. He recollected one other fact. A sickle moon is congruent with the feminine menstrual cycle. Blood.

Those villagers who had not returned to their beds, following the initial excitement of emergency vehicles arriving, resembled the Anthony Gormley statues he'd seen on a rare visit home to Liverpool. One hundred cast iron figures facing towards the sea at Crosby Beach, outside the city. Alfie had been so fascinated by them that he sat on a dune for over four hours. When the tide receded, the sight of the solemn manikins emerging from the waters bewitched him. Located at varying points and distances, each revealed itself according to the will of the sea. Those nearest the shoreline emerged soonest, a revelation of God in their wholeness. Others remained submerged to random degrees; they seemed to cry out for the hand of rescue. Furthest away, motionless heads emanated resolve; refuting the unforgiving mockery of the waves.

Alfie hailed farewell to them, and drove back to theological college. Processing interminably through roadworks on the M6, he struggled to find the single word that might express the spiritual experience he had undergone. Once in his room he sought his thesaurus. *'Colossus'* – man as master? *'Puppet'* – man, alive only at the whim of chance encounters? A cyborg, a Dalek, a symbol. Of what? His eye latched onto *'idol'* – modern man, who has made an idol of himself. None satisfied him, until he saw *'icon'*. Perhaps that was what Gormley was trying to say. Poor mankind. An image sometimes revealed complete in the joyous light of day; too frequently submerged, in part or whole. Snared in the tentacles of fear and anxiety, bitterness and disappointment; head only just above water.

The tiny parcel was handled lovingly by the paramedics. Silence chained the immobile people, broken only by the *'wock, wock, wock-a-wock'* of the magpies gathering to feast on leftovers in the pub garden. The harshness of their call mimicked the bleak autumn dawn. More than one person shared in Alfie's conclusion that it was the heartless cry of *'every man for himself'*.

"Excuse me vicar."

Alfie did not correct the policeman standing before him, but gave him rapt attention.

"We found this on the body."

He took the proffered card from the officer.

"I'm surprised it didn't burn."

"He was at the rear of the building, sir, in the toilets. The brigade managed to extinguish the fire before it got to him."

"Then…?"

"Smoke sir. Not uncommon. Even if the flames do reach them, the smoke has usually got them first. Would you look at the card sir?"

Alfie gave a cursory glance. The best of them. Why is it always the best of them?

"Sir!"

"Yes...?"

"Pete, sir."

"Yes Peter, I recognise him. I issued the cards."

His comments came staccato. Like a sergeant major on the parade ground, but in lullaby tones.

"Kiss me good night sergeant major..."

"Beg pardon, sir?"

"Sorry Peter. Started a youth club last month. Something for them to do. ID card each. Thought it might give a sense of belonging."

Pete picked up Alfie's mode of speech.

"Hesitate to ask, sir. Would you be prepared..." he gestured to the open doors of the ambulance, "might save the parents having...not sure about that."

Alfie inhaled a great draught of the early morning mist, that had woven the village in its suffocating grasp.

"Of course, Peter. He and his parents are my parishioners."

"Living in your parish, or actual churchgoers?"

A thin smile flickered on Alfie's face. He replied with an irony he couldn't restrain.

"Surprisingly, members of my congregation."

"I'm sorry, vicar, I wasn't meaning to be…"

"I know, I know. It's me who's sorry Pete. I beg your pardon. Shall we?"

He nodded towards the ambulance. "Yes sir. One more thing, before we do. Your parishioners, you say. Would you join us when we…break the news?"

"I'll do it for you."

"Very kind of you sir, but there are certain procedures and formalities that have to be gone through."

The stricken crowd parted when the two men approached the ambulance. Their realisation that Alfie was about to identify the body brought a collective gasp and exhalation of breath, that swirled before their faces. The ambulance doors closed on them, and a paramedic unzipped the body bag to reveal the face of an angel, gone to join his Father.

Alfie was rigid at the sight. He reached out and stroked the child's hair then made the sign of the cross on his forehead, before slumping to his knees. His hand rested upon the body, while he intoned with sorrow,

"Oh Arthur, our 'Little' Arthur."

The tears would not stop. Weeping for the son of man. Just as Jesus wept for his friend Lazarus.

Edwina Bowcott was one of those woken by the conflagration, and was joined by Freddie Hargreave. Together they made tea and sandwiches in her kitchen, and served the emergency workers and the villagers throughout the dark night. Their ministry was lit only by the sentinel moon and starlight, as the fire was brought under control. There hadn't been an opportunity to speak with Clem. He was engaged in ministering to his parishioners.

Before Alfie and Pete left the ambulance officers dispersed the crowd to their homes. Hardly anyone was about when they emerged. Edwina was standing across the road, and caught Clem's eye – she could no longer think of him as 'Alfie'. The sorrow and bewilderment in his face caused tears to course down her cheeks.

"You really love him, don't you Teddy."

Freddie rested an arm on a gate post as she spoke. A sense of wonder was in her voice, as if the love she had witnessed in a fleeting look was unfathomable.

"Yes I do. Where does love come from, and so suddenly?"

Even though Freddie stood beside her she only just heard her rejoinder.

"And where does it go to when it leaves?"

Freddie flicked her head to one side, as if looking for the person who had asked the question. She pulled herself together; the model of a stout Englishwoman handling a crisis.

"Time to get back to our men, Teddy. Oh, I am sorry."

Edwina Bowcott embraced her, then wended her way back to the Manor House.

Blind chance tends to lurk over the shoulder. Freddie Hargreave never knew that she had not committed a *faux pas*. Edwina was removing her outer layers and wellies when she heard a noise from the upper reaches of the house. Riding crop in hand, she padded up the stairway. Pausing at the top to listen, she concluded that someone was in her bedroom. Creeping along the corridor, she wished that she had taken a walking stick instead of the crop, but ventured on.

"Blue moon, you saw me standing alone, without a dream in my heart, without a love of my own…"

"Do come in, darling. You'll never make a commando."

Guffawing laughter sullied the air.

"Bowcott! What the fuck are you doing in my bedroom?"

"Well I'd say you already know the answer to that, by the looks of the riding crop. Still turning the old tricks are you, Teddy?"

The same sneering and lascivious laughter of yesteryear.

"Edwina, I prefer to be known as Edwina. What in God's name brings you here, and at this hour of the morning?"

She examined him, sitting up in her bed. He still bore the look of Lord Lucan. The full head of black oiled hair and a moustache like a fox's brush.

Their spry polish could no longer conceal the condition of his features; ravaged by an excess of alcohol, and what used to be charmingly known as *'loose living'*. He looked all of his seventy-four years.

"Hop in old girl, and let's have *'a few fast falls'*.

The last phrase was a perfect impression of Sean Connery in *'Goldfinger'*."

"No longer amusing Bowcott. I'm rather smitten by Daniel Craig these days."

"Huh! What's going on out there?"

"Arson!"

"Oh yes, someone *'arsing'* around?"

She'd never been fond of his braying laugh, but now it positively angered her.

"Not funny Bowcott. I believe a child may have died. Now what do you want, and at this time of day for heaven's sake?"

"Got back from Thailand a week ago. Been in Town since. Got turfed out of the gaming club in the early hours, so thought I'd motor up to see the old place…and you of course, my beloved."

"Tired of Thai girls, are you?"

"Oh, never tire of that, but you know Teddy...beg pardon, Edwina. I say, I'm rather glad you've gone back to your baptismal name. Charming. No, I've been gadding around the world for a dozen years or so. Time to come home."

"This is not your home."

"Oh but it is. I signed on the dotted line to agree that you could stay here in perpetuity; nothing in the agreement to say I couldn't reside here too. It's my property, and we're not divorced."

"I shall see Bernard Hetherington this morning..."

"That old sod still practising? Won't do you any good. My brief has been through it with the proverbial fine hair brush. Quite within my legal rights."

His *'brief'* led a top London chambers. Edwina knew in her heart that he was almost certainly right. Obnoxious as he was to her, she never doubted his qualities of mind.

"Very well. Then I shall start divorce proceedings. I should think after all these years the courts will applaud your generosity when you are compelled to donate the Manor to me."

Bowcott had a rummage beneath the sheets.

"Scuse me darling, just rotating the crops. Ah well, it would appear then that you have me over a barrel. I don't know though; high profile divorce cases can be problematic for both parties. Speaking of parties, we used to have some marvellous times, didn't we? You still in contact with Chad Corbett and his missus? What about the Flexingtons? Get up to North Yorkshire occasionally, do you?"

"Yes, no, no, and what the fuck are you on about?"

"Dear me, Lady Edwina, you should go to church more regularly, and confess your sins."

She blushed heavily and thought, "He couldn't know, surely not?"

"My, my, you are looking flushed. Time of life, darling?"

His voice hardened.

"Now listen to me. We are going to jog along here together. In my safety deposit box at Coutts there is a significant collection of fine photographs and cinematography. If there's any more talk of divorce…"

"You wouldn't dare. It would damage you as well."

"My dear middle class wench. This is not a bungalow in Clitheroe. We are an ancient family, and the lower orders expect to dine on our salacious shenanigans now and again. Frankly, once the dust settles they end up rather admiring us for having the chutzpah to do what they dream about. Besides, if old Sir Rufus Bowcott can drop us in the excrement, footnote Crookback, and come up smelling of roses then I hardly think our sensational divorce will be of any consequence for my family. Now you, however. Your parents are still alive, aren't they?"

Her mother was fading away in a care home, but her father remained all there with his cough drops, and she worshipped her father. Edwina came to a decision.

"Jog along? Agreed, but for public consumption, period. Don't for one minute think I'm going to share your bed, or wait on you hand and foot."

"With all due respect, my dear, you're still a fine looking woman, but my tastes have changed. I prefer spring chickens to old broilers."

She bit her lip, and swallowed the insult.

"You can have my bedroom, Bowcott, now that the sheets are soiled."

"Hang on a tick. Just before you go I'd better unburden my immortal soul somewhat further. I'm on borrowed time. Eighteen months at the most…"

"If you're expecting sympathy…"

"I'm not! That's a minor issue. Fact is Edwina, when I go you go. My son will be master here."

The colour drained from her face.

"Your what?"

"My son."

"Thai, Indian, Filipino?"

"Not at all, my dear. Sound English stock. Couldn't rustle up a pot of coffee, could you?"

Edwina left the room. Halfway along the corridor she put a hand onto the wall to steady herself. An impious voice carried to her.

"She's a lassie from Lancashire,

Just a lassie from Lancashire…"

It resembled the massed choir of magpies in Kelly Hampton's garden. She pulled on her outerwear, and took a shotgun from the locked cabinet.

Mark Hargreave spent the night in Banbury, attending to his other business enterprise. He was minded to wind up his escort business, or rather sell it on. The cannabis trade was minting it for him.

He took the circuitous country route to Temple Weston, avoiding the sterile delights of the M40. While crawling over Bridge Foot, in Stratford-Upon-Avon, he had time to eye up the local talent crossing the river by the narrow footpath. One young lady was Daisy's doppelganger. The traffic was static, so he stretched himself out. It loosened a few taut muscles, brought on by sexual gymnastics throughout the night with the youthful prostitute. She had wittered on again about them having a weekend away. Mark laughed at the delicious thought, sprinkling itself like fairy dust in his cranium. Daisy and Marie, Marie and Daisy. Could he pull that off? The traffic moved, and he nodded in the direction of the Royal Shakespeare Theatre. Mark knew his Shakespeare, and wondered if the sprightly idea had come to him magically through Puck, or maybe Ariel. He nodded to the ugly tower with gratitude, and exclaimed,

"Thanks Bill, old lad!"

"Where in the name of Jesus Christ Almighty have you been?"

Mark did not require the powers of divination that Shakespeare had bestowed upon Prospero to know that his father was in a foul mood. However, his mother interjected before he could reply.

"Benson! I will not have blaspheming in this house. You may no longer be Churchwarden, but that does not relieve you of your Christian responsibilities and duties."

Mark stood in the background, a look of astonishment on his face. He had never realised that his mother was deeply religious. In his surprise he didn't even consider how he might use it to advantage. Beebie was chunnering an apology, and Mark thought it politic to help the old man out.

"Sorry Pa. Spent the last twenty-four in Banbury. Tying up loose ends. I say, I've just heard the news in *'Deux Testicules'*."

"Where? Oh, I see, the pub. What were you doing in there at this time of day?"

"Spot of lunch, Pa. Don't worry, I've not turned into a *'Lockdown Pisshead'*. Soon as I heard about the little lad I couldn't face a thing. Turned on my heel, and came home. Nobody seems to know what's going on."

"I'll tell you what's going on. I was supposed to be interviewed this morning by the local rag, and one of the nationals, to announce myself as the Conservative candidate-to-be. Now they're all out chasing this story. At least the radio interview was pre-recorded. It should be broadcast at half three this afternoon."

There was disdain in Freddie's voice when she spoke, and her tone would have made an iceberg shiver.

"Benson, a child has died. A monstrous crime has been committed, and all you can think of is yourself. Do you consider that you are fitted to be a parliamentary representative?"

Mark thought it was a prerequisite for being an M.P., but didn't much care for the direction the conversation was taking.

"Do you know any more about this sad affair, Mama? I don't even know the name of the child."

She was about to blurt out that she had telephoned Edwina Bowcott. The police were communicating what they knew with Clem Starkiss, and he had spoken with Edwina. The update was shared with Freddie, because they were all on the PCC. Instinct guided her, and she took care not to link Edwina and Clem's names in front of her son and husband.

"I have been made aware that the police are almost certain the arson was committed by teenage vandals who broke into the Hall. Apparently, a petty cash box is missing…"

"How much, Freddie?"

"I really couldn't say Benson. Does it matter?"

"Who told you?"

"Rather not say, Benson."

The old man looked ready to explode. Mark snuffed out the fuse.

"Strange business, Mama."

"What is Mark?"

"Well, why didn't the kid leave, like the rest of them?"

She hesitated. Edwina had put her on oath not to reveal this piece of information to anyone. Caught up in the moment, temptation overcame her.

"You must not reveal this to anyone. It isn't public knowledge yet. He was in the lavatories, and the door was locked."

Mark's expression was quizzical.

"We all lock the door when we're engaged, no pun intended, with, ahem, number two's. Why didn't he unlock and scarper, with the rest of the hooligans?"

"Not the cubicle door, my dear, the external door. Someone had locked him in."

Each dwelt upon the insidious pincers of terror that gripped their minds. Beebie spoke with a sensitivity to which his family was unaccustomed.

"Poor little mite. He were a good lad an' all. How the heck did he get in with a crowd like that?"

"The parents work for you, don't they Benson?"

"Aye Tony and Sandra Archer. Two of my more reliable employees. I see where you're going with this, my love. Not today, and mebbe not tomorrow, but I'll see what I can do for them."

"Compassionate leave, Benson?"

"Of course, my love. On full pay. Perhaps a note to them today won't be taken amiss. It'll be something less to worry over."

"Can't say I know the family, Pa."

Freddie filled him in.

"The Archers live on the estate. Only about twenty-nine years old. I'm told they were a love match at seventeen. Arthur was twelve."

A dreadful unease broke over Mark's features. He walked to the drinks trolley to pour a small cognac. The offer to his parents was declined. It was a day for the unaccustomed. Mark spoke hesitantly.

"Arthur you say, Mama," and he exhaled the name once more, "Arthur, can't seem to place the child."

"Oh Mark, you must remember him. Small boy with blonde hair, and beautiful, fathomless, blue eyes. He read one of the lessons at the Harvest Service. Tony and Sandra were so proud of him. 'Little' Arthur they called him, we all knew him as 'Little' Arthur."

The brandy balloon was of the finest. It crushed and splintered under pressure. Mark's hand spouted blood.

"Oh my darling, what have you done. Quickly Benson, there's a clean handkerchief in my handbag."

Mark peered at his hand as if he'd never seen it before.

"Don't touch your other hand, darling, it will go everywhere. Let me see. It's not too bad. We'll soon have it sorted. Benson, telephone the surgery."

Mark held out his hands, and murmured,

"Sorry Ma, sorry Pa. All very upsetting."

He gripped his hands together, before opening them in an attitude of supplication. The stains throbbed before his eyes, and issued runes of understanding. Mark knew exactly what had happened; he knew who, and he knew why. He looked downwards once again. There was blood on his hands.

Barry Corrigan swaggered towards the greenhouses. It was Friday, and another day sagging school. Out and about tomorrow on deliveries, and pay day to boot. He saw Mark fingering his precious plants.

"Hiya boss. Eh, worr'ave youse done to yer 'and?"

"WHAT HAVE YOU DONE TO YOUR HAND!"

"That's worra said, didn't I."

Mark stood well away from the teenager. There was an almost palpable scent coming off the boy.

He thought that his plants would wither and become lifeless. The bandaged hand rose into the air. Barry's eyes shone.

"Did it hurt?"

He froze. The growling behind him made the hairs stand up on his arse, never mind his neck.

"Wot? Wot 'ave a done?"

"You know very well."

"I never dun nottin. You're always pickin' on me."

"What did I tell you to do about 'L…'" he couldn't say 'Little', "…about Arthur?"

"'e wuz gettin' arsey. You told me to do it. I'll tell 'em you told me to do it!"

Mark clicked the fingers on his good hand, and the dogs noses pressed against Barry's legs.

"Call 'em off, call 'em off! I'll keep me gob shut, promise."

Another click, and the dogs withdrew. Mark pointed at Barry, then at his own feet.

"Sit!"

Barry responded like the Roadrunner.

"Tell me about Arthur."

"Tell you what?"

"Why was he getting arsey? What were you doing to him?"

There was a pause, and Barry cast his eyes downwards.

"You were bullying him weren't you…all the time."

The normally aggressive voice disappeared, and the high-pitched treble of a much younger boy emerged.

"Yeh, but 'e didn't wanna do wot we was doin', so I 'ad to keep at him." His cry was plaintive. "'e would 'ave grassed us up."

Mark towered over the teenager.

"That's makes it alright then, doesn't it…and you like picking on younger kids anyway, don't you Barry? Gives you a kick."

The boy shrugged. Mark squatted in front of him and hissed.

"Don't shrug your fucking shoulders at me! Stand up. Tell me about breaking into the hall."

"It was just a laff, an' I thought I could put the shits up 'im. Keep 'im quiet like."

"And?"

"That vicar's a dick head. Got a cash box, an' flashin' it about in front of everyone. He was askin' to be robbed. There was seventy-five notes in there."

"I will acquiesce to your judgement on the cleric, can't say I know him that well. So, a late night raid, a few bob in your pocket, and everyone goes safely up the stairs to Bedfordshire."

Mark turned to examine new growth on one of the plants. Without warning he swung around, and thrust his face into Barry's.

"Why the fire, dick head?"

Barry's head drooped.

"Why did you lock him in?

"I…"

The denial expired on his lips, and a tremulous silence lay between them.

"I'll tell you why, because you've done it before. Haven't you? HAVEN'T YOU? Answer not required. A little dicky bird told me everything about your exploits in Liverpool. Witness protection my arse. You're here in this saintly village to save your skin from the family of the last kid you maimed. Oh, he didn't die, but first degree burns for life are not exactly a barrel of laughs.

Put you away for a couple of years, didn't they, in some soft-arsed rehabilitation centre, but you're not going to change."

Mark turned his back on the boy, and steadied his breathing. He knew that he was in the presence of pure evil, and it tainted him. He forced down the choking realisation that the essence of evil circulated in his veins and arteries. It had been there for years, and he hadn't flinched from inflicting violence on others.

"I said tell me about Arthur."

"Wot do you mean?"

"What was he like? What sort of things did he do?"

"Goody two shoes. He never even fuckin' swore. Went to church with 'is mam an' dad. *'Did good werks'*.

"What do you mean by that?"

"Sumfin tha' dick head I have to live wiv said. You know, like he helps people. Dick 'ead Jack reckons that's good. Wanted me to start doin' it. Said I should *'take a leaf out of Little Arthur's book'*. Soft pair of friggers. You gotta look after number one, that's wot my real dad sez. Wankers!"

Mark leant against a bench, and crossed his arms to support his injured hand.

"Did he help anyone in particular?"

"Oh yeh, 'e 'ad 'is regulars. There was…"

"Hold on. One more question. Did your other companions in our enterprise accompany you on the hall job?"

"Nah. Liam' ad the wild shites from a dodgy curry, an' Beks said she 'ad the bellyache an' all. Reckon she was *'on the rags'*."

"Barry, the milk of human kindness is a never-ending stream flowing through your veins."

The boy was tempted to follow his instincts and shrug. He restrained himself just in time.

"So who was with you?"

"Nobody. Just me an' the kid."

"Arthur was whiter than white, so I'm told. How did you get him to go along with your little…" he winced at the word, "escapade?"

Barry looked like the cat who got the cream.

"It was fuckin' boss! You know he was dead religious. I mean not just like doin' it cos 'is mum an' dad did. He was always goin' on. Know what he said to me once?"

Mark shook his head. Barry drew himself up, and declaimed like a 19th Century Shakespearean actor.

"The wicked man craves evil; his neighbour gets no mercy from him."

He paused for applause. None was forthcoming.

"That's when I knew 'ow I could put the frighteners on him."

This time he posed as a humble child, and transported them to a hiding place on the school fields.

"Eh, Little Arthur, I've been thinkin' about God and…wot's 'is name?"

Mark swallowed bile, as he heard the perfect imitation of the dead child's voice.

"Jesus, Barry, Jesus our Saviour."

"Yeh, right. He's great, isn't he Arthur. I don't wanna go on doin' wot 'im in the big 'ouse makes us do. I wanna re…re…re… wot is it Arthur?"

"Repent of your sins and be saved."

"Dead right mate. I've 'ad an idea, but I'm scared. Will you go with me?"

"Where?"

"I wanna pray for forgiveness."

"That's fantastic Barry. Come to church with us on Sunday."

"Argh, I don't know. Me mam an' dad won't come, an' I couldn't do it in front of everyone without them. I was thinkin'..."

"Go on."

"Praps we could sneak into the Church Hall, an' I cud do it with you. You cud show me 'ow. That'd be great."

"The church stays open in the week. We could go after school."

"Nah, I don't want everyone to see me goin' into a church." He saw the look on Arthur's face, and hastily posted an addendum. "I mean I will eventually, but like just to get started you an' me together."

"The church hall is locked, unless there's an event on."

"I know how to get in. We wouldn't break anythin', or rob anythin'. Only be in there for five minutes, an' we'd leave it just 'ow it was...an' then I'd be saved."

Mark wanted to ask how he had convinced Arthur to sneak out in the middle of the night, but knew the question was superfluous. Barry's serpent tongue had solved the final difficulty with ease. He walked to the door, and opened it, but the air wasn't fresh. The guiltless part of the market garden was irreparably poisoned.

"From now on you are off the job. You still get paid. The police will be crawling all over this village for the foreseeable future, and you are a liability. Now, before I tell you what you are going to do, get this into your thick skull. Even if they arrest you; even if you get sent down I will bank money for you. But…BUT…if under any circumstances you are tempted to grass…"

His arm shot out. Donald and Vladimir raced towards them. Mark forced himself to push his nose against Barry's.

"Dogs escape from premises all the time. They will rip your fucking throat out!" He let the image sink in. "Don't worry, I'll see you get a decent funeral. Then you'll be going up in flames."

He pulled his face away, and spat.

"I can afford the fine, and a suspended sentence. They certainly won't put me away – forever! Now listen, and listen carefully, *'I shall say this only once'*. The line from the comedy show *'Allo 'Allo* was delivered perfectly. Mark's mordant wit rarely left him for long.

15

'The sights you see when you haven't got your gun.'

Nobody was joking with Detective Inspector Molly McGuire; it was a rare day. Her destination was about half a mile from the primary school, and John Fortune, her DC knew when to remain *schtum*. The rest of the team would meet them there.

Temple Weston was new territory to her. When they reached the church she took a swift left into the churchyard. A surprised John Fortune nipped after her. She moved around the graveyard in a decisive fashion, stopping occasionally to peer at names on tombstones.

Good and evil played ping pong in her cerebral cortex. If only the great British public knew. To most of them evil was something played out on their television screens. 6 o'clock warnings on the news.

"The following report may contain distressing scenes," and afterwards, *"If any of the scenes in the report have given you cause..."*

Followed by signposting to the appropriate support organisations.

Molly was far from being sceptical about this, but she dealt with the victims on the front line; those with immediate and devastating trauma.

She craned her head backwards to view the immensely tall tower reaching up to God. Though ambivalent about religion she knew enough about Christianity to give a confident answer to that most basic question which seemed to bewilder clergy.

"Why does God allow evil?"

When clergy were asked the question they stood rabbit-like in the headlights, apparently unwilling or unable to answer. If those higher up the chain tried to explain their answers spiralled into intellectual obscurity.

Molly ordered the proposition inside her head. If you believed in the Christian God then you knew that He had made you in His own image, and you possessed free will. When Man, *"or should I say Person,"* she thought, fell from Grace in the Garden of Eden perfection was destroyed, but free will remained. God still wanted partners, not cyphers. So imperfect Person, oh bugger it, Man retained the capacity to choose between good and evil.

Working out where she stood on religion was an ongoing process for Molly. She knew from relentless experience, though, that it was those who plump forbade choices who commit evil. God took a decision somewhere along the line to give everyone the free gift of redemption through the sacrifice of His Son. You pays your money and you makes your choice. The only one to blame when evil was done was the human perpetrator, who chose the wrong side of the fence.

   She noted the time. It was insufficient to ponder the atheist proposition that free will is an illusion. Anyway, the sanctimonious ponce who came up with that one couldn't even make his mind up which side of the party political divide he subscribed to; apart from always falling out with his brother. Molly stopped dead. Perhaps political indecision proved the absence of free will? She was confusing herself now, so started walking again. Falling out with a relative was altogether another case. From time to time it injures most of us, but we don't wage vendettas. No, whatever her belief, or lack of it, she had dealt with enough evil to know that it lives next door, not just in faraway lands. One thing she was sure of was that the capacity to do evil is universal. Unwittingly, she subscribed to Original Sin.

"What have we learnt, John?"

"Same thing at both schools. The lad was an angel on stilts."

"They don't need a lift up John, they have wings."

"Sorry ma'am, I wasn't being flippant."

"That's alright John. You know what it's like when there's a child involved. Model pupil at Primary School, and the same at the Comp'. Well-liked by everyone; adored by the teachers."

"Not sure about Arthur's form teacher, the science master. Creepy bugger, if you ask me. Bit too keen. Never stopped smiling and rubbing his hands. Did you see his complexion? I've seen healthier cadavers in the mortuary. Do we keep him in the frame?"

"Hmmm? We won't cross him off the list just yet, but I don't think *'Uriah Heep'* is quite up to murder."

"Uriah who, ma'am?"

"Dear me John, don't you know anything about Dickens?"

"I've never been to one, ma'am."

"Inappropriate John."

"Sorry."

Molly gave her partner a smile of reassurance.

"Bloody clever though, even if I did hear it about twenty years ago. We got something out of the comprehensive school head teacher."

It was more of a question. John was a smart cookie, and she was training him for better things.

"Been a lot quieter over the last couple of months, and I was especially taken by her observation that Arthur seemed tired all the time, and lethargic. *'Spaced out,'* she said."

"So you weren't just ogling her legs."

"They get younger, ma'am..." and together they exclaimed, "like policemen!"

"Here we are, Palmerston Way. The lads have arrived on time. Okay John, big breaths."

John Fortune fought the temptation to say,

"Yeth, and I'm only thixteen!"

Molly placed her hand on the gate. Her keen eyes took in the details of the street. She studied the only detached house. A teenage boy was amassing leaves on the front lawn with the aid of a rake. She wondered why he wasn't in school. The front door opened, and an elderly lady made her painful way towards the lad. She held a plate in her hand. Molly could make out a burger in a bun. There was a short exchange between the pair, with a pleasant smile shared. The old woman traipsed back to the house, but hesitated before closing the door. She looked directly at Molly, tapped her watch, and held up three fingers. Molly gave a vigorous nod. If she'd understood correctly, the old girl wanted a chat with them at three o' clock.

"Interesting Molly."

"Got my attention John. Come on."

"Half a league, half a league, half a league onward, into the Valley of Death…"

He may not have known his Dickens, but he was clued up on Tennyson. She was impressed. Nor was it inappropriate, and first names were always used in front of grieving loved ones; it humanised them.

Tony and Sandra Archer were as anticipated. Huddled beside one another on the sofa. Their complexions were corpse-white; the sort of look a sensitive child expects to see on a ghastly wraith rising above their bedroom window sill. The

Archers couldn't keep food down. When they tried to eat they vomited.

This interview was especially hard. Molly thanked the God she wasn't sure about that they had sufficient questions to ask, which might distract from clunking feet upstairs, executing the search warrant.

John Fortune led.

"I'm sorry about this Tony, Sandra, but the forensic evidence means we have to check."

"Cannabis in Arthur's bloodstream. I will not believe it; we will not believe it."

Sandra Archer spoke quietly, but firmly. She didn't direct anger or rancour at them. Molly McGuire was impressed with the couple. For all the trauma that had wrecked their physical well-being, she knew conviction when she saw it. John continued.

"I'm afraid the evidence is conclusive..."

"Tell us about Arthur, Sandra."

It was Tony who spoke.

"He was remarkable...even to us. It was as if we didn't need to teach him to be courteous and polite, it was in his DNA. School as well. He just loved everything he did. We encouraged him to learn about anything and everything."

"I understand that he was very helpful to people."

Tony was desperate to talk about his son.

"Well he'd been a Cub, and now he was a Scout…"

"It was more than that Tony," Sandra interrupted her husband. "Being part of an organisation was only the polish…the…the…icing on the cake. It was who he was. If someone needed help he would be there, because he knew it was the right thing…"

A gentle knock on the sitting room door halted the paean of praise that flowed in rational sincerity. John Fortune opened the door partially, and listened to the officer in the hallway. He closed the door, and gave a small shake of his head to Molly McGuire. Feet tramped on the stairs, and then the front door closed gently. Before long the sound of a van pulling away was heard.

"Tony, Sandra. We're satisfied that nothing relating to the possession of drugs has been found in your home. You say Arthur was a big help to people. Was there anyone special he looked out for?"

The bereaved parents looked to one another, and exchanged a wan smile.

"Oh yes. Dear Mary Jessop. She and Arthur loved one another. She's in her eighties now, and not so good on her legs."

Tony supported his wife.

"Stalwart of All Souls is our Mary. Been attending since she was a child."

"Mary Jessop, Sandra. Where might we find Mary?"

Tony spoke again.

"She lives in the detached house at the end."

Neither police officer batted an eyelid. Molly picked up the thread.

"Oh yes, I caught a glimpse of her when we arrived. She was feeding a teenager who was raking up the leaves on her lawn. Surprised to see a lad of school age out and about at this time of day."

"It's community service week at the school. Arthur would have…"

Tony was stricken and his chest heaved, desperately sucking in air. There was no noise, but his face flooded with rivulets of tears. Sandra held him to her, and imperceptibly his breathing returned to normal.

Molly was puzzled. Arthur's death was barely two days old. Surely the old lady hadn't sought out a replacement so quickly. That would be heartless, and from the brief description it didn't appear that Mary Jessop would act in cold blood.

"Do you know the…" She was about to say the new boy, but refrained. The word 'new' would be insensitive. "Do you know the boy who's tidying up Mary's garden?"

The Archers caught each other's eye. There was a clear message that prohibited them from speaking their mind

"His name is Barry Corrigan. Next door but one…that way." He pointed.

"Thank you Tony. I'm a little confused. We got the impression that Arthur helped Mary on his own?"

"He did Molly. Apparently, Barry pitched up yesterday and offered his services. With…with…without her usual help Mary would struggle. The whole street is surprised; out of character."

"Tony!"

"I'm sorry Sandra, and God forgive me, but we're here to tell the truth. The Corrigan's are not the best of neighbours, and as for Barry..."

"Jack's alright, Tony."

"He is Sandra; a decent man, but as for Barry and his..."

"Tony!"

Molly jumped in quickly. She knew there wasn't any danger of a 'domestic', because she could see where the Archers were coming from. Even amongst churchgoers they were a rarity. Convinced Christians, and that excluded gossip. She chose her words circumspectly.

"I understand your reluctance Sandra, but we need the fullest picture of the people around you. What's wrong with Barry and his mother."

Sandra steeled herself, and kept it short.

"Barry is...was a year above Arthur. I don't think the poor boy has had much of an example set for him in his life. He has a dreadful reputation at the school and in the neighbourhood. His mother...Tony."

"His mother, Marie, is much younger than Jack. We don't approve of gossip. There's been a rumour in the village that she's having an affair. No one knows who the 'gentleman' is." As an afterthought he added, "They're from Liverpool originally." It was for information, not a pejorative remark.

"Thank you. We appreciate your frankness. I'd like to leave it there for the moment. You need time and space to yourselves. However, I do need to ask two final questions. Have you any idea how Arthur could have got access to cannabis, and more to the point, why he should have started using it?"

The Archers shook their heads in misery.

"One other matter puzzles us, given Arthur's normal pattern of behaviour."

"That's three!"

"Pardon me, Tony?"

"Three questions, Molly."

"Of course, my apologies. Why did Arthur leave the house so late at night? Had he ever done that before?"

They were held in a freeze frame, as if tranquilized. Tony's mobile phone bleeped a notification, and he glanced at it. He had recovered his fragile composure, and his voice rang out.

"We have a visitor arriving. No! No, Arthur had never done anything like that before. We're puzzled too..." He let the sentence drift into the air.

The doorbell chimed.

"Our guest has arrived early, I think. May we see you out Molly, John?"

They reached the tiny hallway, and Tony's fingers clutched the latch.

"Arthur was determined to be a priest. Perhaps he went out to help someone."

John wanted to reply to Sandra, "In the early hours," but caught his boss' warning look.

The front door opened to reveal a clergyman.

"Thank you Sandra, thank you Tony." Molly acknowledged the dog collar.

"Vicar."

"These are the police officers leading the investigation."

The cleric smiled benignly in response to Sandra's introduction.

"God bless you and guide you in your endeavours," he said.

They stopped outside Mary Jessop's gate, scanning the lawn and its borders.

"He's done a tidy job, ma'am."

"Show me that list John. The one the head teacher drew up."

She gave it the once over.

"Look at that John." Her impression of Cilla Black was immaculate. *'Surprise, surprise!'* Come on."

He trailed Molly to the door, whistling the chorus of Dublin's unofficial anthem. Whilst they waited for Mary Jessop to get to the door, she threw him an arched, but amused, look.

"Alive, alive, oh

Alive, alive, oh

Crying, 'Cockles and mussels, alive, alive, oh'."

Within the fraternity of police officers it passed for wit to nickname the senior investigator of murders *'Molly Malone'*.

16

'You know what thought did? Followed a muck cart and thought it was a wedding.'

Clem felt a prickle between the shoulder blades.

His Rector was sat behind him in the priest's stall. Rufus Coleridge would participate in the funeral rites for Arthur Archer by leading the prayers.

Chance brought the fact to his notice that his senior had visited the Archers. Roof had not bothered to mention it, and it resulted in an awkward conversation.

"I offered Alf, or should it be Clem nowadays?"

The enquiry was hardly germane to their discussion.

"The Archers were quite firm on the matter. They wish you to lead the funeral service. I offered."

His repetition of the phrase was revelatory. Rufus was miffed. It was only later that Clem mused upon the idea. Whichever way he sliced and diced it, he couldn't dismiss the conclusion.

He wondered if Roof was so enmeshed in celebrity that he believed he possessed the inalienable right to be always centre stage. During the previous month he had disappeared from the benefice on numerous occasions. Recording his appearances on the TV quiz show *'Pointless'* had occupied a great deal of time. Roof let it slip that in the new year he would be participating in *'Bake Off'*.

Clem tried to be placatory.

"The Archer family are a mainstay of All Souls. We have a close relationship."

Roof maintained a sullen silence. Clem tried diplomacy.

"I would appreciate your support at Arthur's funeral. It's going to be a highly charged affair, and your experience would be invaluable to me."

Truth be told, Rufus had little more experience than his curate in this barren field.

"Would you lead the congregation in prayer. I've always admired your intercessions."

So it was they arrived at All Souls together, but not soon enough to avoid the press gathering outside. Clem left Rufus to deal with *'The Kerb Crawlers of Grub Street'*. His mastery of Liberal Democrat platitudes assumed heights of abstraction that surprised even some of the older hacks. Mental health, social deprivation, plus youth services and support under strain were the substance of his peroration. Nonetheless, Rufus was wise enough not to point the finger of blame for Arthur's death directly at the government of the day. It was only when a young blade amongst the members of the Fourth Estate thrust a microphone under his nose that he walked away; the question pursued him down the long path to the church door.

"So what's the story on you and Spencer Hoffman, Roof? Is he ringing your bell?"

The eulogy to 'Little' Arthur was read by his grandfather with strength and with grace. Bill Archer wasn't that old, probably in his early sixties, and he stood tall. He too was a man of faith, and it supplied him with the strength to speak of his beloved grandson with measureless love. The tears he saved for later.

They sang a hymn, and then it was time for Clem's address. All Souls was like a sardine can. The number attending was so great that a loudspeaker was rigged to broadcast the service to those lining the pathway.

"May Almighty God fill me with His Holy Spirit, and the Grace to hear His voice, as I speak his Word in Christ. Amen.

The reading from Paul's Epistle to the Romans was chosen by Sandra and Tony. You will have noted its brevity. I will attempt to emulate that.

"Be not overcome of evil, but overcome evil with good."

There is anger in our village today; there is suspicion and bitterness, even fear. Fear of an unknown evil that has come into our midst. Neighbour looks on neighbour, and thinks, *'could it be…might it be…'*, and the Noonday Devil laughs as he sows the first seeds of hatred. Seeds that grow into disgust with goodness, and drive us away from Christ; from God.

Tony and Sandra have told me that in the midst of their torment they will not turn from their Saviour and hate, nor would Arthur wish them to. It may surprise you to learn that Arthur was determined one day to stand where Rufus and I stand. Yes, at twelve years of age he had heard God's call to him, and was resolved to answer, *'Is it I Lord? Here I am, Lord'*.

Evil took Arthur from us, but could not withhold him from God.

We must speak of evil.

The secular world we live in would have us believe that for every action there is an identifiable cause, but evil – not naughtiness or a bit of bad behaviour – is greater than that. We are not all evil, but the capacity for it lies dormant in each and every one of us. We are only ever a moment from turning that corner. Then neighbour turns on neighbour, instead of loving him. Evil is 'The Destroyer'. Resistance is a hard road, but we must walk it in faith and perseverance. We must love one another, as Arthur loved.

Let our thoughts be positive towards others; let our words be well-chosen to uplift others; let our every action be generous. The Noonday Devil drives us to turn in on ourselves, and serve only ourselves. Then we love nobody…but ourselves.

'Be not overcome of evil, but overcome evil with good.'

Evil shall not triumph…"

The sudden burst of weeping in the sepulchral silence of the church threw Clem off his stride. It wasn't the noise itself, but its odd note jarred on the ear. The crying sounded manufactured. A mother was excusing her way out of the pews holding the hand of a lachrymose youth.

"'Little' Arthur! Our affectionate name for him. He was not little. Arthur was bigger than all of us, and if we wish to honour him and remember him well we must strive to think, speak and act in goodness. Soon we will say together the prayer our Saviour taught us,

'...thy kingdom come, thy will be done, on earth as it is in heaven...'

ON EARTH...AS IT IS...IN HEAVEN!"

He trusted them to understand his emphasis, and nodded for Rufus to lead them in prayer.

Grenville Simons lallygagged amidst the azaleas. It was a practice commensurate with his job as a journalist on *'The Daily Paragon'*. He juggled his work on the political desk with supplying titbits that came his way to Melanie Cleaver, who *'personed'* the gossip column. It was a quid pro quo arrangement. She received nuggets of information from him; Grenville shagged her. They were the up and coming royalty of the left wing tabloid; the Keir and Angela of one-track journalism. They were so Woke they had bags under their eyes.

"Fine service Vicar, and, may I say, fine sermon."

Grenville didn't mean a word of it. He really wanted to say,

"You talk a load of old bollocks!"

Evil! Original Sin! A cartload of doody. Anyone with a brain knew that all wrongdoing is caused by social deprivation, inadequate schooling, and the low uptake of breastfeeding. A transient image distracted him. Melanie's enormous baps swam before his eyes. Grenville wasn't going hungry. Why should he? He needed lots of calories to fuel his righteous campaign. It was an honour to stand in the vanguard with JC. A man ill-done by.

During this short reverie, in the graveyard, he recollected the words of some no account comedian. When the Truss woman became Prime Minister there had been a furore, because the comic said she had a face like a smacked arse. A right wing comedian of yesteryear retorted that JC had a face like a newt licking piss off a nettle. Suddenly, it was no longer funny to call names in the playground. Grenville had gone on a tirade in his column.

"Thank you, Mr…?"

A hand shot out.

"Grenville Simons, *'Daily Paragon'*. Terrible business this. Poor lad. Suppose the family struggles to keep their head above water in these times."

"Er no, I don't think so. Mum and Dad are both employed."

Grenville was well aware of that, but kept his mouth shut. The Archers had resolutely refused to give interviews to any media. Journalists resorted to neighbours. Mary Jessop sent them away with a flea in their ear, and surprisingly so did Jack Corrigan. Kyle and Bianca Bailey were more accommodating. They had a cracking night out in Birmingham on the proceeds.

"Church was packed."

He let it linger, and Clem bit.

"Oh, you know, baptisms, weddings and funerals."

"No Bar mitzvahs then." Grenville laughed at his own joke.

Clem permitted himself a courteous smile.

"No, no Bar mitzvahs, though we never forget that our Lord was a Jew."

Grenville was stumped. He didn't quite know how to respond.

"Brr, getting a bit parky out here."

Clem laughed openly this time.

"'Parky!' My mum used to say that. From the North Grenville?"

"Leeds originally, and if I'm not much mistaken you're from those parts."

"Liverpool."

"Really?" The surprise was genuine. "Hmmm? Now I listen closely I can just pick up a trace. Must have been away a long time to lose it."

"Oh, I never really had much of a Scouse accent."

"How so?"

"My Dad. He was a man full of aspiration for his children. Thought good standard English and received pronunciation were assets."

Grenville's father had been in the *schmutter* trade. The Jewish community in Leeds has a long history in the clothing business. As an egalitarian, Grenville bridled at the idea of changing your accent. Public school boy he may be, but he prided himself on dropping his aitches and inserting the odd *'fink'* instead of think. It was his way of getting down with the kids in the 'hood.

"I see. Teacher was he, your Dad?"

Clem's roar of amusement nearly roused the sleepers from the past surrounding them. He looked around guiltily. It was alright, the mourners had dispersed.

"He'd have loved to hear that. No, he worked on the production line at the Ford Motor factory."

Grenville didn't miss a beat. It galled him to say so, but he remarked,

"Sounds a good man. A man of the working class."

He would have liked to have said, 'Class traitor!' What was wrong with a good Scouse accent?

Clem was also keeping his contemplations to himself. Yes, his father did possess admirable traits, but the darker ones lived in a burrow inside him.

"Let me take a stab at which district you lived in. Childwall? Broadgreen?"

These were a couple of the more prosperous areas of Liverpool.

"Toxteth."

"Are you old enough to remember the riots under Thatcher?"

"Babe in arms, Grenville. Mum and Dad told me about them. Said they only affected two or three streets. I remember Dad was furious about the bad reputation the whole area got, because of the media."

Grenville seethed internally. This was not the legendary scenario of the Left. The oppressed masses rising against their Fascist masters. The smile never left his face.

"Have you travelled far, Grenville?"

"Up from the *'Smoke'*."

Clem concealed a grin. Had anyone but a northerner referred to London as *'The Smoke'* since Bob Hoskins retired from film making?

Grenville rubbed his gloved hands, and stamped his feet.

"Lovely talking with you. Must grab a sandwich and a drink before the long drive."

Clem bit again.

"You'd be more than welcome to enjoy a spot of lunch at my place. See, just over there. A cock stride."

They laughed at the familiar northern phrase.

"Home-made soup, and a cheese roll. Tea or coffee optional."

"Couldn't run to a bevvy could you, la'?"

"Just the one, as you're driving. Pale Ale do?"

Grenville mastered the temptation to grimace. He'd planned on three courses at a nearby country pub he'd checked out on line. They had a good wine list.

"Very kind of you Clem. Love to."

Melanie could always rustle up some receipts for his expenses claim. Grenville hadn't intended to hang around for so long, but his journalistic nose had been vibrating for a while. There was something about this vicar. Keen on talking, that was it.

"Lead on Vicar."

Clem was puzzled. He hadn't revealed his Christian name to his new friend. Oh, the notice board, of course. He'd changed the notice recently to help folks accustom themselves to his new choice of name.

"Actually, I'm not a vicar; I'm a curate."

Whilst they walked to the vicarage, Clem explained church rank.

"How come you're in charge at All Souls?"

He outlined Colin Ambler's health problems. The House for Duty priest was convalescing after an unpleasant operation.

"My boss is Rufus Coleridge. Based at St. Dunstan's, and Rector of the Benefice."

Grenville changed tack, deciding to be upfront about his knowledge of the latter day pop star.

"Ah, the glamorous Roof! Star of stage screen and television. Saw him skedaddling after the service. Did you listen to his music when he was with *'Flatulence'*?"

"Not bad, but Freddie Mercury was my bag…"

"Not The Beatles?"

"Noooo, Queen are much better. More musically sophisticated."

"Stay away from Liverpool. They'll stone you."

"Here we are Grenville. Come in."

"So what about Spencer Hoffman?"

"You know about that?"

"Spencer's a big name. They're seen around Town frequently. Inside track, you know. Met him?"

Grenville's laugh was hearty, as if implying, *'You're a man of the world.'*

"Yes, I've met Spencer a couple of times. Charming man, and very amusing." He shouted up the stairs. "Luke, I'm home, and I have a guest."

Grenville nearly wet himself. Two vicars in one benefice, and both shacked up with blokes.

"Luke's my son. He was at the service. Arthur was a friend of his. Well, a newish friend. Luke only moved in with me a month ago."

He hid his disappointment.

"Your wife out at work is she?"

"Divorced, I'm sad to say."

Grenville decided to let it lie. He sensed there might be bigger fish to fry.

"Come on, let's eat. Luke, are you joining us for lunch?"

Luke came to the top of the stairs.

"No thank you, Dad. I helped myself when I came in."

"Good man. Say hello to Mr. Grenville Simons. He's a journalist with *'The Daily Paragon'*."

"Pleased to meet you, sir."

"Likewise Luke. Are you a fan of *'The Paragon'*?"

"Glanced at it once, sir."

Luke paused, in philosophical reflection.

"It reminded me of *'The Daily Mail'*."

Grenville was on the verge of an apoplectic fit.

"You know, sir, like two brothers who've fallen out over whether or not the milk should be poured into the cup before or after the tea has gone in."

If Grenville's colleagues had witnessed the scene they would have collapsed in a heap on the floor. Astonishment and bewilderment battled for supremacy on his face. Clem broke up this cosy fireside chat.

"Let's eat Grenville. Bring your dishes down when you're done with them, Luke."

Grenville cleared his throat.

"Er, how old is Luke?"

"Thirteen. Here, a good Yorkshire Pale Ale. You look as though you need it."

Indeed he did. Savaged by a bloody thirteen-year-old.

"Where did Luke live before he came to you?"

"Oh, he was at boarding school down South."

Grenville took a slug of the ale. Not bad. Ah, that explained it. Bloody public schoolboy. Safely snuggled once more in the nest of his prejudices, he attacked his Spartan lunch with relish.

"Mmm, good coffee. Thanks Clem."

They reclined in dilapidated armchairs, sipping from their mugs.

"Suppose you watch all the programmes Rufus appears in. Record them do you?" Grenville sniggered.

He managed a wry smile.

"Watch bits here and there, but telly isn't my style."

"Not watch telly? You must be as rare as rocking horse shit. Oh, I beg your pardon."

Clem waved away the mild obscenity.

"So why aren't you a fan?"

"Puerile drivel most of it, and some of it downright corrosive and evil."

Grenville luxuriated in his coffee, and the glow from the log fire.

"Evil? Come on! What's so evil about television? Give me an example."

"Eastenders!"

Grenville raised an eyebrow. He was attacking the perennial favourite of the nation. The best of the soaps that represented and lauded the merits of the working class. This nut job vicar really had come off the rails of his upbringing.

"You see, Grenville, I know Drama is heightened, but is it really plausible that so much murder, rape, robbery, domestic violence, and downright bad neighbourliness should exist in a square mile?"

The pioneer for the New Jerusalem was appalled. Bad neighbours, bad feckin' neighbours. How can working class people ever be bad neighbours? Grenville had a *'nipping next door to borrow a cup of sugar and singsongs round the 'Joanna'* view. Albert Square was a microcosm of all that's best in goodhearted 'real' people.

Clem compounded the felony.

"They're not the working class I grew up with. *'Eastenders'* portrays the lumpen proletariat; the underclass. The genuine working class always despised them."

He alarmed himself by blurting out,

"You don't play with him. Bernie Docherty pisses his wages away over the bar, and in the betting shop. A bad lot, that family."

Grenville was startled.

"What?"

"Something my father used to say. Actually, a lot of mums and dads used to say it in our area."

Clem took a draught from his mug.

"No, if you want real working class people these days you need to look among the immigrant population. The Asians, the Chinese, and the East Europeans. Family values, education, and a strong work ethic are their priorities."

Grenville was perplexed. Philosophically, he couldn't decide whether to shit or tie his shoelaces. On the one hand praising immigrants was admirable; censuring the indigenous working class was not. He gathered his affronted emotions, and placed a seal over them…for the moment.

"What about this estate where that poor little mite came from? I'll bet they're the salt of the earth."

"Decent enough folk, most of them."

"Most of them?"

"Like any area, there are some bad apples. A gang of teenagers is the worst…"

Grenville pounced.

"Ah, nothing to do with their time. No facilities for them."

"*Au contraire.* The comprehensive school has a community sports hall, and we have – well we did have – our Church Hall. We created a sort of youth club for them. We also run a Tuesday morning club for mums and toddlers. Unfortunately, the teenage tearaways seem to enjoy themselves far more in the Memorial Garden at the rear of the church."

"What do they get up to there?"

"Cans of cheap booze, smoking, littering, breaking the benches, and…"

"And? Go on."

"The scent of something exotic often caresses the air when they've departed."

Grenville was relishing the conversation. The article was virtually written.

"I expect there's not much money around on the estate to pay for subscriptions to sports halls and the like?"

Alfie shook his head vigorously.

"Pretty much full employment in the Hargreave factory, and their rents are around ten per cent lower than market value. I'm told Sir Benson is very generous to his workers. He even paid for the redecoration of our hall, and for equipment, before we opened the youth club. You should see the number of Sky dishes on the estate. It looks like Jodrell Bank."

"Yes, I've heard of Sir Benson Hargreave. Know him well do you?"

"Well enough. He was my Churchwarden until recently. Resigned. Apparently, he has a much greater responsibility to take on in the not-too-distant future."

"Did he tell you what it is?"

Clem shrugged, in a manner that would have impressed Barry Corrigan.

"Don't you listen to the news either?"

"Not much."

A voice came from the doorway.

"He's the next Conservative candidate for Dunsmore-by-Napton. Not sure I approve. Isn't paternalism a thing of the past?"

Grenville beamed a warm smile at young Luke. My word, he was a bright lad. Public School eh. Well, they're not all bad. Plenty of Labour M.P's went to one; even Eton for a couple of them. Why, JC himself went to private prep school.

"Paternalism Luke?"

"Housing the workers, Dad. Bit 19th Century."

"At least they don't have to worry…"

Grenville interjected.

"Until the job goes tits up, or they have to retire."

It was Clem's turn to be confounded. All he could come back with was,

"Well he didn't turf Mary Jessop out."

The doorbell rang.

"Would you mind answering that for me, Luke. Make my excuses."

Luke disappeared, and Clem continued with his enthusiastic dissertation.

"You see, what the nub of the problem is, Grenville, is spiritual poverty…"

An instantly recognisable voice broke in.

"Forgive my persistence Clem. I really must speak with you…Oh, how awful of me, I didn't realise you have a guest."

"Don't mind me, I must be going."

Grenville looked at Clem amiably.

"Oh yes, Grenville Simons…Lady Edwina Bowcott."

Grenville rolled out his oleaginous version of *savoir faire*, and impersonated his notion of *'The Scarlet Pimpernel'*.

"Charmed milady."

Edwina guffawed heartily, and played the game.

"You're very kind, sir. However, I'm just a lassie from Lancashire who made good. Clem, I must have a word."

Grenville clocked the slight bitterness in her tone, and the hand that lingered on the Curate's arm.

"I really must be on my way. Thanks for lunch and the fireside chat. Very stimulating. Bye

Edwina, cheerio Luke…keep up the good work with your Dad."

"Luke, would you look after Edwina while I see Grenville off the premises."

They shook hands in the hallway. Clem was about to close the door when Grenville revolved on his heels.

"Why were you christened Clem?"

"My middle name, Clement. Named after Mr. Attlee; mum and dad were big fans. Temple Weston knew me as Alfie when I arrived. Clem started as a private arrangement between Edwina and myself, now we've…I've gone public."

"It certainly bloody will be," Grenville thought

"Can't think of a finer name." Well, perhaps Jeremy. "See you…Clem."

He sat in his Porsche. The first thing he did was examine the tape recorder in his pocket. Still running. Good, it had got the lot. He decided to take a swift turn around *'The Sir Benson Hargreave Estate'*. Pretty respectable, and yes, there was a forest of *'Dole Dishes'* clinging to the houses. Why shouldn't they have their bit of fun and entertainment?

Grenville marshalled his ideas as he tootled down the M40. There were two stories here. The Curate, who sounded like the Tory Party at prayer; plus associated goodies. Rufus Coleridge and Spencer Hoffman could be added to the recipe, and the sweetie on the top; the lady of the manor was having a ball...with the Curate. Probably holding a pair too. More research would be needed for the second story, and a bit of investigative journalism. Grenville knew a fair bit about Hargreave and his factories. A couple of them were located in West Yorkshire, the county of his birth. Paternalism, that's what the kid had said, and a *'bit 19th Century'*. Good on yer son. Mind you, he hadn't forgiven Luke for *'The Daily Mail'* crack.

When he passed out of Warwickshire, into Oxfordshire, the oddity occurred to him. The Curate, Hargreaveand Edwina Bowcott, if what she said was true about being a Lancashire girl made good, they were all from modest backgrounds. Now arrayed as parasites of privilege, but sucklings of the working class...he liked his inventions...and class traitors. They deserved all they were going to get. So did his readers, the great unwashed.

Grenville addressed the rear view mirror.

"Stout yeomen...yeopersons of England you may be, but you must listen to us; the educated. And bloody well do what we say. There'll be no *'Red Walls'* turning blue next time round."

17

'Giving up the ghost.'

Sunset loomed. Its inflamed face was forbidding, glaring at him like a displeased headmaster. He lingered by the stream, hoping that time alone would wash away the tempest of mixed emotion he'd emerged from the meeting with.

Clem had answered the summons from the Diocesan Bishop. When he entered the room he was unsurprised to discover Rufus present. He was perturbed that Rufus remained a silent onlooker, as the discussion unfolded.

Her Grace kicked off with prayer. An appropriate beginning for all of life's activities. When she got down to brass tacks she adopted a sympathetic mien, but a scintilla of aggravation seeped through.

A copy of *'The Daily Paragon'* was in her hand, and Clem could see the coloured highlights.

"*'The Case of the Curious Curate who Barked at Poverty!'* You are also said by Mr….er, oh yes here it is, by Mr. Grenville Simons to *'relish hobnobbing with the rich and well-heeled'*. He notes especially your favourable comments concerning Sir Benson Hargreave, who he likens to Dickens' Mr. Gradgrind. Are you familiar with *'Hard Times'*, Alfie...or is it Clem?"

Clem considered retorting, "Know *'Hard Times'*, you're giving me one aren't you?"

Circumspection prevailed.

"No, no I don't know that particular novel. Sorry about the name. Yes...it's Clem from now on. My middle Christian name is Clement."

"Recalling the studies of my youth, I can tell you that the soubriquet does not compliment Sir Benson. Gradgrind's philosophy was rationalism, self-interest and cold hard fact. Sometimes he is described euphemistically as *'an eminently practical man'*. It's some years since I read the book, but I also recollect that he prevented his children from developing their imaginations and emotions. I digress. Did you say these things?"

"Not at all, your Grace..."

"Marion."

"It's a complete misrepresentation of our conversation. Yes, those people and topics were discussed..."

Clem hesitated. He realised that it hardly constituted a discussion. Simons had led him up the garden path, allowing him to rabbit on and on. He had revelled and rejoiced in espousing his opinions.

"Sorry your…Marion. What that…that journalist has done is to select disparate phrases and passages and link them together to give an altogether different construction."

Marion and Rufus exchanged a meaningful look. She returned her attention to Clem. The aggravation had disappeared, and was replaced with sympathy.

"Have you encountered the press before Clem?"

He shook his head.

"Ah, we have. Rufus in his former life…"

Another mischievous imp leapt onto Clem's shoulders. He bit his lip to prevent himself from saying, "I thought we didn't believe in reincarnation?"

"…and as for myself, it is one of the crosses of office. You see, Clem, the media operate on the principle of the sin of omission. It's not what they say; it's what they don't say; consciously disposing of that which does not fit. In that way they create the complexion that suits their agenda."

She paused, to allow the lesson to sink home.

"May I ask if this quotation, ascribed to you, is verbatim? *'Spencer Hoffman rings the Rector's bell...ding dong?'* The headline is also rather clever, if offensive. *'CAMP-ANOLOGY AT ST. DUNSTAN'S.'* Do pass on my best wishes Rufus. I'm an avid fan of *'Ring My Bell'*. Spencer seems to be a charming man, and very amusing."

High office requires many talents. Soothing hurt feelings, and smoothing ruffled feathers are accounted amongst them.

Clem was angry.

"That is a total fabrication. You and Spencer were hardly mentioned, Roof. In reply to his question, I just said that I hadn't seen much of you on telly, because I hardly watch the TV."

Rufus appeared to accept the explanation, but managed to give the impression that he was pained by Clem's viewing habits.

"Alfie...apologies, Clem. I am satisfied that your interview with..."

"I invited him to lunch, because he was cold and hungry, and had a long journey ahead of him. It was a casual chat, not an interview."

"Quite so. I am satisfied that you were not malicious, just manipulated. However, that still leaves us with the potential for disruption in both of your parishes."

"I can understand why that applies to All Souls, but why St. Dunstan's?"

"Well, there is the thorny issue of by association, and there…there are other issues which I'm not at liberty to discuss. I wonder Rufus, would you give us five minutes alone. Daphne does rather good coffee."

Rufus retreated in good order.

"There is one further matter we must address, Clem."

Bishop Marion didn't need to look at the newspaper, she had memorised it.

"Is the Lady of the Manor having a ball with the Curate?"

She waited for his response. It was difficult to articulate.

"Lady Edwina…Edwina and I discovered a mutual attraction for one another, and we are…we were taking time to see how it developed."

She peered at him intently. He divined the unspoken question.

"Nothing untoward has passed between us, and it isn't likely to."

"You said you *were* taking time…?"

"My assumption that Edwina was divorced turns out to be erroneous. She isn't, and after a twelve-year absence her husband, Lord Bowcott, has turned up out of the blue to claim the ancestral home."

"Oh dear. What do you intend to do?"

He looked so sorrowful that her heart went out to him. She believed absolutely that the pair of them had acted honourably.

"We don't know."

Without realising it he repeated Bowcott's words.

"Jog along."

"I wish you both the very best. Place it in God's hands. It will be resolved, in His time. Now, I want you to make an appointment with our press department. They will give you a short course in handling our journalistic brothers and sisters. In the meantime, if they circle, and they will until something juicier captures their attention, you simply refer them to our media people. I've had an idea."

Marion picked up her telephone.

"Daphne, would you see if Jonathan David is available?...Jonathan, are you available this Sunday to preach at All Souls Temple Weston? No, no, no, not a command...well yes it is."

She laughed joyously, and Clem could hear it reciprocated down the line.

"Okay with you Clem? Let's put the Archdeacon to work. Put on a show of support. Bags of swagger, as my late husband used to say. He was military you know, I lost him in Afghanistan."

"I'm sorry...sorry about your husband, and for all the trouble I've caused."

"Noooo, worse things happen at sea."

"My Dad used to say that."

"Wise man. Thanks for dropping by. Jonathan will give you a tinkle. Chin up, and don't throw in the towel just yet."

"Persevere and run the race."

Clem couldn't simply walk past Rufus. He sat next to him in the outer office. Rufus folded *'The Church Times'* meticulously. His face did not betray his feelings one way or the other. Daphne concentrated on her computer, and tried not to listen.

"Can you forgive me Roof?"

His Rector didn't hesitate, and the reply was genuine.

"I already have done."

Then he slumped in the chair, looking defeated. Clem waited.

"You see Clem…you see…what it is…what Marion said she couldn't disclose…there's trouble at St. Dunstan's. There has been since I arrived. You know my Churchwarden?"

"Marjorie Knighton? Not very well, but we've run across one another."

"She's not a happy lady. I'm told by members of the PCC that she never has been. Complicated story about a relationship years ago. Marjorie is notorious for undermining others."

"I think you've just described the entire world, Roof. I concluded long ago that most people who bully or threaten others do so because they're miserable with their own lives. Poor unfortunates. They don't possess the courage to challenge their own failures and shortcomings, so they pick holes in everyone else. A sort of displacement of unhappiness."

Rufus became animated.

"I'm sure you're right. Thing is, everyone else in the parish, in all the parishes of the Benefice, seem to be at ease with who and what I am. Or at least those who disapprove of me have the grace to rub along. Those two make it clear that having a gay rector is an abomination."

"Two?"

"Oh, sorry, Marjorie's partner in crime is Jennifer Morton."

"Ah, retired Primary head' isn't she?"

Rufus nodded.

"They obstruct everything I try to do, and the problem is that the rest of the PCC are either frightened of them, or prefer a quiet life. They are the reason Spencer never stays at my place. It's like having the KGB watching my every move. Anyway, that's going to change."

He sat bolt upright, and his demeanour altered. Rufus' face was radiant with joy.

"Spencer and I are to enter into Civil Partnership. We will be living together permanently. Spencer will commute up and down the M40 – God help him!"

"That's marvellous Roof. Congratulations. Here's an idea. What if I lend you the awkward member from my PCC – no names, no pack drill. We've got a cauldron somewhere in store from last Christmas' pantomime. The three of them could form a sub-committee, and meet on Blackstone Heath."

Rufus chuckled, and Daphne tried to keep a straight face.

"Hey Roof, I am so sorry. I can see how my big mouth might have queered your pitch."

Roof howled with laughter, and Daphne joined him.

"You might choose your verbs a little more carefully, Clem."

"Oh God forgive me," and he added his own mirth to the proceedings.

"Excuse me gentlemen, sorry to interrupt the floor show. The Bishop is ready for you Rufus."

He stood up, and Clem did likewise.

"Everything alright there, Roof?" he gestured towards the Bishop's door.

"Just tying up loose ends. Listen, I'm going to give your charity do a miss. Just until the dust settles. But we're tight man."

They embraced each other with warmth, and genuine love.

A noisy rustling in the bushes shook Clem out of his self-examination.

"I say, this is my pitch for the night. Do me the favour of buggering off."

The received pronunciation was incongruous, emerging from the mouth of a grubby and dishevelled figure, thrusting his way out of the undergrowth.

"No problem, brother. I was just about to leave."

"If you were my brother I'd push you into that stream. Arse of the first water he is."

There was no malice or aggression in the words, more an amused detachment.

"I say, you're a vicar!" A grubby forefinger pointed at Clem's dog collar.

The homeless man dropped his pack to the ground, and sat on it.

"Do me a favour, old chap, explain the meaning of life to me."

Clem was inclined to laugh, but restrained himself. He joined the man on the dank earth. His extended hand was taken.

"I'm Clem. All Souls, Temple Weston."

"Hugo, life *'gone West'*!"

Clem could see that the amused eyes were not unkind, but he was being tested. How, in the name of all that's holy, could he unravel the meaning of life? He wasn't patronising, and a sixth sense told him that if he launched into theology it would be understood. But it wasn't appropriate to the circumstance.

"The meaning of life…"

A flashback illuminated the louring clouds in his mind.

"Perseverance, or as Churchill put it, *'KBO – Keep Buggering On!'* That's what we're made for."

The wind was picking up, and it was becoming colder. Without warning Hugo rolled off his pack and laughed.

"Not bad! Not bad, your reverence. Couldn't spare me a fiver could you?"

"No! I can do better than that."

Clem was well aware that clergy must be very careful about whom they invite into their homes. Christian charity is all very well, but it's hard to administer if someone hospitalises you, or polishes you off.

"How about a shower, a fresh set of clothes, and a hot meal? While you're enjoying those I'll ring around to organise a bed for the night."

"Shall we dance, Vicar? *'Lead on MacDuff'*."

They found the footpath, and Clem let Hugo chatter away at will. Suddenly, he pulled up.

"I say Clem. It's Bonfire Night, isn't it?"

"It is."

"I look like a blasted 'guy' in these rags."

"Not for much longer. We're about the same size, and I have a three-piece suit I never get to wear these days."

Hugo performed a jig as he sang,

"Dance, dance, wherever you may be. I am the Lord of the Dance said He…"

Clem's resolve had returned, but he knew only too well that it's hard to waltz with the Devil on your back.

18

'There's more than one way to skin a cat.'

The *'Cock with Two Balls'* was throbbing. It was Country and Western night. Landlady Kelly Hampton loathed the music. An evening of emotionally stunted men weeping over their dead dogs, and a woman that dun gone wrong. Sentimental tossers.

Kyle Bailey slammed his whiskey glass onto the counter.

"Give me two fingers."

Kelly weighed up her options. The traditional salute, or an especially vigorous prostate examination? Business is business, so she rammed the glass under the optic.

"Clint Eastwood is it, Kyle?"

The shirt factory operative attempted the steely gaze of *'cotton-eyed Clint'*. An unlit cheroot was clamped between his teeth.

"That's right lady."

The cheroot fell to the floor.

"Oh shite!"

Kelly withheld a snort of amusement, and slammed the glass on the surface with a force equal to Kyle's. She leant over and whispered,

"And if you light that cheroot anywhere on my premises, except for outside, you'll be through the swing doors quicker than you can say *'Jack Palance'*. *Comprendez*, you slim motherfucker?"

He understood, and didn't take offence. Kelly was entering into the spirit of the Old West, he thought. She looked fair old fucking tasty, for an older woman. He peeked over the bar to catch a glimpse of her legs. The short buckskin skirt showed them off to advantage, as she retrieved a bottle of Budweiser from a low-level cabinet. He wouldn't have said no to Kelly tugging on his lariat.

Kyle had another reason for not replying to her insult. Life was moving on very nicely. He leaned back against the bar, and perused the group of tables all gathered together. Lots of their friends, his wife Bianca, and the Corrigans. Even Jack was having a good time, boosted by his success. Kyle was well-oiled already. It had been pints with a whiskey chaser to commence, but now it was Scotch on its own. Not such a bad bloke, Jack.

Alcohol generally propels the drinker into one of two directions; aggression or sentimentality. Kyle's outward appearance represented, arguably, the toughest hombre ever to walk the West. Inwardly, he was putty. Yeh, Jack was okay, and he looked good dressed as *'The Man in Black'*.

Marie excused herself from the table, and sashayed towards the Ladies. Kyle gave her a head start, and then pimp rolled in the direction of the Gents.

"Oright, give us some quick."

Kyle extracted small packages from his Duster coat, and transferred them to her handbag rapidly. Barry Corrigan was a very naughty boy. Whilst active in Mark Hargreave's service, he had sequestered ten per cent of the cannabis each week for private enterprise. Kyle was stunned when Barry offered him some; he had never done drugs. The next day he collared Barry.

"How much have you got?"

Barry thought he was on for a sale. How wrong can you be.

"As much as that? Right, we're partners. I can shift that lot easier than you."

"I don't fuckin' think so…"

"It's that, or I split on you to your mam and dad."

Barry cried with laughter.

"Me Mam already knows. She's in on it. You tell Jack, an' I know someone who'll burst you."

Kyle assumed he meant whoever supplied him. He withdrew to worry away at the problem for a week. There was a shit load of money to be made. He was tired of the pitiful handouts he got from his boss. It also made him angry. Every time he left his office, after their 'conferences', he felt belittled and humiliated. Hargreave was taking the piss, and Kyle didn't want to play ball any more. The solution was easy. He closeted himself with Marie during their break at work. She saw the sense of it. Together, or separately, they could work the pubs and clubs whenever social opportunities arose.

Kyle stood at the stall taking a leak. There was one other person in there. When they'd finished they washed their hands side-by-side.

"Alright mate. Having a good time?"

"So, so."

The guy wasn't in fancy dress.

"Great music."

"Not to my taste."

Fuck me, this was hard work.

"Haven't seen you around these parts. You from out of town?"

The man spoke over the noise of the hand dryer.

"You could say. We live here weekends."

Kyle's interest in Temple Weston barely extended beyond Palmerston Way.

"Hope you don't mind me saying, mate, but you look a bit down. You know, tired. Could do with a pick-me-up."

"What do you have in mind."

Kyle dipped a hand into his pocket.

"How about a nice relaxing smoke? Sumfin for de brain!"

The mock Caribbean accent was inconsistent with his attire. The man paused, apparently indecisive.

"No, no, thanks for the offer. Trying to give it up. Enjoy your evening."

Henry and Siobhan Norton had intended to finish their drinks, then open a bottle at home. After a brief explanation, she agreed to another large glass of wine. Husband and wife were seemingly engrossed in one another, but Henry managed to keep an eye on Kyle Bailey's progress. He also clocked the young woman, noting that they retreated to the loos at the same time on two further occasions. When he could find a moment in his busy schedule he would drop a word in the ear of his local colleagues.

Henry would have echoed Kelly Hampton's views on Country and Western music, had he but known them. However, he was mildly amused when some ageing dawg, with his out of tune guitar, wailed a rendition of *'Folsom Prison Blues'*. Johnny Cash, *'The Man in Black'*! Now there was an hombre who made a fortune out of pretending to be a rootin' tootin' son of a gun!

The reason for Jack Corrigan's unexpected ebullience in the pub was trying to negotiate his Bentley into a tight parking spot.

"I don't know why we had to travel by car, Benson. We could have walked here in five minutes."

"I don't know why we have to go at all when I've got a crisis on my hands."

"Oh Benson. Hardly a crisis."

"The buggers are on strike."

"Yes, my own, but it's only one factory. The others are still functioning, as per."

"They bloody won't be if I give in to this lot. They'll all want a slice of the cake."

"Benson, be careful!"

The sensors screeched in proximity to a white van.

"Bloody Kelly Hampton, and her theme nights. Village is like a car park."

"I say Beebie!"

Freddie rarely used the term of endearment these days, so it got his attention. He peered at the figure, sloping his way towards the Vicarage.

"That's him, isn't it? I know young Starkiss said fancy dress, but that's taking it too far."

Beebie's sensitivities were not so blunted as to be unmoved by the sight of Jimmy Saville strolling through Temple Weston. Freddie was appalled.

"Really! Lord of the Manor he may be, but evidently good taste is not hereditary."

Bowcott jingled and jangled as he turned into the Vicarage drive.

"Got a bloody brass neck coming dressed like that, and on foot to boot."

"Old money is a law unto itself, my own. Come along."

Clem Starkiss encountered a vision of hell on his doorstep. Regathering his composure he welcomed his guest.

"Good evening Lord Bowcott."

He waggled his over-sized cigar.

"Now then, now then, Bowcott will do. I understand you've got my wife locked away."

"I beg your pardon?"

"Chained to the sink is she? She'll like that. Any chance of a drink?"

"Please, go straight through. Lady Edwina is dispensing drinks. The butler is otherwise occupied."

Bowcott eyed him, and then exploded.

"Hahaha, nice one young man!"

He lurched his way through the hall to the main reception room.

"Sir Benson, Freddie, so good of you to come."

They entered the crowded room together. The atmosphere was subdued. Noses were buried in drinks. It wasn't merely that Jimmy Saville was a pariah, even in fancy dress, but given the charitable nature of the evening it was tasteless in the extreme. A low and angry voice was discernible through the open kitchen door. Folk chattered on quietly, but strained to hear.

"Bowcott, you are contemptible. To dress like that at all is insensitive. On a night like this it's disgusting. I told you about the child."

Subsequent to the death of Arthur Archer, Clem had decided that a Bonfire Night celebration was out of the question. He rearranged the date, and altered it to a charity drinks party instead. They would raise money to rebuild the Church Hall, which would be dedicated to Arthur's memory.

"Why didn't you stay away Bowcott?" Her cry was plaintive. "I have to live in this village."

"Not for much longer, old girl. That is, unless you intend to shack up in someone else's pad."

Bowcott was an anachronism. He clung to his ancestral rights, but spoke like the hippies he'd mixed within Kathmandu decades before.

"Bloody hell! He's got a bloody cheek!."

Beebie had spied the Corrigans entering the room, with the Baileys hard on their heels. Clem ensured that the gathering was not just for the great and good.

Bowcott re-entered the room, where he watched and waited. It didn't take him long to perceive something of interest. He wandered towards a handsome young man who was lounging against the enormous fireplace.

"Giving her the high hard one are you?"

Mark Hargreave's jaw went slack. Bowcott nodded in the direction of Marie Corrigan.

"How on earth…?"

"I can smell it, my boy. It comes off people like musk off a deer." A hand shot out. "Bowcott!"

"I know who you are." He took the hand, and introduced himself. "Mark Hargreave."

"And I know who you are." Bowcott allowed the knowledge to percolate, then added. "Hope you don't spend your life holding on to your father's shirt tail."

Mark bristled, but remained polite.

"Certainly not sir. Got numerous irons in the fire, and all doing rather well."

Marie Corrigan caught Bowcott's eye.

"She's a brazen one, and no mistake. There was a time, Mark, when I'd have suggested a threesome, and her husband could operate the video camera."

"I'm sure you could still raise Cain with the ladies, sir."

"I can barely raise an eyebrow these days. As the sadist put it, *'The thong is over, but the mammary lingers on'!*"

Mark gave an appreciative chuckle.

"Love your outfit, sir."

Mark had dressed more conventionally. He was attired as the Archbishop of Canterbury.

"Good of Lady Edwina to act as hostess for our fresh-faced young cleric, sir."

Bowcott did indeed manage to raise an eyebrow, before heated voices silenced the room.

"You think you can put one over on me, Jack Corrigan. I'll fight you to a standstill."

Jack retained his dignity, and did not deign to answer. It infuriated Sir Benson all the more. He let loose with a second barrel, but its aim was more widely spread. Quite a few of the guests worked for him, and they all lived on the estate.

"You're putting jobs at risk, and if they go then homes go."

He kept his eyes on Jack, but the next comment was for general consumption.

"Mebbe the law won't allow me to evict, even though the housing is tied to the job. It's in black and white in your tenancy agreement."

His grammar had gone to pot, and the hard-nosed Yorkshireman of his youth was speaking.

"Aye, 'appen. But I'll tell you this for nowt. Rents will go up to market price. I'll not be subsidising you any longer."

The smell in the room was no longer the perfumed aroma of romance. Edwina Bowcott took a firm grip, rapping the ladle against the punch bowl.

"Ladies and gentlemen, we arrive at the main purpose of our gathering this evening. May I hand over to our minister, Clem Starkiss."

A few people still hadn't heard that Alf was now Clem, but their neighbours set them right.

"Thank you, Lady Edwina. We are all aware that originally we intended to be out of doors celebrating Bonfire Night. Following recent tragic events I decided that would be inappropriate…"

Everyone's thoughts turned to Arthur Archer. No, a blazing bonfire was out of the question.

"Still, we have had a few fireworks…"

The tension broke. Everyone laughed politely, except for Beebie.

"Before our *'Auction of Promises'* begins, which Sir Chaddesley Corbett has agreed to conduct, we will assemble in the Vicarage garden to remember Arthur."

From the large terrace they viewed the expanse of the grounds, lit by flares. The Bowcott's gardener, Clarence, was shining a torch on an immense rocket. Clem stood in the middle of the lawn, and spread his arms wide. He looked upward into the immensity of the night sky. Deuteronomy 1: 10 filtered through his mind:

"The Lord your God has increased your numbers so that today you are as many as the stars in the sky."

Whilst he remained transfixed in silent prayer, Bowcott scanned his fellow watchers. His yellow eyes revealed the state of his liver, as they lit upon two ladies. One stared at Mark Hargreave;

the other at the distant minister. He saw that the longing in both was painful with desire.

"Almighty God, it has pleased you to take to your eternal home our beloved Arthur. We know that he rests with you in peace and in joy, and that when you call each one of us to you we will meet with him again in love."

Clarence passed a taper to him. The end glowed, and it was an ember of hope in Clem's heart. The firework detonated. Its contents galloped towards the heavens, and opened out into a prodigious flower.

At the rear of the crowded terrace Bowcott's lips moved, but no sound emerged. He was reciting inwardly the old rhyme:

"Remember, remember the 5th of November.

Gunpowder, treason and plot!"

He knew he was being observed, and exchanged a knowing smile with Mark Hargreave.

19

'With a bit of luck, and the help of a few policemen.'

A significant amount of manpower from the Warwickshire Constabulary was enjoying a day out in the country. The second arrest was not made in Temple Weston. A picket line, with statutory brazier, was assembled outside the factory, *'personed'* by half a dozen striking workers. A large force of strikers was unnecessary; the walkout was solid, apart from management.

The patrol car eased its way smoothly to the side of the road. A brace of constables emerged, and walked unhurriedly towards the pickets. Jack Corrigan confronted them with suspicion and truculence.

"This is a lawful picket under the *'Trade Union and Labour Relations (Consolidation) Act of 1992'*..."

"I'm sure you're right sir, and as long as you continue to act in a lawful manner we will have no interest in your activities. We understand, from his wife, that you have a Mr. Kyle Bailey amongst your esteemed assembly."

The officer's sarcasm was not lost on Jack, but he ignored the provocation.

"What do you want with Kyle?"

"Ah, I regret to say, sir, that the matter in question is not covered under the *'Trade Union and Labour Relations (Consolidation) Act of 1992'*. It's personal, sir. If you would be kind enough to point out Mr. Bailey."

Jack shouted to the group around the brazier, warming their hands. It was a frosty November morning.

"Kyle, these gentlemen would like a word with you."

Kyle detached himself from the group. He was met halfway by the police officers.

"Kyle Bailey of 69 Palmerston Way?"

"Yeh."

"You are being arrested on suspicion of dealing in controlled substances. You do not have to say anything. But, it may harm your defence if you do not mention when questioned something which you later rely on in court. Anything you do say may be given in evidence."

Kyle Bailey lived his life acting out the persona of *'Jack the lad'*. In reality he was all mouth and trousers. He had never been in trouble with the law, and he crumbled.

"It wasn't me! It was Marie that got me into it."

Jack Corrigan's ears pricked up. He raced over to them.

"Marie! What Marie? Whose Marie?"

Kyle hung his head in shame, and muttered,

"Your Marie."

Jack raised a fist to strike Kyle, and suddenly found himself on his knees with both arms behind his back.

"Calm down sir, calm down. It won't do you any good to struggle. Tell me your name, sir."

He spat it out.

"Jack, Jack Corrigan!"

The officers exchanged a look.

"Would you be married to Marie Corrigan of 71 Palmerston Way?"

"Yes."

"I'm sorry to inform you, sir, that our colleagues arrested your wife half an hour ago."

Jack slumped forward; all the resistance went out of him.

"Same charge as him?"

"I believe so. Are you ready for us to release you, sir? No aggravation?"

Jack nodded.

"No aggro." He stood up, and turned his back on Kyle.

"Which station is she at?"

The posse that arrived outside *'The Cock with Two Balls'* was team-handed, and they arrived early. Kelly Hampton heard the noise of the cars and van, and rolled out of bed. She peeked through a gap in the curtains.

"Bloody hell!"

Kelly recognised a raid when she saw one. Life in the backstreet clubs of Birmingham had taught her that. She sized them up. Uniform, plain clothes, and a dog.

"Police! Get your arse out of bed. No! Put your overcoat on, and leave your clothes. Back door, turn left. Footpath in far corner of the lawn…"

"I know, I do live here."

"If you hurry up you might just make it. They're still comparing notes out there."

The elderly man sorted himself out as quickly as possible, and she led him down the stairs. He gripped her on the doorstep, and squeezed a breast.

"What have you been up to, you naughty girl?"

She heard him chortling to himself, as he plodded towards the hedge and the obscurity of the footpath.

"Mad, he's bloody mad!"

She closed the door, as Bowcott disappeared from view. The hammering at the front was almost simultaneous. Kelly sat at the foot of the stairs, and counted. A minute to get out bed and down the stairs. The banging increased.

"Oright, oright, let me get my dressing gown on."

She composed herself, and went to the door.

"Who is it? What do you want?"

"Police. Open the door please."

"Need to get my keys. Won't be a tick."

Kelly jangled them in her hands, and gave it thirty seconds. The door was opened wide in a trice.

"Goodness me, you lads are up and about early. I'd offer you a drink, but it's out of hours. Wouldn't want the police calling on me."

She flashed them a big smile, but Detective Constable Andy Harbury, from the Drugs Squad, didn't return her endearments.

"Mrs. Kelly Hampton?"

"Ms, dear, I got rid of him years ago."

"We have a warrant to search these premises. We have reason to believe that the sale of controlled substances has been taking place in your establishment."

He held out the warrant, but she did not look at it. Kelly affected shock, and adopted a soft and gentle voice. She looked very tearful.

"Controlled substances! Do you mean drugs? Here in Temple Weston? Oh my goodness. Yes, yes, of course you must search. I understand entirely. Come in, come."

They all traipsed into the main bar.

"My apologies for the mess. We haven't cleaned up from last night yet…"

"We?"

"Me and my cleaner. She's due in half an hour."

The detective was disarmed.

"I'm sorry Ms. Hampton, she'll have to wait. We may be some time."

"Of course, of course, and do call me Kelly. I can't offer you a pint, but would you like a cup of coffee?"

"Very kind of you Kelly, but we must press on."

"Can I go and get showered and dressed?"

"Dressed yes. I'm afraid the shower will have to wait."

"Okay, ta. I'll stay in my bedroom until you're finished."

"This is PC Helen Aston, she'll accompany you. We'll need to examine your bedroom at some stage."

Kelly assumed that the policewoman would remain outside the bedroom door, but she entered the room with her. Helen Aston stared at her so intently that she began to wonder if she was a *'beanflicker'*. You never knew with women in uniform. Not that it bothered Kelly, nor did she disapprove. In her years on the game she advertised her services for both men and women, and was quite partial to a threesome; whatever its composition.

"Those are men's clothes."

"You're quite right, Helen love."

Kelly had put on Bowcott's trousers, and was tucking his shirt into the waistband. Fortunately, he had shrunk with age and illness, and she was a curvy and well-stacked middle aged woman. Mildly alarmed by the policewoman's observation, she explained herself.

"My ex-husband's clobber. Never got rid of it. I put these on when I do all my dirty jobs. He was a right git. Used to knock me about and all that. I try to get them as filthy as possible."

"They look expensive."

"Oh, they were. It would upset him no end to see them in this state. Vengeance may be the Lord's prerogative, but I'm having a bit as well. Tell you what luvvie, do you fancy that cup of coffee?"

"We can't use the kitchen."

"I've got all the gubbins here. Saves getting out of bed in the morning."

"You've got two cups."

It was a statement, not a question.

"How can I put this delicately. I'm not exactly Julie Andrews in *'The Sound of Music'*. Do you have a boyfriend luvvie? I bet you do. Lovely looking lass like yourself."

When the coffee was brewed they chattered away amiably, waiting for the boys in blue to mount the stairs in their search. Kelly wasn't worried. The product she sold was well away from the premises, but it looked like some other bugger had been engaged in private enterprise.

Kyle Bailey was as meek as the Passover Lamb. He unburdened himself of his misdemeanours. The blame was apportioned to Marie Corrigan, and he thought that only just. She had given birth to that monster of a son. He wasn't entirely stupid, and he didn't mention Barry. From the little that he understood about women, he was pretty certain that Marie would keep her boy out of it, and shoulder all the blame. He suspected that if they both came clean in this way they'd get away with a fine or something.

Her Scouse accent was pronounced in the interview room next door.

"I only did it because he keeps me short. There's never enough money to go round."

DC Andy Harbury was sympathetic.

"That's your husband Jack?"

"Yeh."

"Does he mistreat you in any other way?"

"Eh? Oh, I see what you mean. No, no, he doesn't knock me about or nuffin. He's just as tight as a nun's chuff…an' 'e's a lot older than me."

"So you decided to make an extra few bob for yourself and your lad. Well, I can understand that. Coventry you say?"

She looked bashful.

"Yeh. We have a girls' night out occasionally, an' I get a small supply from the club we go to…"

Marie was nearly as sharp as Kelly Hampton. She selected the name of a Coventry nightclub, and invented a commonplace name for her supplier.

"Do you have to give this man a percentage from your sales?"

"Nah. The people in Temple Weston are better off. I've been charging extra to make a profit."

"That's unusual Marie. These people don't normally do favours."

This time she looked coy.

"Yeh, but you know...I sort of do favours for him. You know, like payment in kind."

Andy Harbury understood completely.

"Where does he take you? Could you identify the premises?"

"What? We don't go anywhere. Like we do, but it's an upstairs room in the club. He, he..."

She burst into tears.

"It's not just 'im. There's two or three others."

It was a bravura performance. Not so much *'The Cock with Two Balls'*, more a cock and bull story.

Andy Harbury mulled over the evidence with his boss.

"It looks small beer to me boss. Bailey and Corrigan have admitted dealing, but it's nothing out of the ordinary. The dog picked up the scent in the pub toilets, but nowhere else. Looks like your informant got it spot on."

Detective Inspector Phil Brooks remained tight-lipped about his source. It wouldn't be wise for it to be known that a Royal Protection Officer was involved.

"Think you're right, Andy." He tapped his spectacles lightly on the desk. "Bugger! I thought this might have moved us on a little. The amount of *'Afghan'* out there is increasing exponentially. Where the fuck is it all coming from?"

Kelly Hampton sat with him in his private quarters in Banbury. He had received her short text message.

"I'm out of this Mark. I've had enough grief in my life. Temple Weston is my home now, and I intend it to be permanent. So, I've given you your stash back, and we'll call it quits."

Mark said nothing for a while. It didn't matter to him if Kelly was a conduit for sales or not. Small beer were the words that came to his mind as well. His profits came from distribution in the nearby towns and cities. She'd also implied that she still knew some very hard men in Birmingham.

Mark believed her. Money interested him, not getting into turf wars and fights with people.

"Kelly, I think that's eminently sensible. Thanks for everything you've done, and we'll call it even Stevens."

She was relieved, and waggled her empty glass at him. He topped it up with Rosé.

"Who'd have thought it, Mark? Kyle and Marie. I'd have understood it if it had been that little bugger of a son of hers. Wonder who was supplying them?"

Mark was wondering exactly the same. It was too coincidental.

"Ah, they'll just get a slap on the wrist. Come on, drink up and I'll take you to lunch. Tell you what, Kelly, you don't fancy a comeback do you?"

"What?"

"Join the girls downstairs. You're still a very attractive woman."

She didn't take offence, and laughed it off.

"Give over, you little charmer. I'm past all that."

He leant across, and clinked his glass against hers.

"What about a one-time special for a friend? After lunch of course."

A young lad carried the shopping bags without effort. The back door to Mary Jessop's was always open. He placed the bags on the floor; all except one.

"Is that you Barry?"

"Yes Mrs. Jessop. I got everything. I'll start putting it away. Okay if I do the toiletries first?"

"Wait for me."

She came into the kitchen.

"Thank you luvvie. You are a treasure. Can of Coke and a slice of cake?"

"Yes please."

He clutched the carrier bag to his chest, and ascended the stairs. The few toiletries went into the bathroom. Standing at the head of the stairs, he listened. Nah, she wouldn't hear a thing.

Barry carefully opened the door to the small bedroom. The old-fashioned wardrobe would do just fine. It gave the faintest of creaks, and he paused. No worries. It was packed with all sorts. Bags and photo frames, clothes and board games.

Swiftly and silently he rearranged the contents. He discovered an empty back pack in the wardrobe. A remnant of the glorious days when Mary and Eddie had scaled many a peak in the Lake District and Scotland. The packages were transferred. Now he didn't have to explain where the carrier had disappeared to. The old bag might be going doolally, but she had a thing about recycling and plastics.

"Here you go luvvie. Sit yourself down. One Coca Cola, and one big slice of chocolate cake."

"Ta Mrs. Jessop, an' 'ere's the plazzy bag for you. Got to save the planet, 'aven't we?"

20

'Who wants stuffing?'

Rain was not conducive to his main task, but it would assist other elements of his mission. Hargreave's shirt factory had security signs posted, but they were meaningless. A few out-of-date CCTV cameras, which were rarely serviced, and not a soul on site. Mark had visited his father there only a month before, and was startled by the ease of entry to the premises. He had expressed his view to Beebie.

"Waste of money, son. There's never been any problems here. We're only a shirt factory. Who'd be interested in us?"

The striking pickets were long retired to their beds, and the braziers out front gave off only a residual glow. Not that it mattered to the intruder. He was at the rear of the complex, and had found a hole in the wire fencing large enough to squeeze through. The piece of equipment he carried was small enough to follow.

He knew the route he was taking like the back of his hand. Hugging walls all the way, he was unseen by the cameras. The fire door looked secure, to all intents and purposes. It was not. It had been opened surreptitiously, and a sliver of wood placed between the two doors before they were drawn together. He opened the largest blade on his pen knife, and pushed it into the join. With a little pressure, the doors swung open easily.

There wasn't time to stand around admiring his handiwork. He could do that from a distance later. Before he knew it he was in the main space; it was enormous. Great bolts of cloth were stacked to dramatic heights. Without further ado, he took the cap off the jerry can and showered petrol over the flammable material. The can was placed with majesty in the centre of the room. It was awkward, holding two items in the same hand, but necessary. Once the match was struck and ignition occurred he would have to leg it sharpish.

   He went to the furthest point from the exit, and set the cloth ablaze. As he ran, he dropped a cigarette lighter. Soon he was at the fire doors, and a mobile phone fell to the floor just inside. Putting distance between himself and the impending conflagration he nonetheless heard the growing crackle of fire. He was through the hole in the fence in no time at all, and into the small copse that bordered the back of the premises.

Commonsense told him that he should scarper immediately, but he wanted to watch. The rain had stopped, but the sky was heavy with clouds. Suddenly, there was a shattering of glass, and the first licks of flame stuck their tongues through the open apertures. What happened next surprised even him. An enormous explosion tore the factory apart.

"Fuck me backwards with a tube of Smarties!"

He picked up his bicycle, and was off.

It was half past three in the morning when he got home. Noiselessly, he returned the bicycle to the shed, and clasped the padlock shut. The work boots were removed, and placed in their usual position. Before he knew it he was in bed and asleep. His features were in repose, but the ghost of a gleeful smile caressed them.

"I am so sorry, Pa."

Mark Hargreave had an arm around his father's shoulders. It was seven in the morning, and not yet sunrise. The factory was still burning, but the fire service had it under control.

"Come on, Pa. Nothing we can do here. Let's get home, and get some breakfast inside you."

"Aye, you're right son. Just a word with the fire chief and the police."

Beebie was informed that they were unlikely to have any news for him before the next day at the earliest. However, the police had searched the perimeter, and had discovered the probable point of entry and a set of footprints.

"Find the bugger, and make sure he falls down the station steps!"

Beebie stalked away, and Mark gave the senior officer a sympathetic smile before following his father.

Nobody had given a thought to telling the striking pickets what had happened, and they turned up at the gates for their daily stint.

Jack Corrigan stood amazed.

"What are we going to do, Jack?"

"I haven't a clue, Kyle. No point in hanging about here."

An opinion was expressed in an accent from the Sub-Continent.

"Ve must call off the strike. There is no purpose in continuing with it. If we do so Sir Benson may continue to pay our wages."

Jack wasn't at all sure about that, but he saw the sense of the proposal.

"Okay. I'll try to get a meeting with him."

In between dealing with the financial aspects of having his premises burnt to the ground, Benson raged all day long about the destruction. Freddie was tired of hearing about it, as the three of them ate dinner. It was a relief to be interrupted by the doorbell.

"Of course gentlemen, do come through. We'll be with you in a short while."

She escorted the two police officers to the comfort of the drawing room, and was soon back there with Beebie and Mark in tow.

"Chief Inspector Parker, sir."

Beebie spoke brusquely.

"Wasn't expecting you until tomorrow. That's what your lad said."

"A stroke of good fortune, sir. Well, for us but not for the arsonist who set your premises ablaze.

It would appear that he gained access through the rear fire door. In his haste to depart he dropped his mobile telephone. I shouldn't say too much more, sir, but I feel sure that I can rely on your discretion. Our lads did a sweep of the area. We're fairly sure the perpetrator gained access to the compound through a hole in the fence, at the rear of your premises. A wider search found footprints…"

"I know that. One of your lads told me."

"Quite so. We also had a look around the small wood, and discovered tyre tracks…"

"A car? A van?"

"A bicycle, Sir Benson. Lady luck has smiled upon us further. We obtained a search warrant, and whilst we interviewed the owner of the mobile telephone our search team located a pair of boots and a bicycle. We are confident that they will match the evidence found at the site."

"By the heck! Well done, well done. You'll have a drink?"

"Very kind of you, Sir Benson."

The two senior officers accepted a Scotch.

"Go on then."

"Pardon me, sir?"

"You've got him. Who is it?"

"Discretion Sir Benson, we can rely on your discretion?"

The Chief Inspector included Freddie and Mark in his question. Mark answered for them.

"Absolutely."

"Subject to the tread of his boots and the tyres of his bicycle matching those we found; I think we can say yes. Yes we have found him."

"And." Benson was beside himself with excitement.

"We have arrested the owner of the mobile telephone on suspicion of committing the arson. I understand that he is your Foreman, sir. Jack Corrigan!"

There was a look of wonderment on his face, as he spoke to his companion. Briefly, he looked into the boy's eyes, but they were unfathomable. It also made him feel uncomfortable, and he lost the staring contest.

"You really are a little beauty, aren't you. Graduated to the big time now. No going back. So now you've stitched up your stepfather, there's just one thing left for you to do."

Barry Corrigan affected a look of sublime innocence.

"Don't come it Barry. Where's the gear you nicked from me?"

"I told you. It's in a bag in the old girl's wardrobe. No flies on me."

"Right, soon as you can – end of the week at the latest – I want it back here. Then you get paid for doing the factory job, and we'll ease you back into the weekend work. Be nice to get out and about again, instead of being stuck in the village all the time."

Barry didn't hesitate. Weekends in Coventry, Warwick and other towns, and money burning a hole in his pocket.

"Deal!"

Mark was tempted to say that it wasn't a question of a deal; he would do what he was told. He felt cold, standing outside the hot greenhouses in the late-November air.

"By the end of the week. Beat it."

Mark watched the cocky stride, with Donald and Vladimir panting beside the boy. He was no longer afraid, and Barry chatted to them as he went. A genuine shiver went through him, and it wasn't caused by the cold day. He realised that they were tied to one another. Barry had as much on him, as he had on Barry. The boy was without any moral scruples. He was a danger to Mark. Somewhere along the line the umbilical cord would have to be cut.

21

'Who do you think I am, Soft Mick?'

Grenville Simons slithered back into the area.

Clem Starkiss was no longer his target. In fact, he was aiming for three bulls eyes in one visit. His first arrow from the oche would be launched at the pop star vicar.

A splendid country hotel was the venue for Rufus Coleridge and Spencer Hoffman's civil partnership ceremony, followed by the reception. They took the wise decision not to ask the management to corral the press off the grounds. A coterie of selected photographers were invited to take a few snaps of the happy couple and their guests, accompanied by their journo colleagues.

"One question each, please."

Spencer's agent, Peggy, took charge. Virginia from the celebrity mag kicked off. They had paid handsomely to do a complete spread.

Virginia's Chelsea tones asked about the inspiration for their matching velvet suits and accessories. Likeminded others explored a similar vein.

"Yes darling, you."

"Grev Simons *'Daily Paragon'*."

It did not escape Grenville's attention that Clem Starkiss was one of the witnesses, and on hearing his name had whispered into Rufus' ear. In for a penny, in for a pound.

"Roof, there's a rumour doing the rounds of your parish that not all of the congregation are happy with you and Spencer getting hitched. Care to comment?"

Peggy tried to intervene.

"It's alright Peggy. Under the circumstances it's a fair question. Mr. Simons, Spencer and I have not, as you so colloquially put it, got hitched. That would require a wedding ceremony. We have joined ourselves to each other through civil partnership. Her Grace the Bishop gave approval, as you can see."

Bishop Marion was standing to one side with other guests.

"I…we understand Church policy on clergy in civil partnerships, and we will abide by that rule."

Roof was referring to the celibacy rule within civil partnerships for gay clergy. Grenville knew he had to be quick, with only one question permitted.

"What about your Churchwarden, Marjorie Knighton?"

Peggy Roughsedge asserted herself.

"Next question. Jamie, yes you Jamie."

Grenville had what he wanted, and didn't hang about. He thanked his pagan gods for Rufus' phrase, *'We have joined ourselves to each other…'*. There was mileage in that, used as a *double entendre.* Far better was the transcript of the interview with St. Dunstan's Churchwarden Marjorie Knighton, and her acolyte Jennifer Morton. Sodom and Gomorrah was always a useful gobbet from the Bible to cast the Church of England in the light of intolerance. That was his objective. Not for one teensy weensy moment did he intend to cast aspersions upon Roof and Spencer; that wouldn't be PC. Their celebrity status and newly sanctioned union were mere tools with which to bash Christianity. He would, naturally, omit the fact that their new state was approved by the Bishop.

His next interview was in Temple Weston, but he was hungry. Grenville parked opposite the pub.

He grabbed a couple of shots of the sign, using his mobile phone. It was really quite amusing, but a more important idea sprung to mind. He must ask his photographer to superimpose the image of *'The Cock with Two Balls'* behind a photograph of Rufus and Spencer.

"Yes my love?"

"Would it be possible to get lunch, please?"

Kelly Hampton was all smiles.

"Course you can, bab. Only you two in. Where would you like to sit?"

"I'll take the table in the corner, if I may."

"Made to measure for you. Drink?"

He selected a large Argentinian Malbec. Usually a safe bet in all parts outside London. An elderly gentleman, perched on a bar stool, remarked.

"Wise choice, sir. Kelly's cellar is not too noteworthy for the discerning palate."

Kelly wasn't at all put out.

"I bow to your vastly superior experience, milord. Just got to get a fresh bottle, me ducks."

Grenville gave his companion at the bar a friendly nod.

"Some sort of in-joke is it?"

"What?"

"Milord."

"Not in the slightest, old boy." He took a gulp of his wine, and shivered like a wet dog as it went down. "I am, for my sins, a peer of the realm."

Kelly bounced into the room.

"Here we are, last one in the cellar. Been going rather quickly of late."

She cast a wry eye in Bowcott's direction.

"Will you have one, sir?"

"Very civil of you, old boy. Fill her up Kelly."

Grenville and Bowcott were situated at either end of the bar, but he heard her concerned whisper,

"Are you sure Bowcott, you've already downed one bottle."

"Pour!"

"Good health."

Bowcott responded with a weak smile to Grenville's salutation.

"Grenville Simons, sir." He walked the length of the bar, and offered his hand. "Only Lord I've heard of in this village is the one who used to live at *'The Manor',* Lord Bowcott. I understand he disappeared from the picture some years ago. I've met his ex-wife though."

"Have you indeed. The Lady Edwina."

"Yes, that's right. Do you know her?"

"Intimately. My dear fellow, you meet a ghost turned flesh. You have been received by my wife you say, now you encounter the spouse. Husband mind, not ex-. Where did you foregather with Edwina?"

"Oh, I was interviewing the local Curate, believe his name is Starkiss, something like that. She turned up at his door unexpectedly."

Grenville decided to fly a kite.

"I…er…I made my excuses and left. I could see they wanted to be alone. I expect it was some sort of pastoral issue requiring intimacy between them. Would you excuse me, I need the toilet."

He didn't hear Bowcott's mutter.

"Lavatory, you shithouse!"

Grenville heard the raised voice as he returned, and hid in the corridor.

"Is that God botherer shagging my missus? I've had my suspicions. You know everything that goes on. Is he Kelly? Is he?"

"Care to add any further comment, Lord Bowcott?"

Grenville emerged from the shadows of the corridor.

"Kelly says you work for that left wing piece of arsewipe *'The Paragon'*. Well your governor, Lord Fleet, is an old pal of mine. You watch your step Simons. I've got it right haven't I? Simons you called yourself. Of the *'Faith'* are you? Now fuck off, you lavatorial rodent, before I take this bottle and ram it up your arse. I daresay you'd enjoy that."

Grenville threw a twenty-pound note onto the counter.

"To cover the drink, and the lunch. Feed it to his lordship. He looks as if he needs it more than I do."

So overjoyed was Grenville at the outcome of this unexpected encounter that he took the unusual step of walking to his next appointment. He followed directions on the *'Street View'* app, and soon arrived in Palmerston Way. His step was positively jaunty. Gold dust, pure gold dust. He laughed aloud. Lord Fleet retired eight years ago. Where had Bowcott been?

Barry Corrigan answered the door.

"Wot?"

"Not at school, young man?"

"Wot the fuck's it got to do with you?"

"Oh eh, Barry. I'm sorry mister. Are you...?"

"Grev Simons, *'The Paragon'*. I telephoned."

"Yeh. We woz expectin' youse. Come in."

Grenville sized up the living room, whilst she made coffee. It wasn't in bad condition, but the decoration was cheap and garish. As the late Liverpudlian comedian Kenny Everett would have pronounced with irony it was,

"All in the best possible taste!"

They settled to their coffee. Barry plonked himself on the arm of his mother's chair glugging Coke.

"It must be terrible for you Marie. I understand that Jack has been denied bail."

"I'm destroyed. So's Barry, aren't you Barry?"

"Wot? Oh, yeh."

Grenville looked askance at Barry's rendition of sincerity.

"And you say he couldn't possibly have committed arson?"

"Arsin', what does that mean?"

"ARSON! It means someone who sets fire to things for fun."

The sideways glance at Barry did not escape his eagle eye.

"How can you be so sure, Marie?"

"Cos we sleep together. Wot I mean is, we sleep in each other's arms. We always have done. It was luv at first sight for me an' Jack. I'd 'ave known if he'd left the bed for one second."

Grenville began to formulate mental notes; Romeo and Juliet, *'Two households both alike in dignity'*. He would use Shakespeare to compare the Corrigan and Hargreave households, but ascribe dignity to the lowly Corrigans alone. He already knew everything about the strike. His old informant Kyle Bailey had filled him in on that, for a small consideration.

"And you mentioned earlier that you've got to keep Barry away from school. Why's that?"

The lumpen teenager stirred himself.

"They're pickin' on me."

"Who, the teachers?"

Marie interrupted.

"They pick on my Barry all the time, but the kids have joined in now."

"Why would they do that?"

"Cos they say his dad 'as put everyone out of werk, burnin' the factory down..."

"He's not my dad, he's my step-dad."

Grenville suppressed a grin at the pathetic resentment. Another note. Bright child denied his education.

"Oh yeh, but he's a good step-dad, isn't he Barry."

Barry took a swig of Coke, and burped.

"Barry, your manners. Say pardon."

"Pardon. Yeh, the best."

Grenville loved the kid. He said everything you wanted to hear, but with undisguised disdain.

"He's a good lad, is Barry. His grades 'ave bin smashin' recently. Changed lad, aren't you, ever since you started helpin' Mrs. Jessop."

"Who's Mrs. Jessop, Marie?"

Barry got there first.

"Old girl, lives in the detached 'ouse at the end of the road. Gives me cake, and Coke, an' sarnies."

"And what do you do in return, Barry?"

"Oh, 'e's ace, aren't you love. Shoppin', cuttin' the grass, cleanin' an' all that. Barry's a star; my little star. Give us a kiss."

The teenager acquiesced, with a squirm.

Grenville's admiration for them was towering. What an act. Clearly an utterly dysfunctional family, and the kid was a shit. By the size of him, Grenville suspected that if anyone was being picked on it was the other kids, by Barry. Still, the story would be of a loving working class family torn apart. An honest man driven to a criminal act by desperation. He was curious about Jack Corrigan. Everyone spoke well of him. Maybe it was true. Perhaps the wicked and intransigent employer had driven Jack over the edge. Whatever! The story Grenville would write would be consistent with his political mantra. It was just a question of how he interpreted the facts.

He took at quick shufti at his wristwatch. Speaking of Benson Hargreave, he was due to meet with him in ten minutes.

"Marie, Barry, you've been terrific. Rest assured, *'The Paragon'* will tell your story with sympathy and compassion. I wouldn't be surprised if by this time tomorrow you weren't national celebrities."

"Oh eh, go way! Er, you said somethin' about…"

He dipped a hand into his overcoat pocket.

"Here we go. Treat yourselves; you deserve every penny. No, don't move. I'll let myself out. Bye."

They held their breath until they heard the door close.

"'Ow much, Mam?"

"One, two, three…oh my God! Three hundred and fifty notes. 'ere you go luvvie, there's fifty. Can you get your own dinners this week. I'm gonna be out shoppin'. Eh, I tell you wot. Bet I can get free drinks in the pub all week. They'll be comin' out in sympathy for me this time. Another twenty for you if I have to buy a drink before Sunday."

Barry thought his mum was dead tight, only giving him fifty quid, but said nothing. He had plenty of dosh anyway, from what Mark had given him.

"Can't apologise enough, Grev. Okay if I call you Grev? Do call me Mark. Got a rather nice Scotch here. Could I interest you?"

"Just a small one, Mark. Driving you know."

"Hang that. Join me for a spot of lunch. Here we go. Cheers."

"Thank you. I did intend to have a bite at the pub, but…"

"Ah, *Deux Testicules*. Not bad grub."

"Had to exit rather sharpish. Upset your lord of the manor."

"You met Bowcott? What a character. Recently returned from extended leave in foreign parts, and causing quite a stir."

"Anything in particular?"

Mark laughed.

"I shouldn't really say, but he caused a terrific kerfuffle when he turned up at the Curate's fancy dress party dressed as Jimmy Saville. Rather insensitive, considering it was a charity evening."

Grenville rolled the delicious whiskey around his mouth.

"Bit of a lad, your Curate."

Mark wasn't taken in one bit by Grenville's hail fellow well met act.

"Is he?"

"One or two rumours that he and the lady of the manor are…"

"Oh yes, I read that in your article. Well, can't say I can help you there. Mind you, Ma and Pa told me that some years back the Bowcotts held rather interesting and intimate parties at the Manor. Don't have any inside info, unfortunately."

Grenville didn't push the envelope. That could go on the back burner for research later.

"It's a shame Sir Benson had to leave for London so suddenly. I could have interviewed him there."

"I don't think that would have been possible. He's going to be occupied with high finance all day, and Conservative Party business in the evening. Hope I'll do as his deputy. Let's take lunch. Let's get rid of your glass. There's a rather decent 2005 St. Estephe awaiting consumption."

Mark insisted that they didn't spoil lunch by talking shop. Instead they swapped reminiscences of public school days; Mark boarding in Hertfordshire, and Grenville's halcyon days at UCS in Hampstead.

"Here's your coat Grev. Want to show you my market garden. We can chat about Pa on the way."

"I expect Sir Benson is pretty cut up about the factory?"

Mark restrained himself from saying, *"With a trite question like that your old man should ask UCS for his money back."*

"Coming hard on the heels of the strike, you'd have thought so…"

He let it dangle.

"Isn't he?"

Mark halted, and adopted a pose redolent of Rodin's sculpture of *'The Thinker'*.

"Bit odd really. He was beside himself for a week, but once the insurance company confirmed they'd pay out he was as calm as the Dead Sea."

Mark sniggered.

"Something funny?"

"Actually, yes Grev. Typical of my dear salty old Pa. It's like he's spent his entire life swimming in the Dead Sea. However much people try to push him under he always finds a way of floating to the surface."

Grev's nose did its bunny act.

"How was the business before the recent hiatus?"

"Oh, I don't know much about his business, other than what he sounds off about over the dinner table. Dear Ma switches off; she's heard it all before. I lend a sympathetic ear."

"And?"

"Oh, you mean what do I pick up. Not so sure I should be disclosing this."

"Off the record."

"Promise?"

"Promise."

Grenville was deadpan. He was aware that there was a trade-off going on, but couldn't figure out what was in it for Mark.

"Not much to tell really, Grev. I understand that the northern factories are underperforming.

Business hasn't really recovered since the Pandemic, and..."

"Off the record."

"Well, I think Pa has overstretched himself a little playing the benevolent knight with his Hargreave estate properties."

Mark had said all he wanted to say, and Grev didn't notice his right hand flick upwards.

"Fuck me!"

The Rottweilers came galloping towards them.

"*'Don't panic Mr. Mainwaring'*, I've got them under control."

Grev stared at the panting hounds.

"Yours?"

"Oh no. I inherited them temporarily. Donald and Vladimir belong to Pa."

"Interesting names. Meant to be a joke?"

Mark did his Rodin act again.

"Hmmm? Maybe, maybe not. Might be Pa's act of homage to their namesakes. What do you think of my garden?"

"You set this up?"

"Not registered as a charity, but created with charitable intent. I've made my money, want to put something back into the community. Free fruit and veg for the village. Well, to be absolutely truthful. Free to anyone receiving benefits, in work or not, and rock bottom prices to those who can afford. Mind you, only to those living on the estate. The rest of the village is very well-heeled."

"What's behind those screens?"

"Greenhouses."

"I see. Tomatoes, cucumbers, that sort of thing."

"Yes, but I'm only allowed access to a small number of them. Pa cultivates the rest."

"What's he growing?"

"Not the foggiest. Closely guarded secret. No one is allowed to see; not even family. Says he's working on experimental crops with the RHS. I think it's wonderful. Such a busy man, and he gives of his time to promote the welfare of the wider community. Goodness me! I am sorry Grev, but I've got a meeting with my foreman about distribution. Let me see you off the premises. Wouldn't want you to get lost with Donald and Vladimir roaming the range."

He walked the journalist to his car.

"You know Grev, it's been a real pleasure. You've been a breath of fresh air to me, what with the never ending upsets we've been having in the village."

"Never ending?"

"You know. First the death of the child and the destruction of the Church Hall, then two of Pa's employees arrested for selling drugs, then the drugs raid on the pub, then strikes and another fire…"

"Drugs raid?"

"Oh, didn't you know about that?"

Grev was so excited he wanted to fly. He would garner information later about the drugs bust.

"Got to love you and leave you, Mark. Thanks ever so much."

Mark held an iron grip on the proffered hand.

"Sometimes I think I'm living in '*Midsomer Murders*', there's so much going on in our quiet corner of England. Cheerio."

Mark hurried into the house, and swept the open bottle of Bordeaux off the table. His long strides took him into one of the greenhouses, where Marie was lying naked on the carpet. He knelt over her and poured the remains of the wine over her lips and breasts. Slowly, he licked every drop from her skin. He bore an uncanny resemblance to a pariah dog slurping blood from the corpse of a plague victim.

22

'Next Preston Guild'

Manufacturing opportunities to meet each other never entered their heads. Edwina and Clem were mature human beings. They held a short conversation about their situation, created by Bowcott's return, and decided that they would not attempt to create an artificial life. They would, however, limit their encounters to within the confines of church business.

The PCC meeting had ended, and the two of them were alone in the Vestry, poring over the parlous state of the finances.

"Well if this ain't a frosty Friday!"

Clem didn't look up; he was scribbling figures on a scrap of paper. He maintained concentration, but laughed aloud and said,

"Burl Ives in *'The Big Country'*, I believe."

Silence compelled him to see who had entered the room.

"Good afternoon, Lord Bowcott."

The sheer malevolence on Bowcott's face startled him.

"What sort of priest are you, young man?"

Clem recovered his composure.

"I'm not sure I understand your question."

"Do you consider it appropriate to be engaged in an affair with another man's wife?"

"Highly inappropriate."

"Then why are you such a hypocrite?"

Edwina attempted to intervene, but Clem raised a hand.

"Let me be categoric, Lord Bowcott. Whatever rumours you may have heard, they are untrue. Nothing has passed between Edwina and myself which constitutes an affair."

Bowcott rested on his walking stick. He looked tired, but there was a troublesome spirit in him which wouldn't let go. He glared at them. Without warning his features changed. Understanding illuminated his face, but it fled to the shadows. He was mourning for what was lost.

"I believe you; I believe you both. An affair, a conventional affair hasn't happened...it's far worse than that. It's an affair of the heart."

He took hold of a wooden chair, and scraped it across the floor. Bowcott eased himself onto it, painfully. His clasped hands weighed down on the top of the stick. An aura of defeat swirled around him, like a miasma dwelling above a swamp.

"You have betrayed me Edwina."

She too felt the need to sit down. Instead, she placed one hand onto the table. Giddiness had overcome her.

"How can you say that Bowcott; how can you even think it? You walked out on me years ago without a second thought..."

"I should leave you two alone."

"No Clem. I want you to hear this."

"Lord Bowcott?"

He waved a hand in response to Clem's enquiry. It signified, *"Do what the hell you please."*

"Bowcott, I have put up with years of your sarcasm, your rudeness, your disdain, your bullying, and..."

She hesitated, and Bowcott lifted his eyes. They sparkled with amusement. A message was transmitted to her. It said, *"Go on, I dare you. See what lover boy thinks of you then."*

"…and the demeaning practices you led me into, and luxuriated in. Now you are the wronged party. I sympathise Bowcott, I truly do. For all the ill you have done to me, I don't want to see you wasting away like this, and I will mourn you. But you, you of all people turning sentimental because you are dying."

Edwina hesitated, and took slow breaths to calm her heaving chest.

"Bowcott, I intend to instigate proceedings for divorce…"

"I warned you what…"

"Whatever the consequences!"

She bowed her head, before embracing her courage. Her eyes were fixed on the man she loved.

"Clem, my husband's warning is that if I divorce him he will expose me before the world. He has in his possession photographs and video tapes of me in intimate and compromising positions…not with him alone…but…with numerous men. We used to hold *'parties'*." Plaintively, she added, "It was years ago."

Clem didn't move a muscle. Sexual jealousy was nonsense to him, the moral aspect was of more concern. He searched her face, and recognised true repentance. Quietly and sincerely he said,

"It doesn't change how I feel; it doesn't change what I hope for."

Unexpected strength coursed through Bowcott's sickly body, and he almost leapt to his feet.

"I won't have it! You're my wife, and my wife you stay. I'll fight you all the way Edwina, and I'll ruin you young man. Wait 'til your Bishop hears about your goings on. Divorce...never! Hell will freeze over before I give you a divorce."

His stick tapped the floor, as he departed from the Vestry. The ominous echo created the same sort of fear that the approach of Blind Pew generated in *'Treasure Island'*. Pew was the fictional character who handed the *'black spot'* to others, signifying that they would die.

Clem cleared his throat.

"Now Edwina, I think we can justify paying for the Tower repairs out of the Trust Fund."

Detective Constable John Fortune fulfilled his guvnor's faith in him. Molly McGuire beamed, like Mother Goose witnessing her first born laying a golden egg. She was one of a group assembled in the Chief Superintendent's office. John was delivering his treatise.

"We've been getting nowhere fast with a number of cases. There was the death of the child Arthur Archer in the church hall fire; then the drugs raid on the pub, and the arrest of two locals for dealing, and now the arson attack on the shirt factory…"

Chief Superintendent Melvyn Woodward interrupted.

"I thought that was cut and dried? Suspect in custody, and solid forensics retrieved from his property."

"So it would seem, sir, but Jack Corrigan is dogged in his denial of any involvement. The odd thing is that his wife swears he never left the house."

"What's odd about that, John?"

"Well sir, we know from neighbours that the couple are not on the best of terms."

Molly McGuire stuck her two pennorth in.

"Elderly lady, boss, one Mary Jessop, well-respected locally. Called us in for a fireside chat, after we'd visited Little Arthur's parents. Gave us the lowdown on the neighbours. Apparently, Marie Corrigan, that's Jack's wife, is having an affair with someone in the village. No one knows who. That's why it's odd, her sticking by her husband when she could be rid of him."

Melvyn Woodward sat forward with a sudden movement. It didn't escape the notice of those in the room. He waved at John Fortune to continue.

"We've overlooked a common factor. Easily done when different teams are investigating different cases."

"And?"

"Well sir, all the crimes are associated with the village of Temple Weston."

DI Phil Brooks, from the Drugs Squad, was puzzled.

"How does the arson at the shirt factory fit? Isn't that located near Dunsmore-by-Napton?"

John Fortune was triumphant.

"The owner, Sir Benson Hargreave, is a leading light of the village. Jack and Marie Corrigan work in his factory, and live in one of his houses. It's Jack who brought the factory to a standstill with a strike."

Phil Brooks stroked his chin.

"Fair enough John. Don't see how it helps us though. The rate we're going at it'll be next Preston Guild before we find out who's flooding the county with *'Afghan'*. Can't see much mileage coming out of a well-heeled place like Temple Weston."

The Chief Super's voice was authoritative, and they sat bolt upright.

"What I tell you doesn't leave this room. The Corrigans, they have a teenage son, Barry by name. The fair city of Liverpool is their hometown. Corrigan is not the real family name, and since they were relocated we have been keeping a watchful eye upon them; for their sakes."

"May I ask why, boss?"

"You may, Molly." Woodward leant back in his chair. With a terse brevity he informed them of Barry Corrigan's propensity for pyromania, and the scarred child he'd left behind in Liverpool.

Molly tried not to sound aggrieved.

"Wish we'd known that earlier. Barry was flagged up by the school as a troublemaker, and Mary Jessop wasn't too complimentary about him at first."

"At first?"

John Fortune took up the tale.

"Apparently, he saw the light, not long after Little Arthur's death. Can't do enough for Mrs. Jessop, or so she says, and rapidly becoming a model pupil at school. Apart from too many Fridays off."

Molly continued.

"We had an informal chat with Barry, parents present. Butter wouldn't melt in his mouth, and Marie provided yet another alibi. Says he was up all night being sick when the church hall went south, and the poor little lad with it."

She added a non sequitur to herself.

"Still can't fathom out how Arthur had cannabis in him."

The Chief Super' ignored the remark.

"How's Barry getting on with his father these days? Correction, stepfather."

John and Molly exchanged a mutual look of surprise.

"You know about that, sir?"

"I do John. The briefing from our colleagues in Liverpool preceded their arrival, and gave a blow by blow account of family discord."

"Funny boss, Mary Jessop described it just like that. Sounds as though matters haven't improved."

Woodward leaned on his desk and mused.

"I met the family twice. He was a big lad for his age, was our Barry. Must have grown a bit in the last few years?"

John Fortune laughed.

"Got big feet, as I recall. Nearly as big as Jack's…Are you suggesting what I think you are, sir?"

Woodward spread his arms; palms visible. He moved them up and down, like a pair of old-fashioned scales alternating their balance.

"Jack Corrigan doesn't have a record. I can remember my oppo in Liverpool telling me that he couldn't understand why Jack put up with it all. Apart from the obvious delights of a young wife. Now what do we know? Barry is off his rocker when it comes to pyrotechnics. Take my word for it, there's a very detailed psychiatric report. Though the shrink concluded that he was a good way along the path of improvement. We know he can't stand his stepfather…"

"Sorry to interrupt, boss."

"Go on, Molly."

"I can see the connection with the death of Arthur Archer, but the shirt factory. Why?"

"An opportunity to revenge himself on Jack. I'm not surprised he's doing better at school. The shrink's report says he's of exceptional intelligence, and becoming goody two shoes all of a sudden puts folk off the scent."

"Or someone put him up to it."

"What's that, Phil?"

"Sorry boss. Just thinking out loud."

Phil Brooks was also processing his cogitations internally. Cannabis in Arthur's bloodstream; Barry's regular Friday absences from school. It was all fairly intangible, but there were tenuous connections. He also couldn't discount the information he'd received about the pub. Phil had run a check on landlady Kelly Hampton. She'd used her married name to apply for a licence. If her maiden name had come up she'd never have got past the magistrates. She had a charge sheet as long as your arm for soliciting.

"I think a formal interview this time, Molly. Other agencies will have to be informed. We need to put young Barry under the spotlight. Be warned, his shrink says he positively relishes being centre stage."

"What about Jack and Marie, boss?"

Woodward organised a few items on his desk that were out of alignment.

"Jack's been charged, hasn't he?"

A nod of confirmation was given by the only officer in the room who hadn't spoken. He was handling the arson at the factory.

"Okay. Let due process run on that. Your problem is Marie Corrigan. What do we reckon? A genuine alibi for Jack, and a false one for Barry? Phil, keep plodding away at the drugs end of the business. I know this meeting hasn't been that much help to you…"

"Not so, sir, a few fresh thoughts have jumped up and saluted. Wouldn't want to elaborate just yet. Need to let them ferment."

The Chief Super' laughed.

"You do that Phil, and when they're ready pour me a glass. Try to make it before the next Preston Guild. I've a feeling that only comes round once in twenty years."

The meeting between Barry and Mark Hargreave was short, far from sweet, but very much to the point.

"I've fucking told you, Barry, I want that gear back that you nicked from me, and I want it now. Don't piss me about."

Barry felt he was in the ascendant. Mark no longer frightened him. He could create just as much trouble for Mark, as he could for him. Still, he would play it cool for a while.

"Okay, okay, you'll have it before the end of the day. I've got to do the old witch's shoppin' later. I'll retrieve it from the wardrobe then."

"Wow, 'retrieve' eh Barry. You have started paying attention at school. Just you remember, arse me around and word will get back to the police about the church hall and my old man's factory. Not to mention how unhappy Donald and Vladimir will be."

Barry adopted a submissive demeanour. After tonight the dogs would no longer be a problem.

He wondered if their flesh smelt the same as that of a burning human being.

"I'll get goin' then. See you."

Barry walked away jauntily, accompanied by the dogs who were content in his company. He had formulated a plan days ago. Mark could wait until *'Kingdom Come'* for the bag of cannabis. He would return later horror-struck, and inform Mark that Mary Jessop had done a big clean out, and the rucksack was long gone. The dustbin men had been the day before, and by now its contents were no doubt scattered to the four winds. He would retrieve it, after doing the shopping, but relocate it in the churchyard. There was an old shed full of broken down rubbish. It was never locked, and rarely visited. The place was water tight, and the gear would be safe there.

"Mrs. Jessop, Mrs. Jessop!"

Barry wandered back into the kitchen from the foot of the stairs, and laid the shopping out on the work surfaces. The deaf old witch was probably taking a slash, and couldn't hear him. He helped himself to a can of Coke from the 'fridge, and sat on the kitchen stool. He'd wait until she came downstairs before putting the foodstuffs away.

She liked everything just so. Wouldn't do to annoy her.

A sharp paring knife lay on the table beside him. He picked it up, and began tossing it end on end, pretending to throw it at the distant cupboard.

"Yeh, yeh, take that motherfucker...and that, asshole..."

He heard Mary Jessop's heavy tread descending the stairs, and quit his circus antics. Innocently, he sipped his drink, and the knife idled in his hand.

"Hello, Mrs. J. I've got..."

Barry recognised the bag in her hand, and just about swallowed, *"Oh shite!"*

"What's this then?"

"Wot?"

She dangled the bag in front of him.

"Don't you come that with me, young man. What's dead long ago and pardon took its place!"

"Looks like a rucksack to me. Where d'you get it from?"

"Don't soft soap me, laddie. I can see that. I meant what's in it?"

"I dunno, nuttin' to do with me. I never sin it before."

"You may think I'm old and stupid, but I was young once like you. I was a lass in the Sixties, and I didn't always behave as I should have. I've had a good sniff inside this bag, aye and seen the little packages. I know what this is, and I know what you've been up to. Just you wait until I tell your father."

She stepped forward, and thrust the bag under his nose. A rational and calm Barry might have continued to talk his way out of it, but he saw red and bellowed.

"He's not my fuckin' dad, an' I've sorted 'im for good. Now give me the fuckin' bag, you old bag, or I'll fuckin' do you!"

Barry's hand whipped up, and threatened her with the knife. Each could feel the hot breath of the other on their face. Mary Jessop was enraged, and old as she was a flare of temper energised her.

"Why, you little bugger!"

She dashed the bag against his hand, and the knife dropped between them.

"Here, have it, and much good may it do you. Now get out of my house."

Barry gripped the bag, and turned his back on the old lady. He couldn't resist a quick peek inside, to see that nothing had been taken. It was part of his creed that everyone was as dishonest as himself. He was satisfied, and glanced over his shoulder. Mary Jessop had picked up the knife, and was waving it wildly.

"Get out! Get out!"

Barry laughed hysterically.

"Worra youse gonna do with dat? Make sure you don't cut yerself shavin'."

"Get out! Get out!"

"For fuck's sake, put it down an' I won't 'urt you."

Her arm was extended, and the point was aimed at Barry.

"Right, right, I fuckin' warned you."

He grabbed her wrist, but she braced it with her other hand. Barry was hampered by his hold on the bag of cannabis. They wrestled for possession of the knife. Mary gave him a small shove against the end of the kitchen table. Barry lost his balance, and spun off the edge of the table. He fell, and dragged Mary to the floor with him.

She lay on top of the teenager. All was silent. Her head lay beside his, and her eyes were closed. Time seemed infinite, but eventually a body moved. Mary rolled off him, and lay on the floor staring at the ceiling. The tick tock of the kitchen clock measured out their lives.

Mary rotated her head ninety degrees. For a long time she remained quiet, fixated on the hilt of the knife. The blade was buried in the centre of Barry's throat. It was only when she noticed his open eyes that her staunched emotions flooded forth. A look of hellish glory bored into her. She began to keen for the dead boy. When she flopped onto her back the sound changed. It rose to a primitive ululation. A crescendo was reached and sustained. The sound of her wailing was heard the length of Palmerston Way. By the time the emergency services arrived she was catatonic.

23

'Icky Ben Douhl, the American Eyeball Tickler.'

Bowcott was not struggling to pay his electricity bill. He emulated the Sun King, and the Manor House shone as brightly as the Palace of Versailles at one of Louis XIV's more extravagant parties.

The Lord of the Manor rarely bothered with his internal life. He was not insensitive to the need for personal reflection, but didn't agree with the modern penchant for spending eternity dissecting the contents of your rectum. He held the exquisite brandy balloon to the chandelier. Why had he insisted that every room in the property should blaze with light? The Harley Street man informed him that death was imminent. He cast his mind back to those halcyon sixth form days at Eton. Wasn't it the old Kraut polymath Goethe whose last words were a call for more light?

'Mehr Licht, Mehr Licht!'.

He was unaccustomed to a brace of insights in short order. Temple Weston was agog with the news of Barry Corrigan's death. Apparently, at the hand of a knife-wielding old woman who dealt in drugs. Bowcott supposed that he'd better appear at the boy's funeral. Got to be seen to be doing the right thing. An ironic snort escaped from him. Might be a good idea to climb in the box with the child, and get it all over and done with.

Kelly Hampton told him, over a lunchtime sharpener or three, that nobody could get a handle on the dead lad. To all intents and purposes he'd been known as thoroughly bad lot, but had recently undergone a transformation.

Bowcott wheezed again.

"I know that my Redeemer liveth!"

The empty salon resounded again to a rasping voice.

His early years as Lord of the Manor were spent in fulfilling his duty. Each Sunday morning he attended All Souls, to sit resplendent in the ancient family pew. It had never really been his thing. Truth be told, he was not so much scornful of religion but of the Church of England. Another thought leapt out at him; it was already turning out to be a night to remember. Did his ire about the state of his marriage emanate from residual love for Edwina, or was it something else? Maybe the greater offence was caused by the involvement of a man of the cloth. Bowcott was old school in matters of faith.

The family was Pre-Reformation, and at heart he was a recusant. Roman Catholic ceremony held him in greater awe than that of Low Church humility. No, he wouldn't be sharing a wooden overcoat with Barry Corrigan, because he had converted to Roman Catholicism. His final rites would be administered by a celibate priest. That would give Edwina something to think about.

Not that he cared anymore. On his way to lunch with Chad Corbett, he'd spent twenty minutes with his solicitor. He went into the meeting boiling with fury. Sir Lionel convinced him that contesting the divorce was futile. Whilst weaving through London's streets to his club he exchanged God knows what feelings for Edwina to one of utter indifference. The revelation came as he entered the club's dining room. The opposite of love is not hate; it is indifference.

Bowcott raised his glass to the teenager he'd never known.

"Cheers Harry…Gary…or whatever your name was. See you soon."

"Excuse me sir."

An attractive young woman stood in the doorway. He only required one servant for the evening, and a very tasty one she was. Mark Hargreave had been good enough to recommend her. He was out of the swim on that sort of thing, and it was hardly appropriate to approach Edwina for help. Anyway, she wasn't invited to the party. Buggered off somewhere for the evening.

"Your guests are just coming up the drive."

"Thank you Daisy. See them into the Drawing Room."

Bowcott poured a small refill, and pondered how the evening would turn out. He was startled as he gazed absentmindedly into the glass. Nanny's face swirled in the liquid, as clear as day. He heard his own childish voice.

"Who's that Nanny?"

The imperious young woman, who tended to his every need, would always reply,

"Icky Ben Douhl, the American Eyeball Tickler!"

Nanny was always dashing hither and thither, and she had no time for casual enquiries from little boys. She did, however, explain why she used the strange name. It was someone she'd heard of in her own childhood, but never ascertained if he really existed. Consequently, it was shorthand for anyone she'd never met, or knew nothing about.

Periodically, Bowcott undertook research attempting to track down the origin of the name. Icky was obviously an abbreviation for Isaac, and Ben Douhl was decidedly Jewish. Perhaps the guy been some obscure and bizarre speciality act in Music Hall, but he couldn't be definitive. It finally occurred to him that the name was irrelevant. What mattered was knowing your own identity, and being secure in it. He headed for the Drawing Room. Tonight would sweep away the topsy-turvy decades of his life; the wanderings; the pursuit of every ephemeral fad. By the end of the evening he would be rooted in his true identity.

"Good evening Lord Bowcott."

"Bowcott between friends. Good evening Beebie. I may call you Beebie, mayn't I?"

The owner of the nickname beamed, like a dog with two dicks. Bowcott focused upon his other guests, proffering a hand.

"Good evening Freddie."

She accepted his hand with a light touch, finding it difficult to meet the charming expression on his face. Freddie had not wanted to come, but Beebie had insisted.

"Be good practice for you, my own. My sources tell me that the old boy is ready to drop off the hooks, and Teddy is a bit short on the readies."

His barking laugh aggravated her.

"That's called something in English, isn't it?"

"Assonance," she mouthed unwillingly.

"Aye, that's it. Anyroad, she'll be selling up before you can say *'Jack Robinson'*, and we will be living the grand life in the Manor."

"Good evening Roddy."

Beebie looked surprised.

"What's all this then? Who's Roddy?"

Bowcott possessed a reservoir of *savoir faire*, and dazzled Beebie.

"Bowcott to the chaps, Roddy to the ladies. Roderick actually. Bally awful name. In the lineage you know, so one has to put up with these things. Good evening Mark, delighted to see you."

He closed in on Mark, who was reclining against the fireplace. They held hands firmly, and Bowcott smirked. In a quiet voice he said,

"Can't thank you enough for the dolly who's waiting on. Understand you've arranged for her to stay the night. Tidying up and all that; spot of brekka in the morning."

Mark was equally hushed.

"She'll cater to your every whim, sir."

Beebie had arrived full of bonhomie.

"Think you've met my lad before, Bowcott."

He walked over to them, and wrapped an arm around Mark's shoulder.

"Can't tell you how proud I am of him. The leading light of our little community with his good works."

"What good works would they be, Mark."

Beebie's enthusiasm was in full flow, and while they talked Daisy distributed glasses of champagne.

"The Monty Don of our village is my son."

Bowcott had been out of England for so long that he had no idea who the famous television gardener was, but smiled.

"Converted my eleven acres to a market garden to feed the poor and needy."

Bowcott's face was an unreadable mask.

"Noble of you Mark. Almost *noblesse oblige*, rather my territory."

"I say sir, I hope you don't think I'm treading on your toes."

Bowcott rested a hand on Mark's arm.

"Not in the slightest, my boy. Must cost a pretty penny."

Beebie was in again.

"No worries there. Clever lad is Mark. Already made his fortune, and I lend a helping hand with the endeavour."

Bowcott gave him a winsome smile of stupendous insincerity. It went right over Beebie's head.

"My dear Freddie, we've been neglecting you."

"That's alright Roddy. *'They also serve who stand and wait'*."

Mark and Roddy chuckled their appreciation. There was an inane grin on Beebie's face. The barb had not been understood by the target.

"You remain a fan of Milton, after all these years?"

It can be distressing to witness someone making a fool of themselves, but it rather amused the present company.

"Don't they make sterilising fluid for babies' bottles? Very good on coffee mugs as well."

Freddie exhaled her social angst.

"John Milton, my own."

"Oh aye, of course, just my little joke," he lied.

"Any good on bed sheets?"

"Eh?"

"Just my little joke, Beebie. Now, Daisy, refresh our glasses, would you. Supper is prepared?"

"Yes sir."

"Thought we'd have an intimate supper. Chance to get to know each other. Full dinner with the village worthies at a later date. Do come through."

The conversation was pleasant and wide-ranging. During the space of two hours they mulled over a variety of topics. Beebie held forth on business and his status as a man of the world, but Bowcott diverted him frequently to ease the tedium. He teased Freddie out on her good works for the church; noting that it must run in the family. Mark was encouraged to speak of his days doing VSO, and Bowcott dropped in bonbons of delight about his years overseas.

Now that they were well-fed and watered they repaired to more comfortable surroundings. The room was furnished with old sofas and leather armchairs. Daisy provided liqueurs, and retired to the kitchen to load the dishwasher.

The remorseless Beebie was in his cups, and still leading the charge.

"Funny affair, looking backward, seeing where you've come from and where you've been. I was looking in an old diary the other day…"

"You keep a diary, Beebie?"

"Been doing it for years, Bowcott."

"What a fascinating coincidence. Why just yesterday I was going through one from over thirty years ago. I didn't realise it was that long since I last fucked you Freddie."

Beebie's mouth moved like that of a goldfish stranded on the carpet, but nothing came out.

"Roddy, don't," she murmured.

"I'm going to be dead soon, Freddie. It's time he knew."

Beebie jumped up from his chair.

"Too bloody right it's time..."

"Not you!"

Bowcott came to his feet. Sick as he was he went toe to toe with Beebie. It seemed to take an aeon until Beebie sat submissively. Bowcott's lineage did not intimidate him; it was the implacable force in his eye that did the job. All Beebie could manage was to splutter,

"How...when?"

Freddie rested one hand upon the other, and sat forward demurely. She finally lifted her head, and addressed both husband and son.

"It was the year you went on a two month buying trip in the Far East. We were new to the village. Edwina and I became friends; she took me under her wing. Before I knew it I was invited to the Manor for drinks, for dinner, then parties."

"And what parties they were, eh Freddie."

"Your memory fails you a little, Roddy. Perhaps you should consult your diaries. I only ever attended two of your so-called parties. You may have talked Edwina into your nasty practices. In fact, I know you did, and she regrets every minute of it; she told me."

Bowcott almost pleaded for her approval.

"But on those two occasions it was just you and me. I didn't invite anyone else to participate in our liaison. You were so grateful to be loved, and...so was I."

The look she gave him was baleful.

"How dare you Roddy. You never loved me for one minute."

"I...I don't know. Maybe...possibly. Please accept my apology."

The three old folk sat in silence, each tracing their imaginings into the rugs. Mark walked across to the drinks trolley, and opened a bottle of champagne. The pop made them jump. His face was filled with fascination, as he prepared fresh glasses and handed them round.

Bowcott had drunk like a fish for decades; that was what was killing him. He set the glass down on a side table, walked over to where Mark was and stood beside him.

"You told me all those years ago Freddie, and I respected you and kept it secret. I was foolish to believe that it meant so little."

His vehemence made tears trickle down her face.

"It means everything. That he and I should know each other."

Only Beebie remained seated, a portrait of misery.

"Mark, it's true...Roddy...Lord Bowcott is your father."

Mark's words ripped the heart out of Sir Benson Hargreave.

"Well thank God for that!"

Bowcott's skeletal hand gripped his son's arm.

"This is your home now."

Mark smiled in assent.

"Freddie, you're welcome to make it your home as well, if you want to. No strings attached."

Her voice was stentorian and dominated the room.

"No thank you, Lord Bowcott. I know my duty. My place is beside my husband."

She held out her hand, and spoke gently.

"Come along Benson. Let's go home."

It was midnight before they parted at the bedroom door. Daisy was already inside, waiting for Mark.

"No thank you son, kind of you to offer."

Mark had enquired if his father would have liked to join him in his extra-curricular sports with Daisy from Banbury.

"I'm content, son. Content that I can call you son to your face."

"Thank you father."

The old man hugged him, and kissed his forehead.

"Now I know…now I know…"

He repeated it over and over, as he shuffled along the corridor. Mark needed an answer.

"What do you know, father?"

Bowcott continued walking.

"Who I am son, who I am."

He was no longer Icky Ben Douhl.

The strangeness of the house, and the excitement of his new-found status woke Mark at 04:30 hours. Daisy was sleeping soundly, worn out by a combination of waiting on and sexual frolics. The ancient building was far from warm, but Mark stood naked before the window. He drew back the heavy curtains. A powerful moon illuminated the property; his home. He was about to return to Daisy's side when the hooting owl breached the solemn night. It went on and on with ominous regularity, but try though he might it was impossible to spot which tree it was perched on.

Impulse carried him out into the corridor. Naked as a warrior, undergoing some ceremonial ritual, he padded along the corridor. Bowcott's bedroom door was ajar. It gave off an apologetic squeak when pushed. The curtains were open here as well. Moonlight fell onto the bed, making it glow like a spaceship about to disappear into space and time. There was no doubt.

"Wake up Daisy. Wake up!"

She looked through bleary eyes at his naked form.

"I'm tired. What do you want Mark?"

"Lord Bowcott is the correct form of address."

Edwina departed from the Manor House twenty minutes before Bowcott's guests arrived. She'd intended to spend the night in her bedroom with a book. When she sought it out in the Drawing

Room she discovered it in Bowcott's hand. He held it before him.

"*'The Way We Live Now'*. Somewhat apposite."

She removed the Anthony Trollope novel from his outstretched hand, and he added,

"But that way is over Teddy. My son will arrive shortly. A new life, a new generation will perpetuate my line."

Wordlessly she left him. In the hallway she composed herself. Edwina knew that his guests for the evening were the Hargreaves. Bowcott's son was…A fleeting thought made her laugh, as she strode up the stairway. Her friend Freddie. Looked like there would be an additional trollop in the Manor tonight.

Clem peeped through the spy hole in the front door, and opened it with alacrity.

"Hello Edwina. Don't stand out there in the cold."

She hesitated before accepting his invitation. When she placed the bulging holdall on the parquet floor their eyes lingered upon each other. Edwina described events at the Manor tersely.

"I went to the pub to see if Kelly had a room for the night. Nothing doing until tomorrow. A stag party in residence."

Clem didn't hesitate.

"This rackety old place has more bedrooms than I need. Come on, give me your coat. Into the sitting room, and a large glass of something."

"It's only for one night. Kelly can put me up long term while affairs are sorted out."

She wished she hadn't used the word 'affairs', but it seemed Clem accepted it in context.

He was in the doorway to the sitting room, and she smiled at the image of his profile.

"Yes," he breathed to himself. Then rousing himself he said,

"In you come. We can sort the details later."

Edwina went to him in the night, when she could no longer bear staring at the ceiling. It was a night for leaving curtains open. Their love was bathed in generous moonlight.

She would not permit him to accompany her to the Manor. It was a short journey, and dragging a couple of suitcases back to the Vicarage was no hardship. Besides, she didn't want him present when she laid out her terms to Bowcott.

Edwina hadn't expected anyone to be about. Bowcott was not an early riser. The hearse nearly knocked her over, as she entered the drive. It appeared to be empty, but she knew better. When bodies are collected the temporary coffin is placed in a lower compartment out of view. That's the unseen cavity that has to be fumigated most regularly. In the trade, the lingering smell is known as *'The Death Sweat'*.

She walked out onto the grass verge, watching the hearse until it disappeared. This put an entirely different complexion on affairs. That word again. If she was correct, about who was being transported to eternity, who had informed the authorities? Oh, of course, that pretty young thing who was waiting on for the evening. Bowcott had delighted in telling her that the young woman would be staying the night. Perhaps she had polished him off.

The lock responded to her key, and she was in the entrance hall. No need to rush. This was now her domain, for the foreseeable future.

"Good morning, Lady Edwina. Out and about early."

She panned round, and saw the new master framed through an open doorway. Paintings by Vermeer came to mind. She remembered, from her art history lessons, that Dutch interior paintings focused on the themes of love and the virtues of domestic life.

"Good morning, Mark."

"Do join me. Coffee?"

"Yes please. He's gone?"

Mark didn't allow his answer to interrupt the pouring of her coffee.

"Father passed away in the night."

He looked at her with a glimmer of satisfaction.

"Peacefully. My father found peace at last."

Mark was not ungracious, and he remained standing until Edwina sat.

"Now, what are we going to do?"

Edwina sipped her coffee, allowing the wheels and cogs of her mind to calculate her next move. She was about to speak when a young woman, clad only in one of Bowcott's shirts, flounced into the room giggling and shouting.

"Mark, Mark, Lord Bowcott!"

Daisy quailed under Mark's fierce response.

"Go away Daisy. NOW! My apologies Edwina. I think you were about to say?"

She had to pause, processing the title with its new owner.

"Your late-…, Bowcott and I entered into a contract. I am permitted to reside at the Manor until my death, or until they cart me away gaga."

"I'm sure both of those things are a long way off. If that's the legal standing then I will abide by it. We can draw a demarcation line between the east and west wings, and live happily ever after."

It was not ideal, but Mark didn't want to start a conflagration. Not just yet. He couldn't resist it.

"Perhaps we could get someone to police no-man's land. How about a clergyman? They're always reliable."

"I have no intention of living beside you," she forced herself to say it, "Lord Bowcott."

"Really? Got yourself a billet?"

He saw wondrous opportunities if he could get her out of the house immediately.

"This is what I propose."

She outlined her terms for leaving him alone in the Manor, while Bowcott's affairs were settled.

"If that is agreeable to you, I will ask Bernard Hetherington to draw something up today. Once our signatures are on it I will vacate my home. Be warned though, I do not surrender my rights easily."

Now she could say it.

"Bowcott was your father, but I am...was his wife. If you will excuse me, I have business to attend to."

She swung around in the doorway.

"Do train up that 'maid' of yours. The coffee is execrable."

Edwina was gone. Mark examined the dregs in his cup. She was right, it was bloody awful.

Bernard Hetherington's clerk expressed it beautifully to his wife over Spaghetti Bolognese.

"Never seen Bernard move that fast in years. Like shit off a shovel."

Edwina spent three nights at the Manor. The agreement between Mark and herself was signed, and she was packed. Two people carrier taxis were required to transport her personal belongings to her new quarters. It was unfortunate that as she stood in the Vicarage drive, instructing the men on what to take where, a gaggle of people passed by.

Marjorie Knighton, Churchwarden at St. Dunstan's, was a stained glass enthusiast. She was leading a party around the Benefice to give them the benefit of her wisdom on all matters pertaining to said glass in the churches. All Souls was second on the list, before lunch in *'Deux Testicules'*. Kelly Hampton became the first resident of Temple Weston to receive the gossip.

"And while the men were taking her suitcases into the Vicarage, they were stood there brazenly. He had his arm around her, and then...and then, he kissed her!"

Kelly was non-committal. If her thoughts were uncharitable they were reserved for Marjorie Knighton. Who did the old busybody think she was? Even Kelly could remember a bit of the Bible. She wanted to say, *"Judge not lest you be judged."* Instead she enquired,

"You all okay for drinks?"

Kelly didn't go in for self-delusion. She was an old hooker turned mine host. No point in regrets; no point having a go at others because you're pissed off at yourself. Kelly knew exactly who and what she was. She could live with it.

Bishop Marion was direct.

"Rufus was obliged to inform me, Clem. I hope you won't bear him any ill-will?"

Clem shook his head.

"Good. Now that I've heard the entire story I can see, and may I say sympathise with, your predicament. However, I understand that Temple Weston, indeed the entire Benefice, is in a state of ferment about your new living arrangements. How is your son coping?"

"He's been getting a bit of stick at school, but he copes remarkably well. At home he has accepted Edwina. We sat down together, and talked openly."

"Wise. Any pastoral support you need, for any one of you, will be available. Call Jonathan David. It's the Archdeacon's specialist area."

Marion steeled herself.

"I'm going to have to put you on gardening leave, Clem. Let me be frank. I think your time in Temple Weston is over, but not, and I emphasise not, your career in the church. Keep as low a profile as possible until I can formulate a way forward for you. Rest assured; I shall not dictate to you. May I ask, do you and Edwina intend to marry?"

"Yes. Divorce is no longer an issue for her. May I ask you a question? Who will run All Souls while I'm...excused duties?"

"Ah, yes, you have every right to know. We were in a bit of a pickle, but the Lord's hand is ever upon us. I have instructed Rufus that he must forgo some of his extra-mural activities. His media appearances are to go onto the back burner for a while. The Rector will lead most of the services at All Souls, and tend to the parish. Colin Ambler is back on his feet, and he will assist with light duties. We have been fortunate that a retired Archdeacon has moved from Stratford to Dunsmore-by-Napton. She will officiate at St. Dunstan's. Sally Markham doesn't take prisoners. Rufus and I are hopeful that she will impact creatively upon the PCC. Luke 3:7."

For the first time in days, Clem smiled.

"...You brood of vipers! Who warned you to flee from the coming wrath?"

"Thank you for coming to see me Clem. When the dust has settled, I will be delighted to meet Edwina."

24

...and I'm the Queen of Tonga!'

No-one likes to admit it at a funeral, but they are glad to be alive. Barry Corrigan's obsequies were observed on the first Friday in December. It was indeed a frosty one. Journalists attended from all points of the compass. Police officers Molly McGuire and John Fortune went out of respect, and they were badgered as they passed through the lych gate.

"Care to comment on why there's no progress on Arthur Archer's murder?"

"Was Mary Jessop known to the police as a drug dealer?"

Chief Superintendent Melvyn Woodward raised a hand to silence the fevered enquiries.

"Ladies and gentlemen. This is a solemn occasion. I ask you to respect the grieving family, and refrain from asking questions which are inappropriate at this time. Later today I will issue a statement to the media about the progress we are making. Thank you."

Molly and John tottered behind their boss, exchanging wry smiles. What progress? Mary Jessop was away with the fairies, and already institutionalised. The death of Barry Corrigan was unlikely to enjoy an extended jury trial. Poor Arthur Archer remained in limbo. The problem was that there weren't any forensics. Not a sniff of DNA. Temple Weston had heard about the cannabis in his bloodstream, and villagers assumed he'd been one of Mary Jessop's victims. They shrugged, and concluded that Arthur had gone off the rails; broken into the Church Hall and, in a drug induced haze, somehow set the place ablaze.

The turnout for Barry was similar to Arthur's funeral. The temporary PA system was rigged and ready for the overflow lining the pathway. Rufus was in his element. Who needed TV when you've got the press clamouring at your door, and the Lord of the Manor to bury the following week? He didn't know that he had the current title holder to thank for that. Mark had seen the will, and his father's wishes to be dispatched left footed. He was having none of it. That might rock the boat, and leave him with disgruntled middle Englanders. Bowcott would receive a funeral worthy of his station at All Souls. Then he would be sealed in the family vault that dominated the churchyard. End of!

Marie Corrigan had Bianca Bailey beside her. Jack was still awaiting trial, and had resigned himself to being sent down. Besides, he couldn't face the antagonism that would be visible in his co-workers, if he turned up in handcuffs. They regarded him as a traitor. Marie didn't care. She'd had enough of him, and once he was inside divorce proceedings would be initiated.

The service was in full flow. Rufus almost genuflected when he announced that Lord Bowcott would deliver the eulogy for young Barry. He had not anticipated that his Lordship would mount the steps of the pulpit. Mark's gaze swept the congregation and settled on Marie's fine legs, displayed beautifully below the hem of her very short black dress. Might it be possible? Well perhaps after the piss-up in the pub.

His voice was mellifluous, and he did a good line in sincerity. The listeners outdoors admired his beautiful enunciation. In the Vicarage garden two figures rested on their rakes. Fallen leaves abounded and needed their attention. It had rained recently, and they were transforming to decayed matter. Clem and Edwina heard everything Mark said.

"Barry had a difficult start to life in his home city of Liverpool. Left all alone, as a single mother, Marie struggled to make ends meet, but she always placed her beloved son first. Barry was constant in loyalty and love towards her. When they came to Temple Weston they were overjoyed, and Barry fitted into our community with exemplary energy. Shedding old habits, he became a model teenager. I have spoken with his head teacher, and she told me that he was one of the brightest students she has ever taught. She was delighted to see the rapid progress he was making during the first term of this school year. An 'A' grade student in the making."

He exhibited a frown, as if unsure about what to say next.

"It would be remiss of me to delve too deeply into the ultimately tragic relationship he entered into with a neighbour. I can say that Barry was a Good Samaritan, and demonstrated all the attributes that we associate with a caring and loving grandson."

The cloud lifted from his brow.

"Many of you may not know it, but Barry worked for me in the last few months. He helped me cultivate the produce of my market garden, which is so beneficial to the village. He was a hard worker, and never shirked the more onerous tasks. Barry gave up many a weekend to travel to Coventry, Warwick and Leicester to acquire materials essential to the success of our project. What more is there to say? We have lost a young life, in tragic circumstances. God bless you Barry, and may you rest in peace."

Mark descended from the pulpit, faced the altar, and bowed to the Cross. The congregation's observance of him was diverted. A high pitched noise whined over the church. Only one person present was certain about the cause of the disturbance.

Grenville Simons arrived in Temple Weston at the crack of dawn. He eschewed hovering around the gate, and was the first to be seated. Small drones are about forty decibels quieter than conventional aircraft, but they are bloody annoying. Today was a red letter day for Grenville. The funeral, the death of one Lord and the unusual elevation of a new one. He'd already got the SP on that. The Baileys relished their role as informants. The noise got less, and Grenville made a note of the time. Oh yes, there was the small matter of a little aerial investigative journalism. Grenville was a whizz at maths, and after worrying away at all the disparate threads, which escaped the police, he ventured to tie a knot. He knew precisely what two plus two makes...perfect sense.

An unspoken thought transmitted itself between Edwina and Clem, as they resumed their labours in the garden. They discussed it over dinner that evening.

"Yes, my love, I was thinking that too. Where is it in the Bible?"

Clem went to a bookshelf. Before he could get there he heard his son Luke declaim.

"*'Do not be deceived: God cannot be mocked. A man reaps what he sows. The one who sows to please his sinful nature, from that nature will reap destruction...'Galatians 6, I believe.*"

Edwina placed her hands in her lap.

"Thank you Luke, that's very helpful to me."

The boy smiled at her. He liked her; he liked her very much.

"Dad, may I ask you a question."

"Shoot!"

"The sinful man who mocks and pleases himself. He sows and reaps his own destruction, right?"

"Right."

"How long?"

"How long will we have to wait before he's destroyed?"

Luke's shoulders shook, ever so gently, and tears filled his eyes.

"I really liked Arthur. He was a good guy. It's not right Dad, it's not right."

Received wisdom informs us that the human spirit is at its lowest ebb just before dawn. It was pitch black for Sir Benson Hargreave. The police went in mob handed. By the time the door of *'The Grange'* was opened to DI Phil Brooks, accompanied by DC Andy Harbury, and PC Helen Aston, the other Drug Squad members, accompanied by a forensic team, were surging through acres of greenhouses.

"Good morning Sir Benson, Lady Hargreave. I am Detective Inspector Brooks, and I have here a warrant which permits me to search your house and grounds for…"

"For what?"

Benson was outraged at the intrusion, and the announcement of a search warrant lit his fuse.

"Prohibited substances sir. It is our belief that the growth, processing and distribution of cannabis has been engaged in on these premises. Is that your drawing room, sir?"

A flummoxed Beebie nodded his head. Freddie looked aghast.

"But that's impossible," she said. "Who could get away with that, right under our noses?"

Husband and wife froze, then snatched a quick look at one another.

"That's what we are here to ascertain. Please wait in your drawing room. PC Aston will accompany you. If you have any, ahem, needs during the period of waiting you will all have to go together."

The Hargreaves were so deflated that they went as meek as lambs.

Their wait was barely twenty minutes. Through the open doorway they saw a policeman in the entrance hall. He was dressed like a member of a South American Paramilitary Death Squad. Phil Brooks approached him, and they went into conclave. It lasted two or three minutes. Freddie's hearing was the sharpest, and she heard the DI say,

"Pass my thanks on to the lads and lasses, Mike. A good job."

Phil paused for moment. He felt the eyes upon him from the drawing room, and strode towards them.

"Sir Benson, Lady Hargreave, thank you for your patience. We needn't disturb the household any longer…"

"I thought so. Bloody nonsense! I shall be contacting your Chief Constable…"

Phil held a hand up, like a traffic cop halting traffic.

"Sir Benson Hargreave, I am arresting you on suspicion of cultivating, processing and distributing a controlled substance. You do not have to say anything…"

The legally required mantra was trotted out, and Beebie was taken into custody. Freddie was caught between Scylla and Charybdis. Even in a crisis she couldn't escape her education and say, *'Between a rock and a hard place'.* She couldn't believe this of Benson; she could believe it only too readily of Mark…but he was her son, her blood.

On route to the police car, Phil Brooks apologised to Beebie.

"Sorry to say, sir, that we had to shoot your dogs. Rottweilers aren't so easily persuaded."

"Dogs, what bloody dogs?"

Beebie wasn't as green as he was cabbage looking, and unlike Freddie he no longer possessed any loyalty towards Mark.

"I tell you, it's nowt to do with me. It's that bloody…" He was about to say 'son', but swallowed the word like a dose of castor oil. "Bowcott, Lord piggin' Bowcott."

The car door was opened, and Phil Brooks held him there. Scepticism, and not a little amusement, vibrated his face muscles.

"I was given to understand that his Lordship passed away recently."

"Not him, you numpty, the new one."

"Being offensive is not advisable, sir. Wait until we interview you formally, and you can tell us anything you like."

Beebie was handled into the back of the car. Phil turned to Andy Harbury, and grinned.

"Including fairy stories!"

Andy Harbury replied.

"Think we now know why Mary Jessop got her nice new house for free."

The Porsche, parked on the other side of the street one hundred or so metres away, did not follow. The journalist at the driving wheel put his belongings into the satchel. Grenville had turned the footage over to the police. His investment in the drone and operator would generate a far greater return than it cost. The quid pro quo for cooperating had been to secure their agreement that he would be the lone journo at the bust. They had been true to their word. He was confident that DC Andy Harbury would stick to the deal, and give him the exclusive on the interview and subsequent action taken. It was early, but he wondered if he could knock someone up at the pub, and solicit breakfast.

"You have heard the accusations made against you. Before we proceed, are you sure that you don't wish to have a legal representative present during this interview?"

"Quite certain, thank you. I wish to assist you as much as I possibly can. With your permission, I will make a statement for the recording. When my darling Mama effected a reconciliation with the man I then thought to be my father I was delighted, if surprised at the ease with which it was accomplished."

"Why surprised?"

"I don't wish to sound vindictive, but Sir Benson has always been a most difficult man. I'm sure that my mother would support that view. What surprised me most was the alacrity with which he jumped at my proposal."

"That was your market garden project. Your charitable good work."

Mark thought he caught a whiff of the sardonic. It didn't bother him one jot.

"Indeed Phil. May I call you Phil?"

"Please do, Lord Bowcott."

"Not going to stand on my dignity. Mark will suffice. Yes, yes it was the speed with which he accepted my market garden proposal which knocked me back a step or two. Hargreave is not noted for his charitable disposition. Evidence the recent strike at the factory. You know the old joke?"

"Tell me."

"What do you call a Yorkshireman?...A Scotsman, without the generosity."

Phil Brooks manufactured a smile. This all seemed straightforward, but he wasn't stupid enough to be impressed by a title.

"Very good, Mark. Do continue."

"Well, this is the nub of the matter. I did all the ordering for infrastructure, tools, seed, plants etc..."

"You bought all the plants?"

Mark laughed loudly.

"Not those particular ones, Phil. Fruit and veg, fruit and veg. Thing is Hargreave and I made a deal. He said he was so delighted by the return of the Prodigal Son that he would stump up for certain things. I insisted on paying for everything concerned with the market garden – I'm not short of a bob or two; currency was my previous enterprise. He paid for the rest, including the greenhouses, of which I was allowed only three."

"Let's come to the greenhouses. You say that you were never allowed entry into them?"

"Only my own. As you probably saw, the bulk of them were screened off. He brought his own people in to work in them. Always said that unauthorised folk had to be kept out. Didn't want to risk contamination of experimental work. Even told me he was working in cahoots with the Royal Horticultural Society."

"What happened to the orders and bills, Mark?"

"It was all done through the accounts department at his shirt factory. That's about it, Phil. Oh, there is one other thing. A few weeks ago I happened to see an electricity bill on his desk. The figure was astronomical. To be fair to Hargreave, he did say that he would foot the bill for leccy, as I believe they call it, but the sum was way beyond what I ever dreamed it might be. My part of the production didn't necessitate paralysing the national grid."

Mark's good nature overtook him once more, and they shared a laugh.

"Right, Lord Bowcott. I think we can terminate the interview. Is there anything you'd like to add?"

"Was a shame about my dogs."

"Sorry about that, but we couldn't have dealt with them any other way. Thank you for clearing up the question of their ownership. Sir Benson was adamant that he knew nothing about them. Curious that."

"Not at all Detective Inspector. Never permitted me to have a dog as a child. He has a phobia about them. I had a phobia about some of the thieving little toe rags on his estate. Kept Donald and Vladimir quiet, and well away from him. Mother didn't even know."

"Interview terminated at 11:36 a.m. Thank you sir."

Andy Harbury escorted him to the exit. Mark did not show any recognition towards the middle-aged man sitting in the reception area. A briefcase was clasped to his chest. The man looked up at him, but simply stared into space.

While Mark made a short statement to the press, gathered at the front of the building, Harry Greenwood was led to an interview room.

"Now, how can we help you Mr. Greenwood?"

"I...I caught it on local radio. I'm Head Accountant at the Hargreave Shirt Factory, or was."

He placed the briefcase onto the table gingerly.

"Most of it's on external hard drive and USB key, there's some hard copy. I think you'll find it helpful. I was concerned about it from the very beginning."

He added hastily.

"Not the drugs business. I know nothing about that. No, it was accounting for stuff outside the factory business that bothered me. Highly irregular. Will this take long?"

Harry was anxious to be away. There was a new car to take delivery of at two-thirty. In an act of true generosity, Lord Bowcott had taken him on to look after the estate accounts. Kindness itself to a man made redundant by arson. Harry had received a most handsome advance payment.

25

'Who wants a bit of the other?'

"**Y**ou can do whatever pleases you with the wing."

"I don't know Mark. Everything is so unsettled at present."

"It's a *fait accompli* Mummy. He's going to prison, and there's an end to it. What sort of life will you have when he's released?"

Freddie sat before the dressing room mirror. This would be part of her wing of the house, if she agreed to come and live in the Manor.

"He's finished in society, and business. What's the point in clinging to some outdated notion of duty."

She looked at him sharply.

"But isn't that the very creed on which a family like yours is founded."

Mark was taken aback. He wandered to the window, and studied the land; his land. It invigorated him, and generated a genuine and truthful response.

"That's all guff, Ma. The Bowcotts are no different to most of the aristocracy in this country. We got where we are because we're turncoats and opportunists. The history books are of England are like volcanoes. The molten lava of betrayals and deals, changing sides and backstabbing cascade from every page."

Freddie was bred to a middle class ideal. It incorporated the belief that some were better than others, and some were better again. She ascribed his statement to cynicism; that was unfair. Mark was not everything she would want in a son, but in this familial parley he was truthful. She was overcome by an intriguing question.

"How have you all got away with it for so long?"

Mark needed time to formulate an answer. He considered her enquiry with absolute sincerity.

"Look out there, Mummy. The Church and I agree about one thing, people are lost. Where we disagree is that I don't believe most people have the gumption or balls to work for permanence. We are accused of self-interest, but what about them? All that tripe about the downtrodden masses; ambitions and talents stifled by wicked Victorian landlords twirling their moustaches. Utter nonsense. What do they crave? Work, and a day that doesn't end too late. Enough money for food on the table and garish clothes; football and ale on Saturday, papers and an obscenely sized dinner on Sunday. Oh yes, and telly every night of the week, with the bonus of a fortnight in Tenerife. We work and persevere, and yes we take advantage, but we also provide what they want. If they want to stake their claim to equality and a share of the pie, let them enter the field and join the battle. The truth is that we are all the same; the same devotees of self-interest. The only difference is in the desired end. We get away with it, because they are complicit in the deal. We've all sold our souls to the Devil."

He looked out of the window again, with pride in his heritage. His eye settled on the church tower.

'God is dead…God remains dead. And we have killed him.'"

Freddie closed her eyes.

"Your capacity to surprise me never ceases, Mark."

She opened them.

"I never realised you had the time or inclination to read Nietzsche."

"A new master introduced me to him. He was my economics teacher. Came to us from UCS in Hampstead. You recall him. Big fellow with a beard and a deafening laugh, and the most appalling halitosis."

Freddie remembered the chap. She hadn't taken to him. A forced bonhomie at an open evening to size up the school. She recollected the look in his eye, as if he wanted to interfere with you. They had considered sending Mark to UCS, but were put off by the pomposity of its self-proclaimed liberalism, and the complete absence of religion. Benson did research. It was asserted that at its foundation, in the earlier part of the 19th Century, *'The Times'* had railed against *'This godless school'*. Sending Mark elsewhere had not, apparently, saved him.

"This is your home Mummy. You will be the Dowager, and you will want for nothing."

"Won't you marry, Mark? I should like to have grandchildren."

He'd wondered when that question would enter the fray, and he trod warily. Freddie forgave him most things, but the revelation that he had already produced a litter, spread liberally around the globe, would not go down well.

"Always on the lookout, Ma. Never against the idea. Haven't met the right girl yet."

He was confident that trite and clichéd phrases would satisfy. Time to go for the jugular.

"I need you with me, Mummy." He buried his face in his hands. "I've been alone for so long."

Freddie leapt to her feet, ran across the room and clasped him from behind.

"My son, my darling son, of course I'll come. Mummy won't leave you alone."

He pivoted one hundred and eighty degrees, and held her to his chest. Mark had been rooting around the Manor, and came across bundles of old photographs. He discovered one of Bowcott in his prime. The newly framed snap caught his eye, as he looked over his mother's shoulder. A frisson of delight went through him. He could have sworn that his father winked.

"Come on Mummy, I want you to meet your new servants."

They swept down the staircase hand in hand, to be met by two young ladies standing in the hallway, demure and proper.

Mark laid out the rubric for them the previous day.

"You do as I say, and you get a new and better life. No more entertaining gentlemen for you, and no more boring husband, when he comes out of prison. Your naff little house will be left behind forever. Lovely bedrooms, decent pay, and going up in the world by working for me. I'll pay for your training."

They agreed without hesitation.

"Mother, Daisy is your personal maid, and Marie will be our housekeeper. They will be happy to provide you, and me, with any service we desire. Daisy, Marie, say hello to my mother. You will address her as the Dowager Bowcott."

Mark knew that 'Dowager' was only applicable to widows. It wasn't quite the right cap, but it was a good fit.

26

'When Nelson gets his eye back.'

He couldn't move. It was as if his muscles were atrophied.

"Tell me again, Edwina."

"His Earldom is in North Yorkshire, but Bobby Flexington has land in Lancashire. There is a living in the Trough of Bowland, and Bobby is the Patron. I'm not going to beat around the bush, Clem, I've called in a favour. It's yours for the taking."

"But how can that be in this age? There are applications to be made, interviews to undergo, and approvals to be given."

Edwina hadn't realised that her younger man was so naïve.

"Influence always prevails, Clem. I understand Bishop Marion and your Bishop-to-be have conferred, and it's a done deal. Remember Clem, when you were ordained you secured a job in a museum. Once you're in, employees rarely get the sack from that sort of institution. Like football managers they merely move on to a new ground."

He was startled.

"You regard the Church of England as a museum?"

"In the way it's run, yes, but Church and Faith are two separate things. They belong together, but if every church building, every mosque, every synagogue in the world were swallowed into the earth right now Faith would still exist."

"Edwina is right, Dad."

He looked at his son with deep concern.

"What about you, Luke? I don't want to uproot you again, so soon after..."

"Oh, don't worry Dad, I like being on the move. It's an adventure."

"There are some very good public schools in Lancashire, Luke."

"That's very thoughtful of you Edwina, but I rather like being with mates in the comprehensive. There are some pains around, but it's up to me to make the best of it, and I intend to, wherever we live together. Hey Dad, have a read of this."

Luke passed a Bible to his father. He had marked a passage.

"What does it say Clem? Read it to us."

"Jesus replied, 'Foxes have holes and birds of the air have nests, but the Son of Man has nowhere to lay his head.' Another disciple said to him, 'Lord, first let me go and bury my father.' But Jesus told him, 'Follow me, and let the dead bury their own dead.'"

Clem smiled at his son.

"You're too clever by half, as your Nanny used to say. You need to get out more."

"I do Dad. You've been rather preoccupied, so I expect you haven't noticed. What do you think?"

"Time to lay down the burdens of the past Clem. We have each other, the three of us. New beginnings, new adventures, as Luke said."

"The thing is Edwina, Luke, I don't know if I want to carry on being a clergyman."

Edwina and Luke were thunderstruck.

"Why Dad?"

"Have you lost your Faith, Clem?"

"No! Not in God, not in Christ...in people."

He narrowed his eyes to focus upon his thoughts.

"The outside world, the millions of unbelievers and non-believers, attack the Church all the time…"

"No-one likes to talk about religion as much as an atheist."

Edwina laughed.

"Where did you get that from Luke?"

"No idea. Must have read it somewhere. Got me into trouble in an R.E. lesson. I quoted it at my teacher. She's an atheist. You couldn't make it up."

Clem was as amused as Edwina.

"What did she say?"

"Oh, nothing to that. It was the next bit that got me into bother."

"Go on."

"I asked her if it can be considered ethically sound to teach principles to others that you don't believe in yourself."

"Too clever by half!"

"Well, she sort of said that. Made me stay behind after the lesson, and called me a public school prat. Anyway Dad, people attack the Church, so what?"

Clem picked up his thread.

"The unfair thing is that, in the middle of all this hoo-ha, I've received, I am receiving, nothing but love and kindness from the Church. The gossips and censors, the uncharitable, are the people who never darken the church door…"

"So they're the ones you've lost faith in? Sorry, your door was open. I didn't mean to earwig. Well actually I did."

"Kelly, come in. What brings you here?"

"You mean I'm one of them that never crosses your threshold." She winked at Edwina. "Got a prezzie for you. Heard that you've got be out in a fortnight. I thought someone should thank you for the work you've done in the village. Couple of bottles of champers. Wherever you lay your head next Christen your pillows."

Clem had already stood, and tears filled his eyes.

"I don't know what to say, Kelly."

"Then listen to a bit of advice from an ex-Convent girl. Firstly, you've no doubt heard the rumours about what I once was. Well they're true. That lot out there can say all they want. I like living here, and I like my pub. If they don't like it, they can lump it. There's plenty of decent folk who don't talk about me behind my back, and most of them, not all, attend your services. I know it's different for you; bridges have been burnt, and you're on your way, but don't abandon everything. You're not daft Clem, and you must have known when you decided to walk this path that it would be rocky all the way. Shake the dust from your feet, and start afresh. You're never going to convince everyone in one lifetime, but you can add a few more bricks to the wall of faith. God knows we need it. Now, give an old prossie a hug, and I wouldn't mind a cup of coffee."

The removal vans departed in advance. Mr. and Mrs. Starkiss and their son took a last look at the Vicarage. The loudspeaker system was doing sterling service again for the dense crowd milling on the path to All Souls.

Bowcott's funeral had been delayed. When the Will was read Edwina contested Mark's right to go against his Father's wishes. She gave up after a while. The recently elevated Lord could afford more expensive lawyers, and time was in his favour.

Rufus Coleridge was intoning prayers from the Common Worship Book for Pastoral Services. He and Spencer were gracious enough to pop in for drinks the previous weekend. It had been civil, despite Rufus having declined their kind offer for him to conduct their marriage ceremony. The date clashed with a recording he was doing for *'A Question of Sport'*. His relief at having them out of his receding hairline was palpable.

A couple of bags were stowed into the boot of Edwina's Audi A5. Rufus' announcement resounded through the cold December air.

"May I invite his Lordship to say a few words about his late father?"

Nothing was spoken as they clambered into the car. Clem sat in the driving seat, staring at the windscreen.

She linked his arm, and rested her head on his shoulder.

"What is it my love?"

"All share a common destiny – the righteous and the wicked, the good and the bad...This is the evil in everything that happens under the sun: The same destiny overtakes all..."

Luke was having none of it. He lay his iPad on the seat. There was a grin on his face.

"Lord, now lettest thou thy servant depart in peace..." He started to sing. *"Follow the Yellow Brick Road, follow the Yellow Brick Road, follow, follow, follow, follow..."*

Life coursed through the powerful engine, and a loving family drove away in song without looking back. They had embarked upon a new adventure. It was a good Friday in Advent.

Printed in Great Britain
by Amazon